The Zook Sisters of Lancaster County

Book Three

Katie's Discovery

By
June Bryan Belfie

Other Books by this Author

All About Grace
Inn Sane – Memoirs of an Innkeeper

The Zook Sisters of Lancaster County
Book One – Ruth's Dilemma
Book Two – Emma's Choice

e-books:

Moving On
The Landlord
A Special Blessing for Sara
A Long Way to Go
The Inn Game
All About Grace
Inn Sane

The Zook Sisters of Lancaster County
Ruth's Dilemma
Emma's Choice

I'm dedicating this book to my daughters,
Lauren Boorujy
Christina Sipler
Jill Poyerd

When I wrote about the three Zook sisters,
memories of my own three daughters came to mind.
The love between sisters is something very special.

I'd also like to dedicate the book to my own dear sister,
Faith Tingley,
who is a writer at heart.
Thank you for your encouragement.

Chapter One

"I can't believe you're married, Emma. It all happened so fast." Katie smiled over at her eldest sister as she poured hot water into their bright yellow teapot. She sat down across from Emma and their *Mamm*, Mary, who took a seat at the white porcelain table to join them.

"I can't believe it either. Now it's up to you, little one." Emma patted Katie's hand.

"And she's going to have the boys line up the way she's slimming down, *jah?*" Mary added as she adjusted her *kapp*.

Katie rolled her eyes. "Now, Mamm, I still need to lose fifteen more pounds."

"No, you'd be a shadow if you lost that much."

"A big shadow," Katie added, her dimples appearing under her fresh kapp.

"Are you and Gabe happy?" Mary asked her other daughter as they waited for the tea to steep.

"Very. He's a wonderful-*gut* man. So considerate and he loves me with such tenderness."

"Were you scared on your wedding night?" Katie asked in hushed tones.

"Katie! You don't ask questions like that," Mary said, her mouth turning to a frown.

"It's okay, Mamm. I don't mind." Emma turned to her sister. "No. Maybe nervous, but not scared. I knew Gabe would never hurt me or expect too much. That part of marriage is nothing to be afraid of Katie."

"Then what part is?"

"No part," Mary jumped in. "Now pour the tea and watch your mouth."

Emma winked at her sister and the subject changed to the weather and then back to the wedding.

"It was nice of the bishop to make an exception and marry you even though it was March and it was short notice, Emma."

"Gabe was determined not to wait, and for the sake of the children…"

"*Jah*, they needed a mother, that's for sure and for certain," Mary said as she poured her tea and stirred a spoonful of sugar into her teacup. The girls poured their own and then sat silently for a few moments enjoying the hot brewed beverage. "Gut tea, Katie. What kind did you make?"

"English Breakfast."

"Jah? We should name it 'Amish Breakfast,' no?" her mother said. "Do you want a piece of the banana bread from yesterday?"

"No, this is fine."

"Katie, you made the bread?" Emma asked.

"Jah, and I didn't eat any yet," Katie said proudly.

Their sixteen-year-old brother, Wayne, entered through the kitchen door. He was working in the fields with their *daed*, tilling the soil. It was a mild, blue-sky day, typical for late March in Lancaster County, and he had on a short sleeved shirt. "Hey, Emma, how's the old married woman?"

"I'm gut. How bout you, Wayne?"

"I'm fine. Great day to work. Daed wants a refill of water, Mamm. He's actually sweating."

"My goodness, I didn't know it was that hot out."

"In the sun, it is."

Mary rose to fill Leroy's thermos with water as Wayne cut into the banana bread. He popped a large piece in his mouth and took the water from his mother, nodding to his sisters as he returned to the field.

"He's gotten taller just this winter," Katie remarked after the screen door banged shut.

"Jah, his trousers are getting short. He's the same size as your brother, Mark, and he's only sixteen."

"His hair is like yours, Emma, so blonde and curly."

"Especially when he sweats. He's so cute."

"Handsome," Katie added.

"Jah, well, I know one particular girl who thinks so," Emma remarked. She sipped her tea and smiled over at Katie.

"Sadie Yoder?" Katie asked.

"That's the one. Those two spend every moment together at the Sings, and I caught them holding hands once."

"She seems like a sweet girl," Mary said, nodding.

"She's smart, too," Emma said. "I had her in my class a couple years ago. Never gave me a bit of trouble. I think she'd be a nice sister-in-law."

"Don't go so fast, Emma," Mary said. "He's a baby, yet."

"I think she's kinda bossy, myself," Katie remarked.

"Oh, jah?" Mary looked over at her daughter.

"She bosses the other girls when we do our quilting. Even tried to tell me my colors were all wrong once."

Wayne's voice pierced the air. He shouted and the women all rose at once as he tore through the doorway, Katie noticed a look of panic on his face. "It's Daed! He's collapsed!"

"Oh, mercy!" Mary ran toward the door, her daughters right behind her. "Wayne, take the horse and ride to your brother's place. We'll need help."

"I will. I'm so scared, Mamm, what if…"

"Hush! Go get Abram. Hurry!"

Katie felt her heart pumping faster than her racing feet and she prayed silently as she ran toward the figure of her father, lying on the ground next to the large horse-drawn tiller. What a relief to see him move!

"*Leroy,*" her mother called out as she dashed over and knelt beside him. "*Are you all right? What happened?*"

"Now, Mary, don't fuss. I just had a spell." His voice was weak, but at least he was talking. "Too hot out here today. I wasn't drinking enough water. I didn't realize."

"You're all sweaty. Are you in pain anywhere?"

"Nee. Just feeling a bit weak, is all."

Katie and Emma lifted his head slightly and Katie tucked her apron under his head. Moments later, they heard the pounding of hooves as Wayne and Abram galloped down the dirt road to the field. Abram jumped down from the saddle-less horse and crouched next to his father. "Daed, what's wrong?"

"Nothing much. Everyone take a breath. I'm gonna make it. Just had a spell of heat—knocked me out for a minute. Let me get some water down and I'll get back to work."

"Not today, you're not. You're coming home with me and then we'll decide what to do about this." Mary took on her authoritative voice, reserved for such occasions.

"I'll tell you right now, I'm not going to any doctor, Mary. I'll be just fine. My goodness, you certainly panic."

"Daed," Abram said softly, "Mamm's right, you need to go and get out of the sun first. It's been a lot hotter than this and you haven't passed out before. Maybe you should check with a doctor."

"Nonsense. All right, I'll go home for a while, but Wayne can't run this farm on his own."

"I can finish this field, Daed," Wayne said. "We're more than half way through it anyway."

"I'll give Wayne a hand. I'll walk you back first, Daed. You need to cool off."

They all walked back together. Katie noticed her father seemed to be staggering, but she kept her thoughts to herself until she and Emma were alone upstairs. "He should see someone, don't you think, Emma?"

"Jah, but you know men. They can be very stubborn."

"Did you notice how he seemed all shaky?"

"He may have twisted an ankle or something, Katie. I believe it was the heat that affected him."

"I hope that's all. By the way, is Ruthie up to going to church tomorrow? Did Mamm say how she's doing with her morning sickness?"

"Apparently, she's feeling better now. She seemed good at the wedding."

"I guess she's over it then. I can't believe my older sister is pregnant already. She's starting to show."

"She's so excited. They're talking about names already.

Katie grinned. "Have they decided on any yet?"

"No, just talking. We'd better go down and see how Daed's doing. He looked so flushed."

"It's the heat, I'm sure." *Was she?*

Around three o'clock, her father insisted on checking Wayne. After Mary allowed him to leave, with the promise of returning right away, she reclined in his chair and closed her eyes. Emma was preparing to leave in order to get home to Gabe and the children and cook a nice meal.

Mary looked over at her daughters. "I was so frightened, girls. I thought it might be his heart."

"He seems fine now, Mamm," Katie said.

8

"Jah, I guess. Go, Emma. You're needed at home. We'll see you tomorrow at the church service, unless your daed is still too weak. In which case, we'll stay home."

"I hate to leave, Mamm, but…"

"Your place is with Gabe and Mervin and little Lizzy."

Emma nodded and leaned over to kiss her mother on the cheek. Then she hugged Katie and left.

A few minutes later, Leroy came in the back door, breathing heavily. "The boy's got it under control. I'm gonna go lie down a few minutes. Just call me for supper, Mary."

"I will, honey. Meatloaf tonight."

"My favorite." He put his arms around his wife and held her silently for several moments. Katie thought she saw his eyes glisten from moisture, but she never saw her daed cry. It was probably her imagination.

Chapter Two

Church was held at the Bishop's house. It was the warmest March on record, so they performed the service in his barn with the food prepared in the house and later set-up on tables in the sun. Katie breathed in the spring earth smells, smiling as the delicious scents of the early forsythia and onion grass reached her senses. Her favorite season was spring and having an early month of temperate weather and blue skies delighted her.

Leroy attended with the family and seemed normal. The episode faded from Katie's memory and she joined her friend, Becky Hosteller, as they carted food out to the serving tables, gabbing as they went.

"Katie, you're getting positively skinny," Becky said as she set down a bowl of potato salad next to a casserole of baked beans. Katie added two baskets of bread beside them.

"You think so?" Katie's grin went from ear to ear.

"I do! I'm jealous. I saw a couple guys looking at you."

"Really? Who?"

"I don't know. But they were looking, I mean it." Becky covered the salad with clear wrap.

"Maybe they were looking at you."

"I don't think so. My face is too fat."

"It is not. You're pretty and you know it."

"Well, it wasn't me they were looking at." Becky insisted.

They started back toward the kitchen for more platters of food. Others were doing the same. The women enjoyed this time of fellowship and the men stood off to the side discussing their farms, future crops, and their upcoming baseball games.

Katie brought up a subject that had been on her mind. "Now that Emma's married, I bet she will want to give up teaching soon. She'll probably get pregnant—that's what everyone does. So I wondered if you've ever thought about teaching."

"Actually, I'd love to teach. I'm getting bored silly. Mamm doesn't really need me that much since I have three sisters still at home. Is it hard?"

"The teaching part isn't, but sometimes the kids give you a rough time. Not that you couldn't handle it, but..."

"Living in a home with seven brothers and sisters kinda prepares me for anything. Yeah, I'd have to talk it over with my parents, but I think I'd like to teach."

"I remember you got good marks in all your classes, even arithmetic. That's one reason I thought of you," Katie continued. "Of course, Emma hasn't said anything yet, but I know she wants to be the best wife in the world for Gabe and she loves his kids so much, she'd probably want to stay home for them."

"They are nice kids. At least, Lizzy is."

"Mervin's a gut kid, too. He's just been through a rough time. You know he lost two sisters and then his mother. It's been real hard on him."

"That's horrible. I'd forgotten about his sisters passing away, too. No wonder he's been a bit of a problem. Who wouldn't be?"

Katie nodded. "So, if Emma wants to quit, at least I know you'll be available?"

"Yah, and thanks for thinking of me. I'll give it some serious thought. It would be fun to work together."

The last of the platters were set on tables and the girls added pitchers of sweet tea and lemonade, along with glasses.

"Girls, call the men folk. We're ready to eat now," Mary said as she placed a stack of paper napkins on the table next to the plastic forks and spoons.

After everyone ate, the women cleaned up. Not ready to leave yet, Ruthie and Emma went off by themselves to have a sisterly chat before heading home. Their husbands, Gabe and Jeremiah were discussing the possible purchase of a large size buggy and several other men had joined into the conversation, adding their opinions on the new features. Since Jeremiah worked at the buggy shop with his brother-in-law, Mark, he gave details of the newer, 'modernized' version.

"I'm glad you feel better, Ruthie," Emma said as they walked over to a sunny area near the horse pasture.

"Me, too. That morning sickness lasted through the evening. It was ever so hard."

Emma pattered her sister's abdomen, lightly. "You're popping out a teeny bit."

Ruth's hand went to her slightly protruding belly and she smiled over at her sister. "We're really excited now, Emma. I think it's a girl."

"Really? What makes you think that?"

"I don't know. Just feels that way I guess."

Emma laughed. "I guess boys feel that way too. Have you felt the baby kick?"

"Not yet. I'm not that far along, you know."

"You can hardly tell you're pregnant."

"Emma, I confess—I kind of stick my stomach out a little." They laughed and leaned against the white rail fence. A warm breeze added to the pleasant moment.

"You heard about Daed?" Emma asked her sister.

"Katie told me about what happened earlier. It must have been scary for everyone. Do you think it was just the heat?"

"I don't know what to think. It's never happened to him before and it's been way hotter."

"That's kind of what I was thinking. He really should see a doctor."

Emma rolled her eyes. "Good luck. He can be stubborn and he doesn't think there's anything wrong."

"Jah, you said that right. Mamm will keep a close eye."

"Jah, for sure and for certain."

"So, dear sister," Ruth started, "how do you like being married?"

"So far, it's wonderful-gut. I love Gabe so much, Ruthie."

"And he, you."

"Jah, that's what he says."

"You don't believe him?"

Emma looked at Ruth with a pout. "Of course. It's just that…well, it's hard being a second wife in a way. I wonder if he's thinking of her sometimes when he seems far away."

"And when you're intimate?" Ruth asked softly.

"How did you know?"

"I guess, I'd wonder the same thing, Emma, but I thought you told me he wasn't that close to his wife. Didn't you say they were sort of distant?"

"That's what he told me once."

"So, why not believe him? He has no reason to lie to you."

"I know you're right. But sometimes he talks about her and then he gets such a dreamy look and—"

"Oh, Emma, you should see his face when he looks at you. Talk about dreamy."

"Really? You're not just saying that to make me feel better?"

"No. I think he's cared for a long time now. I noticed it months ago when I saw you together. Can I give you some sisterly advice?"

"You always have," Emma said with a lopsided smile. "Why stop now?"

"Just relax. Enjoy what you have together. You can't expect he'll never have thoughts of his first wife. You really have to accept that. And let him talk about her if he needs to. I know it will be hard, but try not to be jealous. And in time, you'll feel more secure about your marriage. I just know it."

"Good advice, Ruthie. *Danki.* I'll try—really. I appreciate your honesty. We do enjoy being together as a family. The children are so dear to me."

"You're a wonderful mother to those two. God brought you together, I'm ever so certain of that."

Emma reached over to give her sister a hug. "Danki. I feel better already. Sisters forever?"

"Jah," Ruth returned the hug and said with a smile, "always and forever."

Katie sat on a bench with her friend Becky after they finished their clean-up. Several other friends their age came over to talk about the Sing to be held that night. Priscilla, Emma's flirtatious friend who once had eyes on Gabe, announced she was asked to the Sing by John Troyer, the eligible bachelor who had been smitten with Emma for a brief time.

Katie smiled over at Priscilla. "Now that Emma's married, maybe you stand a chance with John."

"That's a horrible thing to say," Priscilla remarked. "Like I couldn't get a man by myself? I'll have you know—"

"Sorry, that didn't come out just right," Katie said, blushing at her thoughtless words. She hadn't meant to be so catty.

"Humph." Priscilla, hands on hips, stormed off toward the young men, who were observing the girls. John went over to her and they stood whispering. Then John let out a hearty laugh and they walked hand-in-hand over to a table still laden with snack foods.

"I guess I goofed," Katie said, under her breath.

"Big time," one of the other girls said, then they all giggled.

"Has anyone heard from Josiah Stoltz?" asked Ida Mae, a tall, freckle-faced red-head a year younger than Katie.

No one had heard. "I wonder if he'll ever be back," Katie said aloud.

"He said he'd only stay with the English for about a year. It hasn't been that long since he left. He talked about being able to save enough money to buy his own land by the time he returns."

Katie missed Josiah. He had always been pleasant toward her. She had hoped he'd stick around the area longer before heading for the city, and maybe even ask her out, but he seemed upset after Emma made it clear she wasn't interested in him as a boyfriend. Since he'd been rejected earlier by her other sister, Ruth, who could blame him for being discouraged? Perhaps the older Zook girls had been too fussy.

Wayne was standing next to his male friends, but his eyes never left pretty Sadie's. Katie noted his neck turned a scarlet color whenever she talked to him. Goodness, she wondered why he didn't just ask her to be his girlfriend and get it over with. It was obvious the girl liked him, the way she paraded in front of him sometimes and giggled when he talked to her.

Katie hoped she never acted that silly around a boy. Of course, no boy had ever flirted with her. Water rose in her eyes causing them to gleam and she swallowed quickly to prevent them from spilling over. Maybe things would be different now. She wondered if her friend had been honest, saying she'd seen some boys look at her. Anyway, they could have looked and just been amused by her plumpness.

Her Mamm had taken in her dresses by nearly three whole inches, though. Jah, things were definitely improving. She didn't even crave sugar the way she had weeks before. It was actually getting easier to diet and she spent more time reading, instead of running to the pantry for comfort food every time she had time to herself. Katie was sure prayer was helping. Maybe God even cared about how much weight she lost. It seemed ridiculous since He had so many important things to worry about, but she knew God loved her and cared about her, so maybe it wasn't silly to pray about it. Whether it was true or not, she planned to continue to place it before the Lord each morning. Yah, prayer definitely helped.

Chapter Three

The family celebrated Ruth's twentieth birthday at Mary and Leroy's farm. Benches had to be brought in from the barn to handle the overflow of guests. Katie had sewn two maternity dresses for her sister, and Mary had made several sets of underwear for her expanding middle, but she had given Ruth those presents in the privacy of her bedroom earlier in the day.

After opening her gifts—mostly clothing, Ruth arranged the items on a library table in the parlor and set the birthday cards next to them. Her guests sat or stood around in small groups, discussing different subjects. The family loved any excuse to get together.

Katie was chatting with Ruth when she saw her clutch her abdomen and appeared to catch her breath. Katie asked her sister if she was in pain. "No, little sister, I just thought I felt the baby kick again. The feeling of life inside you is so amazing, I try to feel it with my hand every time the baby stirs."

"That must be so exciting. Can I feel it?"

"Place your hand here," Ruth said as she reached for Katie's right hand and placed it over her left side.

"I can't feel anything." Katie looked disappointed.

"The baby is still again. It's very faint, Katie. You'll probably have to wait until it's bigger and stronger."

"Ruthie, do you think I'll ever find a man to love me the way Jeremiah loves you?"

"Of course you will. Why would you even ask such a silly question?"

Katie sighed. "I guess 'cause no one has ever shown interest in me. Not even one tiny bit."

"You're not even eighteen yet. Give it some time. 'Mr. Right' just hasn't come along yet, is all."

"I guess so. Becky said some guys were looking at me at one of the Sings."

"Jah? See? My little *schwester*. Don't *brutz*. Pouting will give you creases in your pretty face."

Jeremiah came up from behind and reached for Ruth's hand. "Hi, Katie. Danki for making Ruthie those nice clothes.

She's going to need them pretty soon." He grinned at his wife and kissed the side of her head.

"Sure. I was happy to. Have you felt your baby move yet?"

"Nee. Every time it happens, I try to put my hand there in time, but then he stops kicking."

"He?" Katie smiled at her brother-in-law.

"Well, 'it' stops. I hate to call our baby an 'it.' You know what I mean, Katie?"

She laughed. "Ruthie thinks it's a girl and you call it a boy. Maybe she'll have twins."

"Waneta had her baby, Katie. Did you hear?" Ruth asked.

"Yah, everyone was talking about it at the Sing. I heard they named him Harley."

"He looks like Waneta already. He's so adorable. I went to see them yesterday. Did you know he weighed almost nine pounds?"

"Wow! That's a big *boppli!*"

"Jah, especially for a first," Ruth said.

Jeremiah squeezed Ruth's hand and then kissed it. "You don't have to have a big one like that, Ruthie."

She laughed and leaned her head against his chest. "I don't have much say in his size, Jeremiah, but I'll try not to gain too much weight. Waneta gained forty pounds."

Wayne's older friend, Willis, joined the group. He smiled over at Katie and nodded. "You look nice, Katie. Different, somehow."

"I've lost a lot of weight," Katie said with a touch of pride.

"Jah, that's it. You trying to look like a movie star?" He grinned at her and she felt her face flush.

"I just want smaller clothes, is all."

"So you'll save money on material?" he teased.

"Oh, jah, and thread as well," she bantered back.

"You like teaching?"

"Jah. I love it. Most of the time."

"Gut. I bet the kids love you. I bet you're easy on them."

Ruth laughed. "According to Emma, she's real tough—doesn't let them get away with anything."

"Jah, they listen—or else," Katie said, her dimples indenting her cheeks.

"My goodness," Willis said with a grin. "You look all soft and sweet. I can't imagine you with a temper."

"I reserve it for bad behavior," Katie added, enjoying the attention of the young red-haired farmer.

"Katie, we can go take a walk together if you'd like," Willis said as he pushed his straw hat back on his head, exposing some loose curls.

Katie felt her heart leap in her chest. She always thought Willis was cute. He had a carefree laugh and never seemed moody like some of the other guys. She had never even considered him as a potential beau, but the perspiration forming under her arms made her wonder if she wasn't interested in his attention. "I probably need to help with the refreshments," she said hesitantly.

"Go, Katie, there are plenty of women here to get things ready. It's a beautiful April day and you could use the fresh air. You look pale," Ruthie added.

"Okay, but I'd better get my shawl. It's still chilly."

Willis followed Katie over to the front door where she reached for her woolen shawl, which hung on a peg. He took it from her and placed it around her shoulders. Katie liked the touch of his hand on her arm as he led her out. They walked around the perimeter of the farmhouse and she commented on the red tulips which were ready to burst.

"Jah, they're beautiful. Do you like to garden, Katie?"

"Sometimes. I like to plant things, but not weed so much."

"Me, too. Planting is work, but rewarding. I love to farm. This is such a busy time at the farm, but a happy time for me. I love the smell of the fresh turned soil and the feel of the warm sun coming through my shirt when I plow. I feel I can almost reach up and touch God sometimes."

"Really?" Katie looked up at this young man, whom she had barely spoken to before. He had a poetic nature—a rarity in her community. Most Amish men she knew were pragmatic and brief in their comments. She smiled broadly and wondered if he'd try to take her hand. Instead, he stopped walking and leaned against the side of the fence railing. He folded his arms, looked out at the field, and took in a long slow breath.

"What are you thinking about, Willis?"

"Just about Him. God."

"What about Him?"

"That He's so gut. He provides everything we need."

Katie stood a couple feet from him and then took her place against the fence rail to rest. She looked up at the cumulus clouds drifting across the bluebell-colored sky and thought about his remark. "Jah, we too often forget to thank Him for all He's given us."

"And all He is. Katie, he knows every hair on your head."

"Mercy. I have a lot of them, too." They laughed softly at the same time.

"I don't know why I never noticed you before. You're the prettiest of all the Zook girls and soft as a gentle rain."

"How do you know? You've barely touched me."

"Jah, true, but I can see your delicate skin." He moved closer and reached over to touch her cheek with his forefinger. "Just as I thought. Like silk."

Katie was afraid she'd have cardiac arrest! No man—no one—had ever said such beautiful things to her. Goodness, could she be in love so quick?

"Katie," a voice came from the back door, startling her. She gave a slight gasp and turned toward the sound of her mother's call. "Come in, you two. We're going to have the cake now."

"We'll be right there," Katie responded. She wished she could spend more time alone with Willis, but it would be rude to remain outside while the festivities were taking place inside.

"So, maybe we'll go to a Sing together, Katie," Willis remarked as they headed back to the farmhouse.

"That would be ever so nice," Katie responded. "Jah, I'd like that."

"How about next week then?"

"Already?"

"Is it too soon?"

"No, no. It's fine. I'll be ready whenever you say."

"How about if I pick you up around six. If we get there too early, we can take another walk together. Maybe it will last longer next time."

Katie agreed to the time and felt her heart palpitating. Maybe he's the one.

Willis tipped his straw hat and held the door for her.

Oh, mercy. So this is what it feels like to have the attention of a man. Hallelujah!

Wayne was the first to notice his sister's cheerful disposition—merrier than usual.

"What's got you so pepped up, Katie?" he asked at supper the next night. Conversation stopped as everyone's eyes turned toward Katie.

"Nothing special. I guess 'cause it's springtime."

"You've had lots of springs before, but you don't usually go around singin' all day."

"Have I been doing that?" Katie felt heat travel up her neck.

Leroy laughed. "It sounds gut. Don't stop now."

Mary looked over at her daughter. "I think our *dochder* is noticing the menfolk and they're beginning to notice her."

"Mamm, you're embarrassing me." Katie held a paper napkin up to her face and giggled.

"Jah," Wayne added, "A certain man took notice of my sister. Right, Katie?"

"If you mean Willis Shrock, I guess so. We're going to the Sing on Sunday night."

"Katie, you never said." Her mother looked shocked.

"I was going to tell everyone. I just didn't think about it."

"Oh, like it's every day a guy asks you out," Wayne teased.

"We'll have them clambering for your sister now," Leroy said with a chuckle. "She's like the white swan. Look at her."

"Stop it." Katie meant it now. She felt like she was on display. Even though it was her family, she hated to be the center of attention.

"Now, Leroy," Mary said, her lips in a frown, "you can see our Katie's embarrassed. Let's change the subject."

"Oh, Mamm, she's so much fun to tease," Wayne said, disheartened by his mother's suggestion.

"Jah, you're right, Mary," Leroy said. "Katie, pass the potatoes, please. So, it's supposed to get into the seventies tomorrow. The ground is warming. It'll be easier to plow."

Katie handed the bowl of fresh mashed potatoes to her father and breathed a sigh of relief. She'd have to slow down on her singing. It was a dead giveaway, yet her heart still soared and she re-lived her few minutes with Willis over and over in her mind, savoring his smile and words like manna from heaven.

Chapter Four

The school children were difficult to control now that the weather had changed and they preferred playing outdoors to the board games, which were set up during the cold months. The older students practiced their German sitting under the trees during recess, but the little ones couldn't be contained. They ran around the schoolhouse perimeter, playing tag or hide and seek.

On one unseasonably warm day, Katie and Emma tried to teach outdoors, but there were too many distractions. They allowed the children an extra fifteen minutes since it was so lovely out. Then the girls went inside and placed sheets of new spelling words at each of the desks for the second and third graders and sat by their desk for a few extra moments before calling the students in for their afternoon session.

"Katie, you know I'll finish out this year with you, but then we'll need to find a replacement."

"You're pregnant!"

"No," Emma laughed. "Not yet, but I'll want to stay home with Gabe and the children."

"Did he tell you to?"

"He didn't have to. I want to stay home. It's where I belong."

"Jah. You'll probably be pregnant by then anyway."

"Not at the rate we're going."

Katie looked over at Emma, who glanced away.

"That doesn't sound gut."

"It's nothing. It's just been difficult lately to find time for each other." Emma twisted a pencil several times between her fingers, without looking up.

"Because of the work load for Gabe?"

"That and the children seem so needy."

"In what way, Emma?" Katie heard pain in her sister's words.

"Lizzy's been getting nightmares. We can't figure it out. She seemed so excited for us to marry, but she calls out almost every night and when I go into her room, she begs for her daed."

"Really? So he goes to calm her down?"

22

"Jah and then he's so tired. It's upsetting. I don't know what to do."

"Do you think she's jealous of you?"

Emma looked up, arching her brows. "Mercy, I don't know. I love her so much. I hate to think that."

"So, do you argue with Gabe?"

"Not really. It's just that…well…he doesn't seem to have time for me like he did in the very beginning."

"Maybe you're imagining it."

"Last week, he slept on the sofa because he said he had a sore throat."

"That was considerate. You don't want to get sick." Did she hear doubt in Emma's voice?

"Jah, but Lizzy was sitting on his lap last night while he read to her and I reminded him about his throat."

"And?"

"And he looked annoyed with me and then told Lizzy to get off his lap. She looked over at me like I was being mean."

"Children don't understand. She's so young. What about Mervin?"

"He's fine. He lets me hug him sometimes and he helps me with the wood. He's a gut boy. Maybe I'm too sensitive."

"I think you should talk to Gabe and see what he's thinking. It sounds like a mis-understanding more than anything."

"You're probably right, Katie. I've been edgy lately myself. Especially now, before my monthly starts."

"Tell him. Men don't understand."

"He was married before, you know. He should know about women." Emma placed the pencil in a tray on the desk and tucked loose hairs under her kapp.

"Jah. I'm more concerned about Lizzy. She seems fine with you in school."

"That's the funny part. She is, and even at home, until Gabe shows up."

"I think that's probably normal," Katie said as she reached across and patted her sister's hand. "Don't forget—she's been the queen for a while and maybe she misses her place now that you're there. How about if I take the children Saturday and give you some time alone with Gabe? We can bake cookies together or go for a picnic."

"Would you, Katie? That would be wonderful-gut. Then Gabe and I can talk."

"And maybe more?" Katie grinned at her sister.

"Now, Katie. Enough." Emma laughed and got up to call the children inside for school.

Saturday, Katie lived up to her promise and took the children back to the house after breakfast where they planned to spend time together baking. Then, since the weather was perfect for picnicking, she decided they'd head out to a local park area with a basket lunch around noon.

After tending to the animals Gabe joined Emma for coffee and fresh-baked sticky buns. They sat together at the kitchen table. "These are really gut, Emma. Even better than…"

"Say it, Gabe. It's okay."

"I'm afraid it might upset you if I talk about, you know…"

"You can't pretend you have no past. I'll be okay, really." Emma reached across the table and placed her hand over Gabe's.

"Emma, you're so understanding."

"I'm trying to be. Sometimes it's harder than others."

"In what way, honey?"

Emma broke off a piece of bun, but set it on the plate without even tasting it. "I guess what I'm trying to say is, it's hard to be the second wife, especially when the first is lost to death…at such an early age and all."

"Why should that matter?" Gabe's mouth was drawn and he looked confused.

"Gabe, surely you must understand. It's just…well…I know you loved her—"

"Jah, I did."

"Well, maybe you just wanted a mother for your children and you—"

"Emma, Emma. How can you even think such a thing. You know how much I love you. I don't like to talk about the dead, but you know things were far from perfect with Beth. We kind of went our separate ways somewhere along the line. Maybe it was the pain we went through. I don't know." Gabe put his head between his

24

hands. He was silent for a moment and then sat back and looked over at Emma.

"Darling, I married you for all the right reasons. You are everything a man could ask for. The fact that the children loved you too was a plus—a wonderful bonus, but it was my love for you that made me want you for my bride. Do you believe me?"

Emma wiped a tear away and nodded. "Jah. It helps to hear the words."

"I've purposely avoided talking a lot about the past, because I feared it might be difficult for you, besides I live in the present most of the time."

"I think that's gut, Gabe. I should, too."

"So now we have that cleared up—"

"Actually, can I talk to you about something else that's been bothering me?" Emma's heart palpitated wildly. This was not going to be easy.

"Anything."

She had his full attention now and she moved back in her chair, removed her hand from his, and pushed her mug to the side.

"It's about Lizzy."

His brows furrowed as he looked into Emma's eyes. "What about her?"

"I'm concerned. She's having so many nightmares."

"She's always had nightmares—since her mother..." Emma noticed his jaw tighten.

"But now, now that we're a family, I thought she'd get over them. And when she does wake up, she rejects me. It hurts, Gabe. I love her so much."

"I know you do, Emma. You're a wonderful mother to her. In time, she'll get over it. Right now she still depends on my being there."

"The thing is, when she's at school or even here at home, we get along real gut, until you join in."

"*Ach.* Think she's jealous of you?"

"I'm wondering that, too. I have to talk with her and let her know your relationship with her will never change."

Gabe nodded and relaxed his facial muscles. "Jah, I'll talk to her too. Maybe we should talk to her together. What do you think?"

"I like that idea."

Gabe poured more coffee and took a sip. "So now that that's cleared up, what should be do today? Anything special? Do you want to go to the shops?"

"No, I don't need anything." Emma looked down at her hands, which she had placed on her lap. She folded them together. "There is one more thing." This was harder than talking about Lizzy.

"Jah?" Gabe looked over with a puzzled expression. "You have ever so much on your mind. What is it, Emma?"

"I...I just hope you're satisfied with me."

Gabe laughed out loud. "Is that all? Of course I am. I told you, you are everything a man could ask for. You're a great cook and housekeeper and you keep me in clean clothes. A gut Amish wife."

"I meant...in our personal life." There it was out.

Gabe rose from his chair, walked over to Emma and reached for her hands. She placed them in his and stood. Then he wrapped his arms around her and kissed the side of her head before answering. "Dear Emma, have I been neglecting you? Forgive me. There's just been so much catching up to do on the farm. I've ignored it for so long. Goodness, you are a wonderful wife in that way too. I couldn't ask for more."

Then he lifted her chin and pressed his lips against hers, gently caressing her back with his other arm. Another tear rolled down Emma's cheek and touched his. He moved slightly back and opened his eyes. "Please, honey, don't cry. God has blessed me so much with you. The thought of hurting you is so painful. I love to be close to you. Come, we go now and I show you how much you mean to me."

"But the farm..."

"Everything else can wait. You are the most important person right now." He took her by her hand and headed up the stairs. Emma felt the excitement run through her whole being. When they reached their bedroom, she removed her kapp. Gabe came over to her and removed the pins from her hair and it fell loosely down her shoulders.

"My beautiful Emma. I never want to hurt you again. Forgive me."

26

Emma closed her eyes, lifting her smiling mouth to his. "You are forgiven, husband. I love you."

"And I love you."

They never left the farm that day. Their bonding was special—in mind, body, and spirit. Now to bring Lizzy and Mervin into this union and make it a true family. That was their mutual goal.

Chapter Five

Katie changed her dress three times before the Sing. "Jah, the black one makes me look thinnest," she said out loud as she hung the others up on pegs in her room. Then she used milk of magnesia under her arms to help prevent perspiration before putting on the dress and apron. She pinched her cheeks until they reddened and licked her lips to make them shiny. Willis would be along any time now, so she cleaned off her black shoes with an old towel and picked out her freshest kapp.

Her first date. How exciting! Now she'd have something to talk about when she got together with her friends. She had always felt left out of the conversation as the girls discussed the young men in their lives. She had seen Willis at the Sings with three different girl friends before, but he had never asked the same girl more than once or twice. She wondered why. Perhaps, he was just waiting for the right girl to come along and perhaps she would be it.

Her daed looked up from his newspaper and smiled. "My little *dochder* looks *lieblich* tonight."

"No one's ever called me lovely before. Danki, Daed." Katie went over to her father and kissed the top of his head. He let out a chuckle and grinned at her.

Mary looked over and smiled. "She's growing up, Leroy. Soon we'll have another wedding to plan."

"Then we'll be on *our* honeymoon, Mary." He grinned and returned his attention to his paper.

"Now, watch yourself tonight," Mary warned. "We don't know much about this young man. His family's only been here a couple years since moving from the other district."

"Don't worry about me, Mamm. I know the rules. No hand holding, definitely no hugging."

"Or kissing."

"Jah. I will keep him far away."

"Gut. We want to get to know him better. You can ask him to come by and I'll make him my special pancakes next week."

"Only if he asks me out again, Mamm. He might not like me after tonight."

Leroy folded his paper and looked up. "Goodness, why not? You are a special girl. He'd have to be *ab im kopp* not to see that."

Katie let out a giggle. "He's certainly not crazy, Daed." Katie walked over to the window to watch for his buggy. He had said six and it was almost quarter after. Still no sign of him. What if he didn't show up? What if it was a joke? Guys sometimes thought it was cool to play jokes on girls. Then she would just find someone else, is all. She gritted her teeth as she paced. Then around half past the hour, she heard wheels on the gravel drive and her heart leapt in her chest.

Willis came to the door and greeted the family. Wayne had already departed for the Sing, with plans to stop first at Sadie Yoder's. Funny, it was also her brother's first "date" tonight.

"Sorry I'm late. Had chores to finish up first."

"That's okay. I hardly noticed the time," Katie said. She noticed her mother roll her eyes. "I guess we'd better get going."

After they said good-by, Willis took her by the hand and helped her climb into the buggy, though she'd done it thousands of times without assistance. Conversation was pleasant, but sparse on the way to the Beiler's barn. The clopping of his horse matched the beat of her heart. Steady and quick.

Once they got to the barn, Katie headed over to the group of girls standing by the refreshment table while Willis took care of the horse and buggy. Priscilla stood off to the side, flirting with John.

"So I'm just waiting for Willis to come back," Katie mentioned to her friends, trying her hardest to sound nonchalant.

Becky's brows rose. "He brought you?"

"Jah. He did," Katie said proudly.

Ida Mae's mouth formed a ring. "Wow! He's taken just about everyone now. Do you like him, Katie?"

"He seems nice."

"He's a friend of my cousin," Ida Mae added. "Johnny thinks he's a girl chaser."

"Jah? So far, he's been a gentleman. Hush, I see him coming. I'm going to go sit with him."

Willis greeted her friends and then nodded toward a bench. "Let's sit over there, Katie."

Wayne was standing over in a dark corner with Sadie and she was laughing at something he had said. Wayne stood a little straighter and pulled at his suspenders, muscles exposed. Though it was chilly in the barn and most of the girls wore shawls, the young men seemed to prefer short sleeves to jackets and Katie wondered if that wasn't in order to look more masculine.

Soon the singing began and at least thirty young people were in attendance. Katie caught a couple of the other young men looking at Willis and her and she prided herself on being with such a nice looking man, though pride was not a gut quality to have. Willis had fine features and coarse red hair and was average in height. Jah, she could have some fine looking children with a man like Willis.

On the way home, Willis commented on the full moon. He pulled his buggy to the side of the road and looked up. "It's a might pretty moon, don't you think, Katie?"

She followed his eyes and let out a sigh. "It is that, Willis."

"It makes your eyes sparkle, Katie. Did you know that?"

Oh my. "Nee, I guess I didn't." Her hand trembled and she placed it between the folds of her skirt.

"Jah. They sparkle like mica or diamonds even."

"Really?" Katie noticed his head was getting closer to hers. Uh, oh. Her heart pounded and she felt weird sensations travel through her body. *Oh, my, this will never do.*

"It's getting late, Willis. My mamm and daed will be looking for me."

"Oh, okay." He returned to his original position and clucked his tongue to alert his horse, which picked up on the cue to return to the road.

"You have a fine driving horse, Willis," Katie said, attempting to break the silence.

"Jah, he is that." His eyes never left the road.

Katie slowed down her breathing and stared straight ahead. This whole thing was moving much too quickly. Surely, he wasn't going to kiss her already. Maybe he was just one of those fellows who likes to see how far he can get with a girl, and Katie meant absolutely nothing to him. He remained a gentleman, took her hand again to help her down from her seat when they pulled in, and walked her to the front door. Her father was standing behind the screen door with a lantern and stepped out to greet Willis and his daughter as they arrived.

"We was wondering if you'd be coming home about now. Your *bruder* got back already."

"It was a gut Sing, Daed. Lots of people showed up."

"Jah? Glad to hear it. *Gut nacht,* Willis."

Willis nodded to them both and headed back toward the road, after turning in the drive.

"Did my boppli have fun?" Leroy asked as they went into the kitchen where Mary greeted her.

"I did, Daed, but…"

"But?" Mary's eyes widened and brows went up.

"I don't know. I might not go out with him again."

"Did he do something wrong, Katie?" Mary asked.

"Nee. But I think he wanted to."

"You're a gut girl, Katie. If he was fresh with you, tell us." Leroy said, his voice even and stern.

"He wasn't really fresh. Just that I think he wanted to kiss me already."

"Tsk, tsk. Much too soon for romance," Mary said, shaking her head. "I'm glad my dochder has good sense and set him straight."

"He was a gentleman. He backed right off, so he didn't actually behave badly."

"Well, the thought shouldn't have been there this soon. I don't think you should see him alone again, Katie. Do you agree?" Mary asked.

"I guess, but it was ever so nice to be there with a guy. My friends seemed impressed."

"Sounds a little prideful," Leroy said firmly. "A touch of *glassenheit* would suit you better."

Katie felt tears forming. She made such an effort to avoid shedding them. What had started as such a wonderful-gut night was not ending well. "I'm sorry, Daed. I'll try to be more humble."

"Jah, that's the Amish way, Katie. Now go to bed." Her father's voice had become gentler, which only made her eyes fill faster. Katie sniffled and removed her shoes before heading to her room.

As she lay in bed, she reviewed the whole evening. When she got to the part where Willis talked about her eyes, she pretended that she had allowed him to kiss her. *Oh, my, I wonder what that would feel like. What if I had bad breath? I'm glad I used my head and not my feelings.* Eventually, she slipped into a restless sleep. At least she had had her first date and that was ever so gut.

Chapter Six

The following Friday after school, Emma took Katie home. Ruth was helping Mary hang the freshly laundered curtains in the living room. When they were done, Mary made a pot of coffee, and the four women sat together to catch up on their lives.

"So, Mamm told me about your first date, Katie. You behaved so gut. We're proud of you," Ruth said as she smiled over at her sister.

"Jah, well. He didn't actually try anything."

"But you suspected and a woman knows those things."

"Jah," Emma said, nodding. "A gut Amish woman waits for kisses. She doesn't give them out free-like."

"Did you ever kiss anyone besides Jeremiah?" Katie asked, turning to Ruth.

"I...I don't think you should ask me that," Ruth said, a blush running up her cheek.

"Oooh," Mary's brows nearly hit her kapp. "My, my. We'd better change the conversation. Ruthie, tell us how you're feeling."

"So much better. Now I'm getting excited. She kicks me a whole lot."

"She?" Mary let out a laugh. "Jeremiah calls it a 'he,' don't he?"

They all laughed and Mary poured more coffee into their mugs.

"I guess I should tell everyone now," Emma said. "I've decided to quit teaching and stay home with Gabe and the children. They need me."

"Are you expecting?" Mary asked.

"Not yet, but I need to be home more. Gabe wants me near him."

"Ah, that's sweet," Ruth said as she placed her hand on her sister's. "You seem so happy, Emma."

"Jah, we are happy. Just a few problems with Lizzy."

Mary looked up, surprise registering in her expression. "Lizzy?"

"I think she's a little put out with me living there. She's been used to having her father to herself."

"Poor baby," Mary shook her head. "Of course, it will take time, but she loves you, Emma."

"Jah, I know and when we're alone we have a wonderful-gut time. But when her daed is there, she wants him to herself. Gabe and I talked about it and we're trying to spend special time with her till she gets used to the idea of us being married. We think it would probably be a gut idea to hold off having a new boppli right away."

"Can you do that?" Mary asked. "I mean…"

"Jah, I know it won't be easy, but it might make it harder on Lizzy if we have a baby right away. It shouldn't be too long before she accepts her new life."

"I know who could replace you at school, Emma. I already talked to Becky about teaching if you leave."

"And she's interested?" Emma added sugar to her coffee and stirred it.

"Jah, she wants to teach. I knew she would. She really liked learning when we were in school together."

"She'll have to go to the board and talk to them first," Mary said.

Katie nodded. "Jah, she knows that, Mamm. When would you leave, Emma?"

"Not until after this session ends. We only have a few weeks left. I hope I don't get bored staying home."

Mary laughed. "Bored? What's that? Believe me, even without a little boppli, there is so much to do."

Emma smiled at her mother. "I know you're right. For one thing, I want to get better at baking pies."

"I'll show you how," Katie offered. "I'm super gut at making pie crusts."

"And eating them, too," Mary said, grinning at her daughter.

"Not anymore, Mamm. I hardly ever have more than one little piece of dessert. Sometimes it's really hard, but I don't want to gain my weight back."

"How much have you lost altogether," Ruth asked Katie.

"About twenty pounds. I still want to lose about twenty more."

"Nee. You'll be too skinny," Mary said, shaking her head.

"Mamm, Ruth and Emma are skinnier than me and you don't tell them to eat more."

"She's right, Mamm," Ruth added. "We're glad she's slimming down. And just because your first date wasn't so gut, maybe next time a young man will win your heart."

"I'm nervous about Sunday church service. I don't know how to act in front of Willis now."

"Just treat him like any other boy," Mary said. "Be friendly, but don't encourage him."

"What if he asks me out again? Should I go?"

"I think not," Emma said. "Next time he might really kiss you. You don't want that."

Ruth let out a giggle. "Maybe she does."

"Nee!" Katie said, glaring at Ruth. "Just 'cause you liked being kissed by guys—"

"Katie, don't talk like that. Ruth is older than you and what she did or didn't do should not concern you. She's a married woman now about to have a baby, so I think you should behave more mature."

Wow, her mother looked upset. Perhaps she should be more upset with her sister, Ruth, who lived life as an *Englisher* for several months! No telling what she did while she was away.

"Katie, I asked you something." Mary said, looking at Katie with her lips drawn down.

"I'm sorry. What did you say?"

"I asked if you'd check outside for the asparagus. We need some for supper."

"I'll go. Just let me put on some old clothes first. Where's Wayne?"

"He's with your daed. You can tell them supper will be ready in an hour or so. We're having rabbit stew."

"Sorry, Ruth," Katie said when she noticed her sister's eyes were downcast. "I didn't mean anything by it."

"It's okay. I admit I did a few things I regret, but I've asked God to forgive me and now I must forgive myself." Ruth rose and took her empty mug to the sink and washed it out, laying it on the drain board. "I must run now. Jeremiah will be home soon and I have to start the chicken."

The girls all hugged and then went their separate ways.

Once Emma got home, she started frying the chicken and put a pot of water on for rice. Gabe came in the back door with a bucket of peas to shell. "That rain last week helped push the peas along. We'll have enough to take to market if we want to."

"I'll make pea soup with some of them," Emma said.

Gabe set the bucket down and went behind Emma, surrounded her with his arms, and kissed the nape of her neck. "Hello, beautiful."

Emma twisted around to face him and returned his amour with a passionate kiss.

"Daed!" They dropped their embrace as Lizzy's voice came from across the room.

"Lizzy, I didn't hear you come in. Where's your bruder?"

"I don't know and I don't *care!*" Lizzy proclaimed loudly as she stomped out of the room.

"Missy, you get right back in here this very minute!" Gabe yelled out to her.

She walked in with a sheepish expression. "Jah?"

"Is that any way to speak to your parents?"

She stood silently, tracing a circle with one foot.

"I'm waiting for an answer." Gabe's voice was softer now, but he stood with folded arms waiting for a reply.

"I guess not, but you shouldn't be doing that."

"Kissing my wife?"

"You never did that with my real mother. It's…it's disgusting!"

Emma lowered her head to hide her amusement.

"Of course I kissed your mother."

"Never in front of me. You never kiss me like that."

Emma saw a tear working its way down the child's face. "Oh, Lizzy, of course your father wouldn't kiss you like that. You're his child."

"Jah, Liz. Kisses like that are for husbands and wives—not children. Come here." Lizzy made her way slowly to her father and he took her by the hand, went into the parlor, and sat her next to him on the sofa. Emma followed them in.

"Lizzy, Emma and I both love you very, very, much. And Mervin, too. But love for your child is very different than the love you have for a mate. You know how you love Peter the cat, who lives in the barn?"

Lizzy nodded without looking up. Her mouth trembled as she sniffed back her tears.

"Well, you love me different, right?"

"I guess."

Gabe smiled over at Emma, who had taken a seat next to the sofa. "I hope you do. So when your mamm was alive, I cared for her and loved her, but she is in Heaven now and I won't see her again for a long time. Your daed was very lonely for the love of a woman and—"

"You had me and Mervin." Her eyes focused now on his.

"Jah, and that was wonderful, but a man needs more. He needs the love of a grown woman. Someone to help him."

"I can cook."

"Lizzy, a man needs a woman not only to take care of his home. Even more than being the mother of his children. A man and woman are bonded like one in a marriage. God made us that way—to need each other. And someday, Emma and I will have another child—maybe several."

"That's okay, as long as they're girls."

Emma laughed softly and knelt beside Lizzy. "Honey, your daed will always love you and have a special place in his heart just for you. Love isn't divisible, it's—"

"What's divisible?"

"Can't be taken apart and divided like a pie. Love just keeps expanding like...like a rain puddle. More water (or love) keeps being added, so the puddle gets bigger and bigger. Your daed's love is like a big giant ocean."

"Jah," Gabe added. "My love is big enough for a whole bunch of people—hundreds maybe. Know what we mean? So I can love you and your brother, my family back in Ohio and all their kids, and still have room for Emma. Do you understand?"

"Maybe. But my other mamm, my real one, told me never to let someone kiss me on my mouth. She said it was naughty."

"That's because you are a child, Liz. She didn't mean ever."

"Then why didn't I ever see her kiss you?"

"I guess we were just in a different room the times we kissed."

"I'm never getting married. It looks so yucky."

Gabe put his arm around her shoulders and kissed the side of her head. "Someday you will not think it is yucky."

"Nee. I will never, ever get married."

"We'll see, little one. Now go put milk out for the barn cats and we'll call you when supper is ready."

As Liz started toward the kitchen door, she turned back and looked at Emma, who had stood up and was straightening her apron. "Emma, can I still call you 'Mamm' even though I was mean to you?"

"Sweet Liz. Come here and give me a hug." Lizzy went over and the two held each other silently for several moments. "You must know I love you like you came from my own body, don't you Liz?"

Liz nodded and smiled as she drew back. "I love you, too, Mamm. I'm sorry I was mean to you."

"It's okay. Let me give you some meat scraps for the cats. Come. And today I made rice pudding for desert—just the way you like it."

"With raisins and cinnamon?"

"Jah."

"Yippee!" Lizzy ran out with the plate of trimmings for the cats and Gabe drew Emma over and kissed her lightly.

"I hope we've made some progress with our little girl."

"I think so, Gabe. She'll be fine. I just have to produce daughters and not sons, I guess."

Gabe laughed and went back out to the barn to milk the cows with his son.

Chapter Seven

Katie thought about Willis dozens of times a day, picturing his bright red hair and his cute smile when he talked. Certainly what she felt couldn't be love, could it? I mean she just had one date with him. No, it was probably infatuation and the fact that he was the first boy who had ever asked her out. He had been a gentleman though, the way he helped her in and out of the buggy. And he didn't force a kiss on her, which was a gut thing. Jah, maybe she would go out with him again if he asked. Trouble was, she wouldn't even see him for a couple of weeks, not until they were together again at church meeting. There were times she wished they were allowed to have phones.

"Katie, I asked if you wanted to have apple juice," Emma's voice interrupted Katie's daydream as she was wiping down the blackboard. It was Wednesday and the children were still on recess.

"Nee." She put the eraser back on the tray and reached for her lesson book. "I'm not eating anything until supper."

"Mercy, you didn't eat any lunch. You'll get sick."

"I want to sew a new dress and I need to get my waistline down another two inches first. Shall I call the kids in yet?"

Emma looked up at the clock. "They have five more minutes."

"Oh, jah. Emma, if Willis asks me out again, do you think it would be okay?"

"That's for you to decide, Katie. Do you want to go out with him?"

"I think so. No, I know so. I like him."

"Then, why not? You said he was nice to you and polite and all."

"He was. Do you think he's nice looking?"

Emma laughed out loud. "What does it matter what I think? People probably don't think Gabe is some handsome movie star, but to me he's wonderful-gut to look at."

"Oh, he is—for an old guy."

"Old? Goodness, he's all of thirty-five!" Emma shook her head and grinned at Katie.

"That seems old to me. Oh, I'd like to stop and talk to Becky on the way home, if we have time. Do you want to ask her about taking over for you next year?"

"Jah, that's a gut idea. I talked to Gabe about it and he was pleased."

"So, you're really going to wait to have a baby?"

"We've discussed it. Lizzy seems better now since we had our talk, though. Maybe we'll just let God take care of the baby thing."

"Are you scared to have a baby?"

"No. Not too much. People do it all the time."

Katie glanced up at the clock. "Let's call the kids in. I want to finish my spelling lesson with the little ones. Lizzy is doing so well now, ain't she?"

Emma nodded. "And so is Mervin. I'm so proud of him. He's getting all *A*'s this term. I haven't told Gabe yet how gut he's doing. I want Mervin to surprise him."

"That's because of you, Emma. You are such a gut mother—I know that."

"Danki. I try. Okay, back to work."

They stopped at Becky's on the way home and she agreed to take over Emma's place at the school the following year if the board okayed her. She hugged Emma as they left. "I hope I can be as gut as you have been. My little nieces love you and they're all speaking English now ever so gut."

"They're adorable *kinder*. So easy to teach."

After Katie was dropped off, she found her father lying down on the sofa. He sat right up as she entered the door. "*Hallo, dochder*. How was school?"

"Okay," Katie answered, as she hung up her shawl. "Don't you feel gut, Daed?"

"I'm fine. Just a bit tired, I guess. Wayne's finishing up for me."

"Daed, aren't you going to see a doctor?"

"Whatever for? Can't a man get tired without everyone getting all excited?"

Mary came into the room with a basket of dry towels to be folded. "Leroy, why are you yelling?"

"Goodness gracious. I'm not yelling. Merely talking loud enough for Katie to hear me. She was after me to see the doctor. That's all you women have on your mind. Maybe you like to make doctors rich or something."

"Ach. We care is all. You look pale. I'm going to make an appointment tomorrow and that's it." Mary plunked the basket down and Katie went to help her fold the towels. They laid them on an empty chair.

Leroy rose and headed for the door, reaching for his straw head as he went. "A man can't get peace in his own house anymore. You can make the appointment, Mary, but you ain't big enough to get me there."

Mary shook her head, letting out a long sigh. "See what I have to deal with? Men!"

Katie reached for a washcloth and folded it. "I think he'll go if you talk to my brothers and they put pressure on him."

"I hope so. I've noticed he seems out of breath sometimes."

"Maybe he's just getting old."

"Jah? You think so? Maybe." Mary put the last towel in the pile and Katie reached for them and headed for the stairs. "I'll be down in a minute, Mamm. I want to change my clothes.

"Oh, I saw the Willis boy this morning at market. He asked about you, Katie."

Katie stopped and looked at her mother. "Was he selling?"

"Jah. His family always has a stand on Wednesday's. I thought you knew that."

"No, I haven't been to market at all for over a year now— ever since I began teaching."

"Of course, I'd forgotten. Anyway, he seems like a hardworking young man. If he asks you out again, you have my permission to go."

Katie's grin spread across her face. "Danki, Mamm. Maybe he will ask me again. I'll help with supper. Don't cook potatoes for me, though. They're too fattening. I'm just eating salad tonight."

"I baked raisin bread—"

"No. No bread."

"Ah well. I hope you don't get sick, Miss Katie, eating like a canary."

"I want to sew a new dress, Mamm, for my next date."

"Now don't you go gettin' all excited before you're asked, Katie."

"I won't. But Willis isn't the only available guy, you know." Katie sucked in her tummy as she passed the mirror in the hallway. Jah, she was definitely slimming down. Things were looking up for Miss Katie Zook.

Chapter Eight

"Daed, we're all concerned about you." Abram twisted his hat in his hands as he watched his father groom one of their horses. It was the first Saturday of May, warmer than normal and Leroy was working in the shaded side of the barn.

"Jah, I know." Leroy didn't look over at Abram, but instead moved to the other side of the horse and began brushing his mane with steady strokes.

"So? Don't you want to find out what's wrong?"

"There ain't nothin' wrong."

"Mamm told me about you coming in early to rest."

"True. I did." Leroy worked his way around the horse's neck avoiding his son's gaze.

"That's not like you and besides, it wasn't long ago you passed out."

"Jah, that's true, too. But I'm fine today. And I'll be fine tomorrow, God willing."

"We just want you to get checked out by a doctor. That's all. If there's nothing wrong, well..."

"Well, we pay some rich doctor to tell us I'm in great health. Is that what you want?"

"For peace of mind—"

Leroy set his brushes on a work bench and put his hands on his hips. "*Sohn*, I know you think you're helping, but I would know if I needed a doctor. I wouldn't be able to farm the way I'm doing. Ain't that true?"

"I don't know. But—"

"I'll tell you what. If I pass out again, I'll go see someone. Will that satisfy you?"

"Jah, but I don't know about Mamm. She's really worried about you."

"Your mother worries about everyone. Now she's worried about Katie because she ain't eating much. She used ta worry cause she ate *too* much. She worries about me if I want a nap. She worries about Ruthie when—"

"I see what you mean, Daed. I'll have a talk with her. But you've made me a promise, right?"

"Yeah, yeah, yeah. Now hand me that saddle. I need to get some exercise. Go tell your mother and get her off my back."

Abram patted his father on his arm and headed back to the house where Mary and Katie stood by the open kitchen window, waiting for his arrival.

"So? What did he say?" Mary asked, as Abram placed his hat on a hook. "Is he going to let me make an appointment?"

"If he passes out again, Mamm, but not until then."

"Next time, he might not come back awake." Mary plopped down on the sofa and put her head in her hands. Katie sat next to her and put her arm about her shoulders.

"Mamm, at least he agreed to go if this continues," Katie said, attempting to reassure her mother.

"What if it's his heart? Maybe he had a heart attack. Maybe he has brain cancer. You don't know, Katie. And he's so stubborn, he's willing to put us all through this, just because he's too worried about spending the money."

"I think it's more than that, Mamm," Abram said softly. "I think he's afraid they'll find something."

"Mercy. That's worse yet. See? He's worried, too. I never met such a stubborn man. He makes our old mule, Harvey, look like a follow-about puppy."

"Do you think *you* should talk to a doctor about him?" Katie asked her mother.

"They wouldn't be able to do anything, Katie, without the patient. They would want to do blood tests and things. No, we'll just have to wait and watch."

"And pray." Abram sat on the rocker across from his mother.

"I do already. Every day." Mary wiped her eyes with her apron as Katie nodded in agreement.

"So how's little Sammy's cold?" Mary asked her son.

"Better."

"Gut." Mary blew her nose in her hanky and stood up. "I'll make tea."

"Not for me, Mamm. I have to get back. I have to finish tilling. Sorry I couldn't get Daed to agree to go to the doctor."

"You tried, Sohn. Take some brownies home with you."

"No, danki. Keep them here. Fannie just baked shoofly pie this morning. Katie, you like brownies."

"I'm dieting, Abram. Can't you tell?"

"Sure, everyone sees you're gettin' skinny."

Katie giggled. "I wouldn't go that far."

"Don't lose much more, though. You'll lose your dimples." Abram reached over and pinched Katie's cheek.

After Abram left, Mary poured boiling water into her teapot. "Go tell your daed that I want him to come in and have tea with us, Katie. At least I can get him to stop working so hard."

"Jah, I'll tell him." Katie did as she was bid and then sat at the table with her mother.

"Here, I cut a brownie in half. Take it."

"No, Mamm. Please. Don't tempt me."

"It's not going to hurt if—"

"Mamm! Stop it! It's hard enough as it is!"

"What's going on here?" Leroy entered the house, removed his shoes, and looked over at his wife and daughter. "I don't like to hear angry voices in my house." He scowled as he went to the sink to wash up.

Katie burst into tears. "May I be excused? I'm sorry, Mamm. I didn't mean to yell. Honest."

"Jah, I know. Go. Go on, Katie. We'll talk later." Mary bit her lip and looked over at Leroy who was watching his daughter ascend the stairs.

"What's wrong with our dochder? She's not been like the Katie I know."

"I guess it's her age."

"Mary, she's almost eighteen. She's too old to be actin' up."

"I don't know, Leroy. I'm concerned about her. I thought she'd be happier now that the young Willis boy showed up."

"Jah, she did seem happier for awhile. She's a gut girl. Someday someone serious will come into her life. She's still young." After drying his hands, he reached for a brownie and popped it in his mouth.

"It's hard having her two sisters, both so happy and all," Mary continued.

"I guess. These brownies are extra gut, Mary. New recipe?"

45

"Nee. I just added extra chips. Do you think I should talk to Katie?"

"Do what you think best. I'm gonna take a rest. That sun's gettin' hot."

"Leroy?"

"Jah?"

"I love you."

"Danki. You know I love you, too."

"Jah. I want you around when I'm old."

"I'll do my best, honey. Let me go rest now and tonight we'll play some cards. Are you up to getting beat by your husband?"

"We'll see. Last I looked, I was a hundred fourteen points ahead."

"I'll try to even the score, tonight." Leroy leaned over and kissed Mary tenderly on her lips. "You're still my special *liebschdi.*"

Sunday during the church service, Katie made sure she sat where she could see Willis, and he could see her. He smiled at her twice and she felt her heart flutter. Of course it fluttered when any young single Amish man showed her any attention, so it probably didn't mean undying love on Katie's part.

While the women prepared the meal after the three-hour long service, Priscilla went missing. And so did John Troyer. Katie and her friends discussed their joint disappearance.

"I think they're going to announce their wedding plans soon," Ida Mae said as she stirred additional sugar into the lemonade.

"It wouldn't surprise me, not even a little bit," Becky said as she folded paper napkins and set them next to the silverware. "I'll be glad in a way."

"Too much competition?" Katie asked with a grin.

"Well, jah. That's part of it."

"What's the other part?"

"Just she makes the rest of us look plain."

"We're supposed to be *plain,* for Heaven's sake," Ida Mae said.

"You know what I mean." Becky grimaced at her friends.

"So, Miss Katie," Ida Mae said, looking over at Katie, "are you and Willis serious?"

Katie felt her face flush. "Mercy, we've only been to one Sing together. That sure doesn't make it serious."

"Are you going out again?" Ida Mae asked.

"Daresn't say. Don't look now, but he's headed over." Katie tucked in her tummy and stood a little straighter. "Hallo, Willis," she managed to greet him in her normal voice.

"Hallo, Katie—girls. I'm a might thirsty. Can I have some lemonade?"

"Of course," Ida Mae grinned and instead of pouring a glassful, handed the pitcher to Katie. "We must be off to get the salads, ain't so, Becky?"

"Oh, that's right. See you guys." The girls left Katie and Willis by themselves as they moved swiftly toward the kitchen, giggling as they went.

"So, are you going to the Sing tonight, Katie?" Willis asked as she poured lemonade into a plastic glass for him, spilling only a few drops as she did so.

"I think so. It's at the Bishop's barn, right?"

"Jah. I go past your place if you want me to pick you up."

"If it ain't too much trouble."

"I'd like to. We had fun last time, remember?"

"Jah. It was. Okay."

After setting a time, Willis returned to his group of young men and Katie walked into the kitchen where her friends were eagerly awaiting the news.

"Jah, we're going! He asked me!" Katie could no longer restrain her excitement and the three girls huddled together and giggled.

"Katie, I'm so happy for you," Ida Mae said. "He's such a cute guy."

"Girls," Ruth said as she passed by with a tray of cold cuts. "Help out. It's getting late and we're still not ready."

Katie grabbed a bowl of slaw and followed Ruth out the door. "Ruthie, I'm going on my second date tonight."

They set their dishes down and Ruth turned to hug her sister. "I'm happy if you are, Katie. See how quickly things can change?"

"Jah. I think it's because I'm not a big fat cow anymore."

"Ach. You never were, silly. A little plump is all. You're wearing a new dress aren't you? I don't remember you in that color green before."

"I made it yesterday."

"In just one day?"

"Well, Mamm cut it out for me and pinned it and I sewed it up myself. It's three inches narrower in the waist, Ruthie."

Ruth laughed. "And my waistline is six inches bigger just in the past couple weeks!"

"Jah, you look like you're expecting now. Not just fat."

"It's so much fun to be pregnant now that I feel gut. Let's check with Hannah and see if we should announce dinner."

The afternoon dragged. Katie checked the clock every half hour or so. She spent time mending, reading, walking, praying, and even singing, but it still seemed like forever before it would be time to prepare for her big date. Her parents seemed amused at her restlessness.

"Katie, you're driving me nuts. Why don't you just sit down and read a book," Wayne said as he whittled at the kitchen table. "Time won't go any faster, jumpin' around."

"I can't help it. I'm just so nervous."

"You went out with him already, so he knows you're a silly girl."

"Now, Sohn, leave your sister alone," Leroy glared over his newspaper.

"It's okay, Daed. I'm used to it. I bet not all brothers are as mean as you are," she added, frowning at Wayne. "I bet Sadie would like to know more about you and I might be the one to tell her."

"You wouldn't dare."

"Oh, no?"

Mary clucked her tongue. "You two will never grow up."

"I'm going to my room for awhile," Katie said to her family. "At least there I can find a little peace."

Katie sat on the bed and went through a book of quilt patterns. She really had no interest in quilting, but there wasn't much else to read. She certainly couldn't concentrate on reading her Bible. Bored with the pattern book, she tossed it on her dresser and laid back on her bed. Would she let him hold her hand if he tried this time? Probably better to wait a few more weeks. What if he didn't like her once he got to know her better? She'd find someone else is all. She liked the looks of Zeke Gingrich, but he seemed proud—not the kind of man she'd marry.

Finally it was time to get ready for her big date. She washed up and then brushed out her hair before twisting it into a neat bun and replacing it under her kapp. She looked at herself in the mirror over her dresser. Even her face was thinning down, thank goodness. Satisfied with her appearance, she made her way downstairs. Wayne had left already and her parents were eating leftover chicken and noodles.

"Katie, did you want anything to eat before you leave?" Mary asked.

"They'll have stuff there. I can't eat now. I'm too jumpy in my stomach."

"You don't eat enough, dochder," Leroy added as he spread butter on a piece of rye bread.

"I eat plenty, Daed. I don't get hungry like I used to."

"Jah? I guess that's gut."

"Here he comes. I'm going to go out and meet him. We'll be late if I don't."

"Have a gut time, Katie, but take your shawl. It still gets chilly in the evening."

"I will." Katie grabbed it off the hook and raced out the door. Willis stopped and climbed down to help her up. "Sorry I'm late. It's hard to get going. My daed was late milking again."

"How come?"

"He's late doing everything, Katie. That's just the way it is. So are you looking forward to tonight?" he asked as he made his way into the driver's seat of the open buggy.

"Jah. It's always fun to be with my friends."

"I don't know why I never noticed you before. You'll be the prettiest girl there." He grinned over at her as he clucked for his horse to move.

"My goodness. That's silly." Silly, maybe, but it was music to her ears.

"I mean it."

"Even prettier than Priscilla?" That might be pushing it.

"Oh, jah. In my eyes. You have such nice teeth, Katie. So straight and white, like seashells."

"I bet you never saw a seashell," Katie teased.

"I've seen lots of pictures. Okay, white like lumps of sugar. Better?"

Katie laughed. "I picture funny bumpy teeth now, all crunchy like."

His laugh permeated the carriage. "Okay, I'll just say nice white teeth and let it be so."

They road silently for a few minutes and then Katie asked him about his family.

"I'm the youngest of seven. The only one left at home. I'll probably stay on the farm since my daed needs help. We have almost three hundred acres, which is a lot for one person."

"What about if you marry?" *Goodness, did I ask that?*

"Oh, the house is big, plus there's a *dawdi haus* vacant. It won't be a problem. But that's not going to happen for a while."

"No, of course not," Katie said with a nod.

"Unless, of course..." The rest of the sentence hung unspoken, between them. Katie caught her breath and asked about his nieces and nephews.

"I have to count again in my head. My one sister-in-law just had twins. Most of my family lives on the other side of Pennsylvania, closer to the Bloomsburg area."

"I have family around there too. I wonder if they know each other."

"Probably. Amish know Amish, that's for sure and for certain."

The evening went well and Willis behaved himself, even on the trip home. So well, that Katie was slightly disappointed. It would have been nice to have him at least try to hold her hand, but maybe next time. If there was to be a next time.

As she prepared for bed, she replayed the whole evening in her mind, grinning when she recalled his comments about her teeth. She ran her finger across her freshly brushed front teeth and thanked God for how straight he had made them. Then she finished her prayers and slept, dreaming of a wedding and she was the beautiful bride.

Chapter Nine

Becky was approved to teach and so she stopped by the school to observe class several times the following week. One afternoon, after the children were dismissed, the three girls sat down to talk before heading to their homes.

Emma was excited to finish the school year so she could concentrate on her new job as wife and mother. She told Katie and Becky that Liz was much more accepting of their situation since they had their talk and that she felt she and Gabe could go ahead and start their new family.

"I'm excited for you, Emma," Katie said as she stretched her legs and removed her shoes.

"Let's go back to my place," Emma suggested. "I made fresh apple cobbler and unless Gabe's finished it up, there should be enough for us. I'll make a pot of tea and we'll just relax."

"Gut idea," Becky said.

"Uh, I have to get home, Emma. Maybe next time."

"Katie, what's so important that you can't visit your sister?" Emma looked over at Katie, her mouth drawn down.

"I just love apple cobbler is all. I don't want temptation."

"I'll cut a teeny piece or give you an apple," Emma suggested.

"Stop tempting me, Emma!" Katie's voice sounded shrill.

"Well excuse me," Emma said, exchanging glances with Becky.

"We can get together another time," Becky said softly, avoiding Katie's eyes.

"I'm sorry, *schwester*. I didn't mean to get upset with you. It's just that everyone keeps saying, 'eat this,' 'eat that,' and I'm just learning to do without."

"Jah, I guess you're right. Okay, we'll do it another day. I need to wash clothes anyway. With all the rain we've had, Gabe gets real muddy and has to change a couple times a day."

"I'm so sick of dull days," Katie said, her voice calmer now. "It's depressing sometime not to see the sunshine."

"Jah, it is," Becky agreed as she stood and stretched her arms in the air. "I hope I do a gut job teaching. You two seem to have so much control."

"Wait till the last week of school. The kids get rambunctious toward the start of summer recess." Emma picked up her notebook and two text books on her way to the door. "You'll close up, Katie?"

"Sure. I'm sorry about before. I don't know what's come over me lately. I just lose my patience over everything. I made Daed mad the other day."

"Maybe you're getting your monthly," Becky suggested.

"I missed last month and this month was hardly anything."

"Well, sometimes we just get out of sorts," Emma said.

"Jah, well, I really am upset with myself. I won't let it happen again. I'll close up in a couple minutes and then head for home." She was glad she had her own buggy today.

Once alone, Katie sat at her desk and closed her eyes. What was wrong with her? She should be happy that her life was improving. She'd had two dates and she'd lost a lot of weight. She loved being in an Amish family and living in beautiful Pennsylvania. She had a job she liked and a huge family and circle of friends. So why was she so unsettled? How come she flared up so easily? *Oh, Lord, help me to control myself. Please remind me when I start to get stressed. Danki for all You do for me and forgive me when I lose my temper.*

Katie opened her top drawer to place her scissors and ruler inside when she caught sight of half a chocolate bar. Her stomach was grumbling since she had skipped lunch. She could almost taste the chocolate melting on her tongue as she folded back the foil, exposing a large square. She broke it off and held it. "Don't do it, Katie," she said out loud. "Think of the calories." With reluctance, she re-wrapped the piece and shoved it toward the back of the drawer, 'out of sight,' and hopefully 'out of mind.'

When she got back to the house, her mother was peeling potatoes. Wayne was working with her daed in the fields.

"Do you need help, Mamm?"

"I'm fine. My world—with only four to cook for, it's simple now. Of course your brother eats for three," she said, a grin forming. "So how was your day?"

"It went well. Becky stopped by again. I think she's excited about teaching."

"I know your sister is excited about leaving. Katie, you look tired. Wanna take a nap before we eat?"

"I might. Yah, I've been tired a lot lately."

"Maybe you don't eat enough. Now don't get mad at me, but I think you're losing too much weight now, too quickly."

Katie let out a long sigh and reminded herself about her temper. "I'm fine, Mamm. Really. Everyone gets tired sometimes."

"Jah. Okay. I'll call you when supper's ready. It will be about an hour or so."

Katie hung up her teaching dress and put on an old faded one, then she lay down and closed her eyes. She placed her hands on her flattened stomach and felt movement as her grumbling, empty stomach interrupted her thoughts. It had been almost two weeks since her date with Willis. Since he lived only three miles away, she wondered why he didn't just come by. Certainly he would if he truly cared about her. She realized how little she knew about him, but of course, it was early in their relationship, if you could call it that, so it would take time for them to confide in each other. She'd ask her sisters how long it took for them to feel close enough to their boyfriends to open up and talk about personal things. She certainly didn't mean inappropriate things. Nee, that would wait for marriage, just things on their minds like problems with the brethren or the old customs versus new. Things that were interesting, but not of a personal nature.

Since the new bishop, things seemed to be loosening up slightly. He knew about Ruthie playing her violin in the privacy of her home and he wasn't disturbed at all. And the fact that the family read the Bible had been okayed. She knew some of the bishops discouraged reading the Bible. Why, she couldn't imagine. Though sometimes she read things that seemed to contradict the Ordnung. Katie knew the rules by heart, but when they seemed to conflict with other things she read, her Mamm just told her 'never mind' and wouldn't discuss it further.

As her hand rose to her cheek to attend to an itch, she felt some skin flake off under her nail. She'd always had soft skin, but now it seemed dry all the time. Maybe she'd put corn oil on it before she went to bed. Katie's mind drifted and soon she was startled by a knock on her door. "Katie, I've been calling you. It's time to eat."

"Oh, my, what time is it?" Katie sat up and looked over at her clock.

"Five fifteen. Your daed is getting grouchy. He needs to eat."

"I'll be right down. Sorry, I must have slept."

"Jah, okay. Be quick."

Katie heard her mother's shoes, tapping down the steps. After rinsing her face and washing her hands, she tucked her loose hairs under her kapp and joined the family. Nothing was said about her being late, but she guessed by her father's expression that it did not go un-noticed.

While Katie and her mother cleaned up the kitchen from supper, Mary reminded her that the family would be celebrating both Emma and Katie's birthdays Saturday afternoon since their birthdays were only three days apart. Emma was turning twenty-two and Katie was going to be eighteen.

"What time is everyone coming, Mamm?" Katie asked as she scrubbed a pot.

"I told them about two. Fannie is coming earlier to help."

"She's such a sweet sister-in-law."

"Jah. Very helpful. So's Hannah, but it's hard with a young baby and three other little ones. She looks tired lately."

"I'd go babysit more often if she wanted me to, but she always says she's fine."

"I know. I offer too, but she'll get more rest once Joseph grows up a little. He still wakes up a couple times at night to nurse."

"I can't wait for Ruthie to have her boppli. Are you excited?"

"Of course. Every new grandchild is a blessing from God. Do you have to do any work for school tonight?"

"I just have a little work left, but I'm going to bed early tonight."

Mary looked over at Katie as she hung up the dishtowel to dry. "Are you getting sick?"

"I don't think so. Just tired."

"You hardly ate any dinner, Katie. I'm beginning to worry about you. Are you upset because the Willis boy hasn't been around to see you?"

Goodness, was she? Was that her problem?

"I don't think about him that much. Not too much, anyway. I guess I just need to catch up on sleep. Last night I was restless all night. Oh, Mamm, I don't know why I'm the way I am." Katie sat down on a kitchen chair and rested her head on her hands. Mary sat across from her.

"What way? What are you saying?"

"You know—grouchy a lot and I'm ready to cry at the drop of a kapp."

Mary placed her hand over her daughter's and gave it a gentle squeeze. "Is it your time of month?"

Katie shook her head and sniffed. "That's another thing. It's not normal. I missed a whole month and I'm definitely not pregnant."

"Merciful day! I would hope not!" Mary's eyes nearly popped out of their sockets at the thought.

Katie grinned through her tears. "You don't have to worry about me doing something like that."

"Katie, I know that. My goodness, I know you are a pure young woman. But I'm concerned. I'm going to make an appointment for you to see a doctor."

"Don't do that, Mamm. Please. I just need to rest and I'll be fine. Daed's the one you should be worried about."

"I've given up trying to get him to the doctor. I can just do so much. He's still tired a lot, but at least he hasn't fainted again. Maybe he just needed to drink more water."

"Maybe so. You know I'll help on Saturday. If Willis does show up before then, can I invite him to the party?"

"Of course. Any of your friends. Right now I'm expecting about fifty people to show up, counting Emma's friends, too."

"Wow! That's a lot of work for you Mamm."

"It's not work when it's for my loved ones. People are bringing casseroles, of course, so it won't be that much work. It should be fun and we don't always celebrate so big."

Katie rose and smiled at her mother. "Thanks for listening, Mamm. If I ever figure out what's wrong with me, I'll let you know."

"You'll be fine, dochder. Just a difficult time is all. Sometimes it's over nothing that we fret. Please come to me anytime to talk."

Mary stood up and surrounded her daughter with her arms. "Now, go rest and tomorrow will be a new day."

Katie dragged herself upstairs and fell asleep within minutes. It was only seven o'clock, but she slept through until morning. Surely, that was what she needed.

Chapter Ten

Emma tucked the quilt under Lizzy's mattress and pulled her shades. "Did you want me to read you some more from <u>The Wind in the Willows</u>?"

"I don't think so."

"Really?" Emma looked over at her step-daughter, whose light brown hair trailed over the colorful daisy quilt. She looked almost lost in her bed stacked with two feather pillows. "Don't you like it?"

"I do ever so much, but I just want you to talk to me tonight. Maybe talk to me about when you were little."

Emma sat on the edge of the bed and stroked Lizzy's hair, smoothing it against the pillow. "Let's see. I'll try to remember when I was your age. Seven. Hmm. Okay, I think I remember that Christmas. That was the year my mamm made me a special doll."

"The one on your bed? With the funny hair?"

Emma laughed. "Jah, that's the one. The only one that survived. Katie adopted all my other ones."

"What's adopted?"

"Took over. People say that when a child has no mamm or daed and a new family takes the child as their own."

"Like me and Mervin? You adopted us?"

"Well, maybe that's right. I have become your mother, haven't I?"

"In my heart, I think you are now. I don't 'member my real mamm as much anymore. Do you think she'll be mad at me?"

"No, no, Lizzy. Your mamm would want you to be happy. She was a gut person and only wanted what's best for you and your brother."

"Would she be mad at daed for kissing you and marrying you?"

"No child. Of course not. Dead people have their own place in heaven. They are so happy up there; they wouldn't be upset if we found some happiness for ourselves down here on earth."

"Huh." Lizzy's forehead creased as she soaked in all this information. "Then I can love you a whole bunch and she won't cry?"

"Nee. No tears in heaven, Lizzy."

"That's gut. So what's your dolly's name?"

"April. I just liked the name."

"It doesn't sound Amish, but it's pretty, like the month."

"I think so. When I opened the box I was so excited. Aunt Ruthie tried to grab it, but I held on so tight. You can't believe it." Emma smiled at the memory. "So what do you think? Was that a nice story?"

"Aunt Ruthie was naughty to try to take it."

"I think she just liked teasing me. She was a gut sister. Still is."

"She's going to have a baby, isn't she? I could tell 'cause she's getting real fat all in the front."

"Jah, she's so excited. So is Uncle Jeremiah."

"Are you feeling bad 'cause you don't have a baby growing in you?"

"No, not really. My time will come. Would you like another brother or sister, Lizzy?"

"Just a sister."

"Well, we can't pick what we want. The gut Lord picks for us." Emma smoothed the pillow case and straightened Lizzy's hair, hoping to prevent snarls.

"I guess."

"You'd love a little brother, I'm sure. Boys can be cute, too," Emma said with a smile.

"How do you get it in your tummy anyway?"

"Oh, it's getting late, Lizzy, we'll have to talk more another time."

"That's always what Daed says too. I'll ask Mammi. She'll tell me."

"We'll tell you, honey, just not tonight. I'm real tired and it really is getting late."

"I'm glad it's gonna be Friday tomorrow. Are you excited about the party?"

"Of course. It will be wonderful-gut. Are you excited?"

"Jah. I love my new family. You're lucky to have so many nice people in your family. Everyone is gut to me."

"Well they love you Lizzy. We all do."

"Danki. Some night if I can't sleep can I take April to bed with me?"

"Sure. Do you want her tonight?"

Lizzy's grin spread across her face. "Jah, I think I won't sleep gut tonight unless she comes with me."

"Then I will get her for you." As Emma headed out the door, Gabe came up the stairs and headed to Lizzy's room to say good night. He stopped first and kissed Emma lightly on her mouth as she went past him. "I'll be right back, Gabe. Lizzy's going to sleep with my doll tonight."

"Goodness, she must have been a very gut girl to get your doll."

"Oh, it's not for keeps," Emma grinned. "Just on loan."

After Liz settled down, Mervin worked on a wood carving of a hawk for awhile and then went to his room for the night, leaving Gabe and Emma by themselves as they read by a kerosene lamp. Emma snuggled close to Gabe on their sofa and closed her book. She prepared him for Lizzy's questioning and they discussed how they would answer. Then Gabe lifted her chin and kissed her, first gently and then with sweet passion. "So we have our little girl's permission to have more family?" His mouth turned up and he raised an eyebrow.

"Jah, looks that way." Emma put her hand behind his head and drew his lips back to hers.

"Maybe we should go upstairs, jah?" Gabe asked softly.

"I think it would be wise."

Gabe checked the doors and turned off most of the lighting, reserving the final lamp for their ascent. Emma smiled as she followed behind. Jah, it would be nice to have her own boppli. Really, really nice.

Saturday started out with a flurry as Mary rolled out dough for her famous lemon sponge pies. She prepared six shells, figuring Hannah's five cherry pies and her mother's apple pies, which would probably number four, would be sufficient for the pie line. Emma and Lizzy were bringing a large sheet cake.

Wayne and Leroy had their breakfast and went out to tend to the animals. It had rained during the night leaving behind a low mist, which made it difficult to see the hills beyond the barn. Mary looked out the kitchen window as she washed the bowls from her baking. Pennsylvania was lovely this time of year. Life was bursting forth in its radiant color and as the mist rose, the grasses glistened from the earlier sprinkling. Of course in Mary's mind, no place could be prettier than this, her own piece of land. She had never left Pennsylvania and it never entered her mind to do so.

Katie came down several minutes after the men left and washed her hands. "What do you need me to do, Mamm?"

Mary looked over, noticing her daughter's pale face. "You need to eat first, Katie, then you can cut up celery for the potato salad."

"I'm not hungry yet. I'll get the celery."

"You always come down ready to eat—"

"Mamm, please. Don't start." Katie looked over with a deep frown.

"Jah, okay. Do the celery."

They worked side by side in silence. Mary noted Katie's hand shook slightly.

"You okay, dochder?"

Katie let out a long sigh, filled with frustration. "I wish people didn't keep asking me things like that. I'm fine. I'm tired is all."

"Did you have trouble sleeping? Was your room too cool?"

Katie shook her head, her mouth firm. "How much celery should I cut?"

"The whole bunch. What we don't use in potato salad I'll use with cut-up chicken. I'll need more eggs when you have a chance to check."

"I'll go now," Katie remarked as she set the knife aside and headed toward the kitchen door.

"You can wait until—"

"No. I need some air!" Katie snapped as she reached for her shawl in case it was cool and then took the egg basket from the shelf.

"With that attitude, young lady, you can stay in the barn to cool off!" How much should a mother put up with, she wondered. Katie's short fuse was beginning to grate on her own nerves. She'd always been such a pleasant girl. What could be wrong? She shook her head and went back to her baking.

60

The pies sent out a familiar aroma as they cooked. The house always took on the scents of good Pennsylvania Dutch cooking, passed down from generation to generation. Mary was known for her lemon sponge pies.

When Katie returned with a couple dozen fresh eggs several minutes later, she placed them on the counter and came over to her mother. "Mamm, I'm sorry I was fresh. It won't happen again."

"Jah well. It better not, young lady. I'm ever so tired of it."

"Will you stop being mad at me, Mamm? It's a special day."

Mary put her dishtowel down and turned to face her daughter. "You're right and anger is not of God. Come give your mamm a hug and we'll put our upset behind us."

Katie and her mother hugged and Katie wiped her eyes. "I guess I'll make some oatmeal. Do you want any?"

"I already ate with your daed and Wayne. You go ahead. I'm gonna take a break for a while since the pies are in the oven. Even with my special shoes to make me straighter, I still get tired quick." Mary sat at the table and sorted through her recipe cards.

"What was it like to have polio, Mamm?" Katie asked as she stirred the oats into the simmering water.

"Not fun, Katie," Mary said, removing her recipe card for raisin cookies that Wayne had requested. "It was bad. I was so sick, but I'm ever so blessed not to be more of a cripple than I am."

"Mamm, don't call yourself crippled. You only have a limp and even that's better now."

"Jah, I know. Your daed tells me that, too. When I was young though, I thought everyone looked at me feeling so sorry for me. I didn't like that."

"No kids would like to be pitied. But look at Daed. He certainly liked the way you looked and I bet he was the most sought after man in the bunch."

Mary laughed. "He was that all right. What a charmer. Oh, my. Well, I'll be back in a few minutes. You can hard boil the eggs when you're done, Katie. Oh, keep an eye on the pies. Hannah should be here soon and Fannie, too. The cookies will have to wait."

"I'll watch for the family. When's Ruth coming?"

"She wasn't sure. Sometime before noon, though. Emma, too."

Mary pulled herself up the stairs to her bedroom. Jah, the polio was a bad thing, but look how God had blessed her with her wonderful family. "Thank you, God," she said as she removed her shoes and rested on her familiar bed.

The day went well. They ended up with over fifty people, including the children, but with everyone pitching in with the food preparation and clean-up, it went smoothly. Katie was disappointed she had not heard from Willis and wondered if he'd ask her to the next night's Sing. If not, she was determined not to be upset. Easier said, than done, she thought to herself.

By eight o'clock everyone had left and Katie finished putting the last of the dishes away while her parents sat with her brother discussing the party. Katie's stomach rumbled and she decided to have a glass of milk before going to bed. She was more exhausted than she realized and began to feel chilly though it was quite warm in the kitchen. When she was done, she took hold of her shawl and cuddled up on the couch next to her mother. "It was fun, jah?" Mary asked her.

"It was wonderful-gut. Danki, everyone, I really loved it."

"So now you're a big grown-up eighteen-year-old woman," Wayne said with a twinkle in his eye. "So what are you going to do about snaring a husband?"

"Mercy, what a thing to ask her," Mary remarked, clucking her tongue.

"What about Willis?" Wayne continued, ignoring his mother. "Think you can hook him?"

"Is he a fish that I need to use a hook?" Katie asked with a grin.

"Might be the only way you get someone."

"Now, now. Stop your teasing, Wayne. I've heard enough," Leroy said, frowning at his son. "When the time is right, our Katie will become a bride. She has plenty of time to find Mr. Right, jah Katie?"

"Absolutely. I'm not in a hurry."

"You're still too big around the middle," Wayne remarked as he reached for a handful of peanuts setting in a bowl by his chair.

Mary shook her finger at her son. "You are being mean, Wayne. Besides, it ain't true anymore. Our Katie is slim as can be now."

"Sohn, I want you to go to your room and say prayers to be nicer." Leroy's mouth was drawn taut after he spoke.

"I just like to tease her, Daed, is all. Okay, Katie, you look pretty gut now. Don't be mad."

"Upstairs. Now." Leroy pointed to the staircase and Wayne sighed as he stood to obey his father.

Katie blinked rapidly to hold back her imminent tears. "Jah, I know I'm still not skinny like my sisters, but I'm trying."

Mary shook her head. "Too hard, Katie. I don't like you eating so poor-like. You're losing too quick."

"I'm okay, Mamm. Soon I'll be just the right weight and then I'll eat a little more sometimes."

"I don't know why girls want to be so skinny anyway," Leroy said, looking over his rimmed glasses. "Girls should look like girls. Not like boys with kapps on."

"Jah, you're right, Leroy. They worry far more than they should."

"Can I go upstairs to work on my mending?" Katie asked, still choking back her tears.

"Sure, if that's what you want to do, Katie," Mary said, a frown forming on her face. "We had such a gut day, jah? And now your bruder had to spoil things. He's to be punished, Leroy."

"Jah. I agree. Tomorrow I'll figure out his punishment. I'm too tired tonight."

Katie leaned over and kissed her father on the top of his head. "Don't be too hard on Wayne. He just likes to tease is all."

"Not hurtful stuff, though, Katie. He has to learn. I'll figure something out and a gut talk will be part of it."

Katie smiled. "That's torture to my bruder. He hates lectures."

Leroy chuckled. "Then I'll make it specially long."

When Katie finished preparing for bed, she said her prayers and then rested her arms across her abdomen. She felt pain running through her lower area and wondered if her monthly would soon start. She was already two weeks late again. She probably should see a doctor. Heaven knows, she wanted to one day have lots of babies, so if there was anything wrong, now was the time to take care of it. Jah, she'd tell her mother to go ahead and make an appointment. Maybe give it another week first, though. She hated to have her parents pay bills on her account and perhaps everything would turn out just fine.

Not only did the pain keep her awake, but she was restless as well. Probably overtired from such a busy day. She thought about Emma, just turning twenty-two and already with a family. Marrying a widower with two young children was a brave thing to do, but then Gabe was a really nice man and obviously adored Emma. God must have brought her into Gabe's life to be a gut wife and a mamm to his two children.

Then Katie pictured Ruth and Jeremiah. How excited they seemed to be waiting for their first child. Jeremiah was always patting her tummy. Most of the men kind of looked the other way, but he was so proud of her. What would it be? Ruthie thought it was a girl, but Jeremiah referred to the baby as a boy. Oh, well, one of them would be right.

Then she thought about Willis. She knew so little about him really. He was a nice person, but didn't open up much. Of course, neither did she. Their time together was pleasant enough, but certainly not what you'd call exhilarating. Lacked sparkle. Still he was available and showed interest. A possibility. Then Josiah's wide grin and hearty laugh came to her mind and she smiled thinking about his cheerful disposition and the fun they had together. She missed him and wondered how much longer he'd stay away trying to earn enough money to buy his own land.

With so many brothers to divide the acreage with, he would need the additional funds if he wanted to remain farming. She could never see him leave his farm animals. Funny, he bored both Ruth and Emma with his talk about his livestock, but she found it interesting. Well, sort of. She found everything about him interesting. Jah, she'd be happy when he returned and she knew he'd be pleased to find her so much thinner, if he noticed her at all.

Chapter Eleven

Josiah heard the buzzer go off which meant closing time at the factory. He didn't think he'd get so tired working as an assembler when he took the job. He'd just been pleased to find something that paid as well as it did. The guy who gave him the aptitude test said he showed remarkable mechanical ability, especially since he came untrained. It meant they started him at a slightly higher wage than the average worker. His Amish roots kept him from being prideful, though he admitted to being pleased with his ability. Jay had gotten him the interview, but had dropped out of the factory himself. Wally left, too. Josiah was pretty sure they'd been fired. He had no idea why, though they weren't the least ambitious. They used to drive in together, so he had to take public transportation now, but since the trolley went right by the apartment, it was simple to get to work.

He cleaned up somewhat before heading home and one of the other assemblers, a guy by the name of Monk, asked if he wanted to go for a few beers.

"Not tonight, but thanks anyway." Monk was a gabber and kept him out till one in the morning once. It had taken Josiah all that time to get the horrible tasting beer down anyway.

"I'll catch you next week, buddy," Monk said as he headed out the swinging door to the parking lot.

Josiah got bored staying home every night in his small apartment, so when Jay and Wally asked him to go to a movie with them, he agreed, though he hated spending even five dollars for a ticket, when it could go into his account for his future home.

As the guys headed over to the theatre complex, Jay mentioned there would be girls meeting them there. "We'll spot them outside the theatre. I met them last night at a club in town. They're hot."

"Yeah? How many are coming?" Wally asked.

"I told them there'd be three of us," Jay said, grinning.

"How did you know I'd come along?" Josiah asked.

"If you didn't, I'd find someone else. You need to get out more. You're gonna end up a recluse or something weird."

"Like that uni-bomber guy – a real screwball," Wally added.

"I'm usually too tired at night. Besides, I read a lot."

"I've seen the junk you read," Jay said with a sneer. "All history stuff. I had enough of that garbage in school."

"I like reading about the early days."

"Probably 'cause you live like them Pilgrims," Wally said, causing Jay to laugh.

"Maybe so." Josiah ignored their digs as much as possible. Sometimes it got to him, but he did need to get out once in a while. Aside from Monk, the men he worked with were either married or had their own friends. Their values just weren't the same as his anyway. Of course, neither were his room mates.

Sure enough, when they arrived, three girls were standing by the movie posters waiting for them. They looked wild to Josiah. Their clothes were suggestive and one girl had bright red hair with spike shoes to match. She was introduced as Scarlet, which seemed appropriate given her choice of hair dye. The girl on her right was Sandy and she was so thin, it was difficult to be sure of her sex. She wore braces, which seemed incongruous to her worldly attire. Her blond hair had streaks of green. She looked like she couldn't be more than fifteen. Josiah had trouble not staring and Wally poked him once and winked.

"So what's your name?" the third girl, a dark-haired girl, and the most normal of the three, asked Josiah. He told her and she didn't laugh, which pleased him somewhat. Usually when he gave his biblical name, he received ridicule or other signs of amusement.

"And you're?"

"Rita. It's not really, but I saw an old movie once with an actress by that name and I liked it."

"What's your real name?" asked Josiah.

"Barbara, after my grandmother. I hate it."

"It's not so bad."

"Thanks. You're pretty cute. What movie are we going to?" she asked as the other four headed toward the cashier's booth.

"I'm not sure. I don't even know what's playing, so I don't care which one. I'll let someone else decide."

"I only go to *R* movies," she added, snapping a wad of gum in her mouth.

"Sometimes they're pretty violent," Josiah said as he walked beside her on the way to join the others.

"Here," said Wally, "I'll treat tonight. Theatre number five. See you two there. I'm gonna get popcorn for everyone."

"Thanks, Wally. I appreciate it," Josiah said as he handed the second ticket to Rita.

"Oh, I saw this one already. Lots of killing stuff. You'll like it." She tossed her jet black hair over her shoulders and walked ahead of Josiah.

It was totally dark in the theatre and it took a couple minutes for Josiah's eyes to adjust. When he was able to see, he led Rita toward the middle of the theatre. There were very few patrons seated and his friends hadn't arrived yet.

"I don't wanna sit this close. Let's sit in the back," she said, turning toward the stairs leading to the top row. Josiah followed and took the seat next to her by the aisle. She continued to snap her gum and hummed along with the music, which was the background to a preview. "I saw this one, too. It was pretty crummy," she said.

"I'll be sure not to go then," Josiah said, wishing he had remained home.

Soon his friends arrived and took the seats directly in front of them. Once the feature film began, they settled down to watch. About half way through, after at least six car chases and five brutal murders, there was an embarrassing love scene. Josiah turned slightly away from the screen and tried to think of something else. He couldn't believe Rita seemed to be enjoying it and showed no signs of being self-conscious. Then he felt her hand on his knee and he literally jumped out of his seat. She gaped and laughed. "You're so funny, Josiah. I swear, hasn't any girl ever touched your leg before?"

"Uh, I don't believe so. That's not something we do in my group of friends."

"What are you? A bunch of monks?"

"We're Amish."

"I heard about them once. You act like you're from another planet and don't even have cars, right?"

"Right." It was difficult to hear her now with the victim on the screen being tossed out of the twentieth floor window, screaming as he soared through the air.

She kept her hands to herself after that. When they left the theatre, she went over to her girlfriends and whispered to them. They all turned to stare at him and grinned.

Josiah feigned a headache and left his friends for home. The whole evening had been a disaster. This was not a world he was familiar with or wanted to be part of. How much longer could he hold out before returning to his people?

Chapter Twelve

Before the preaching service began in Adam Stoltz' barn, Katie and her friends, Becky and Ida Mae, along with two other girls, gathered around the side of the barn and chatted about their week.

"Did Willis ask you out again, Katie?" Ida Mae asked.

"Not yet, but he just got here. I saw him talking to Wayne and John-boot."

"He'll probably ask you to the Sing," Becky said. "You'll go with him, won't you?"

"Probably. There's no one else right now, anyway."

"Priscilla told me she and John are getting married," Martha, a short brunette, who was a year younger than Katie, remarked.

"That's no surprise. They've been smooching behind the barn already this morning," Ida Mae reported.

"Disgusting." "Jah, terrible bad." "I'll never act like that." The girls all nodded in agreement, scowling at the horrible prospect.

"I see Willis now, Katie, he's still talking to the guys."

Katie pulled in her stomach and improved her posture, but avoided looking his way.

"Guess what my brother told me?" Martha asked her friends. Without waiting for a response, she continued. "Josiah Stoltz may be coming home. While he was gone his older brother came back from Ohio with his wife and three boppli. It's gonna be ever so tight in that farmhouse, what with his other brothers."

"When's he coming?" Katie asked trying to sound indifferent.

"No one knows for sure. You like him too, Katie?" Martha asked with a grin.

"Just as a friend."

"Come on girls, time for service," Ruth called over from the driveway. "And Katie, go tell the boys to come in now."

Katie's heart pounded as she made her way over to the group of boys, who were now standing behind a row of blooming lilac bushes and didn't hear her approach. She caught one of the young men speaking her name. She stood still, eavesdropping, though she knew it wasn't the proper thing to do.

"Jah, I guess Priscilla's out of the competition," she heard Willis remark.

"Thought you were hung up on Weighty Katie, anyway," one of the others said. They laughed and without waiting for his response, Katie turned and ran back to the others, her heart pounding and the ache in her heart turning her stomach into knots. It was true. She was still just a fat girl. It was all a farce—Willis being interested in her. He probably wanted to joke about her and amuse his friends. She would never, ever speak to him again. Oh, she wanted to crawl into a hole and never leave. Life was so brutal. Even losing twenty-five pounds didn't help that much. She was fat and that was all there was to it. When she arrived at the door to the barn, Ruth stared at her. "Katie, whatever is wrong? You look sick."

"I am. I have to go home. Please, Ruthie, take me home."

"I...I will, but I should get Mamm first. Are you gonna faint?"

"I don't know. I might. Things are swirling funny-like. Oh, Ruthie."

Ruth supported Katie with her arms as Jeremiah appeared behind her.

"What is it, Ruth? What's wrong with Katie?"

"She's sick, Jeremiah. Go tell Mamm."

"No, please don't cause a scene, Ruthie. I'll be okay. Just let me go home and go to bed please."

"We'll both take her, Ruth. Wait here while I get the buggy." Jeremiah walked swiftly toward the parked buggies.

"Mamm will have to know, Katie. I'll stay with you till the family gets home."

Katie couldn't control the tears any longer. She put her arms around her sister and wept. Fortunately, the young men had not broken up their conversation yet, so she was able to leave without further embarrassment. She cried all the way home as she sat in the back seat with her sister, who caressed her back with one hand and held Katie's hand with the other. "Hush, Katie, you'll be fine." Then she whispered, "Is it your time?"

Katie nodded as she continued to cry into her hankie. "I'm so late, Ruth. Things are so messed up and maybe I'll never have a baby like you and—"

"Nee. Stop that. Sometimes girls just get off schedule. You're a fine healthy Amish girl. We know how to do babies, jah?" she added, trying to lighten the mood.

"I don't want Jeremiah to hear."

"No, we're talking soft enough. He's watching the road real careful—not paying any attention to us."

"I'm sick of being ugly and fat." Katie started sobbing again.

"Mercy, you've slimmed down so much, *Oma* thinks you'll blow away."

Katie let a smile peek through her tears. "Oma always thinks that."

"Jah, but it's true. Look how skinny you are now."

"Don't Ruth. I know you're trying to help me but I know the truth. I see myself in the mirror and besides…"

"Jah? What?"

"Never mind. Willis won't be around again. He took me out…for a joke."

"A joke? What kind of joke, Katie?" Ruth raised her brows.

"I have a nickname. Surely you've heard it. Apparently everyone knows it. 'Weighty-Katie.' I heard it with my own ears."

"I never, ever heard you called that and if I did I'd have to punch them in the face!"

Katie dropped her hankie to stare at Ruth. "Really? Seriously? You'd punch some one? You?" In spite of herself, Katie let out a giggle as she envisioned soft, sweet, Ruth defending Katie's honor with a clenched fist.

"Here we are girls. I'll leave you off right by the door while I put the horse around back." Jeremiah stopped the buggy and waited while Ruth helped Katie down and they headed for the house.

Katie made her way to the sofa and sat bent over. She was extremely pale.

"I'll put on some tea water, unless you'd rather go right to bed."

"No. I feel like I'm gonna kutz."

"Oh, mercy. I'll get a wash bucket. Isn't there one in the storage room?"

"Jah, behind the potatoes. Hurry." Katie tore off her kapp and clutched her stomach. Ruth arrived just in time, as her sister began to retch. She doubled up as she emptied her stomach, and then continued with dry heaves. When she finally finished, she lay back on the sofa and closed her eyes. Her skin was white and pasty.

Ruth reached for Katie's forehead and felt for a fever. "Poor Katie. At least you don't have a fever. Let me get a washcloth so you can freshen your face." Ruth removed the bucket, dumped it into the toilet, and cleaned it out in the tub. She nearly vomited herself from the sight and odor. Morning sickness had been such a difficult time and this was a vivid reminder. When she returned with a fresh cloth, she heard Jeremiah come up the walkway.

He came in but backed away quickly when he saw his sister-in-law's condition and heard she had just vomited. "I'll be outside with the animals, girls. I'm no help in here I'm afraid."

"Jah, go Jeremiah. I'll take care of Katie."

After he left, Ruth asked Katie if perhaps she had eaten something that disagreed with her.

"I didn't even eat this morning," Katie answered weakly.

"Oh, well that is a problem. You need to eat breakfast."

"Jah, jah. I know. Most important meal of the day. Mamm always says that."

"It's true, though. You know that."

"Ruthie, I know you mean well, but I feel too horrible to talk about it. I'm gonna go lie down and try to sleep. You can go back to the service with Jeremiah. I'll be all right now. There's nothing left in me to *kutz*."

"Are you sure? I don't mind missing one Sunday. I'm afraid to leave you alone. What if—"

"Ruthie, I'm a big girl now. Too big," she added bitterly.

"Hush. It simply isn't true. You're nearly the size of Emma now. No one would call you fat."

"I can see."

"Well, apparently not so gut. I'll go, but I'm going to talk to Mamm about you missing periods. That's not right. Maybe you need medication."

"I'll go see a doctor about that. I just wanted to wait a little longer."

"Katie, I'm worried about you. Please don't wait any longer to get help."

"Okay." Katie touched Ruth's hand with hers. "Danki. I love you, Ruthie, and I don't want you to worry."

"Do you want me to help you upstairs? Should I make a pot of tea for you first?"

"No. I don't want anything in my stomach yet. I'd just throw up again. I can go up by myself."

"All right then. We'll head back. I'll try not to get Mamm upset when I tell her, but you have to promise to see the doctor."

"I promise. Now go before you miss anything more and tell Mamm not to rush home. I'm gonna sleep now."

After Ruth left, Katie pulled herself up the stairs by the railing and nearly collapsed on her bed. *Weighty Katie. Weighty Katie.*

Mirrors don't lie. Wayne doesn't lie. The boys don't lie. It doesn't matter that the tape measure kept reducing the size of her waist; she was still fat and would always be fat—unless she reduced the amount she ate even more. That was the answer. No breakfast, a banana for lunch, and half portions for dinner. She could do it. She *had* to.

Chapter Thirteen

Two nights later, Josiah came home from work and showered. As he dressed in fresh jeans, a knock broke his thoughts. "Jah?"

"It's me. Jay."

"Door's unlocked."

Jay shoved the door open and held out a piece of pizza. "Here. We had it left over."

"Thanks." Josiah reached for the lukewarm piece and placed it on an old Rolling Stones magazine, which he had glanced at once.

"You're done work. Why don't you come out with Wally and me tonight? We're going to a club in town."

"I'll pass. Maybe next time."

"You gotta get out more, man. You'll die of boredom. Okay, we won't take you to any more movies. That was dumb, but relax a little."

"I'm pretty tired, but maybe I'll go for a while. There's nothing left in the refrigerator. Do they serve food?"

"Burgers and stuff. It's cheap."

"I guess I'll grab something to eat there and then head home. Is it in the neighborhood?"

"Yeah. On the corner of 14th and Center. The place with the flashing green lights. Come on. Wally's waiting."

Josiah smoothed down his hair and reached for his wallet. The three walked five blocks and turned down Center to 14th Street, a seedy section of town. There were several scantily dressed girls in their late teens standing in the front with a couple of older men, laughing and speaking to each other, conversation sprinkled with curse words. Josiah heard the Lord's name used several times and it wasn't in prayer, but he tried to ignore it as he went through the glass door and followed his friends to a round wooden table with curved benches on two sides. At this point, he wished he'd gone to the hot dog stand instead.

"How 'bout a beer, Stoltz?" Wally asked, as a heavily made-up woman with shorts and a tight T-shirt came over for their order.

"Ginger ale and a cheeseburger, please," he answered, addressing the waitress. She smirked and looked over at the other two.

"Your usual?"

"Yeah. A pitcher of Smithy and two shots of whiskey."

"Got it." She took off and Josiah looked around at the rest of the crowd. Some of the people were already intoxicated and the smell of stale beer mixed with cigarette smoke reached his nostrils. And people from the city found the barn odors obnoxious. At least it was normal animal scent. Not like this filth. Why had he consented to come?

"I met a girl earlier who's coming by in a while with two friends," Wally said, proudly.

"Bet they aren't as great as the girls I showed up with," Jay countered.

"Better. What do you say, Stoltz? Are you up for it?" Wally looked over with a grin.

"I don't know. Depends."

"Sugar's a hot number. I bet her friends will be too."

Josiah's eyes wandered to a couple in the next booth who were lighting up hand-rolled cigarettes.

"I probably won't stay. I wanna write my girl back home."

"Yeah? You have a girl?" Jay asked. "You never mentioned that before. Got a picture of her?"

"No. We don't believe in pictures."

"No kidding. Is she a dog?"

Josiah bristled at the implication. "I don't want to talk about it."

"Hey, man, you're testy. So, she won't know what you do while you're here. Have some fun. Loosen up, Dude."

"Jah. I'm loose, but I still wanna leave early."

The waitress set down the drinks. "Your burger will be out in a few minutes, honey," she told Josiah, and moved on to another table. He took his straw and swirled the ginger ale around, removing some of the fizz. Then he took a sip.

"There you are. Wally, right?" A girl with dyed hair the color of Josiah's favorite lilac bush, stood at the table. Josiah turned away when she leaned over exposing way too much flesh. "Who's your cute friend?"

Wally laughed and moved over to make space for the three girls, who were standing next to the table, glancing about as they waited for an invitation to join them.

"You mean me?" Jay asked with a smile. "I'm Jay."

"No, this guy," Sugar responded, pointing to Josiah.

"That's Stoltz."

"Yeah? Is that your real name?" she asked Josiah. He gave his full name and watched as her crayoned brows hit her bangs. "For real? Are you one of those weirdoes from Dutch country who doesn't believe in phones and stuff?"

"I'm Amish, if that's what you mean. I'm not a weirdo, though, just a regular guy."

"Oh, you sound so cute," her friend Tina said as she squeezed next to him. "Say something else like that. I love it."

Josiah felt his blood pressure rising. He didn't appreciate the attention, especially from this girl. He tried not to look at her, since she, too, could become a temptation. After all he was a young man and his hormones were just as strong as his English friends. "So your name is Tina?"

"Yeah, and our other friend," she said pointing to the third girl who was drumming her hand on the table on the other side, looking for the waitress. "That's Misty."

"Hey." Misty paused her tapping long enough to lift one finger in a weak gesture.

"Hey." Josiah returned the greeting and took a sip of his drink.

"So, you promised me some grass," Tina said, turning to Wally.

"I have something way better, but it'll cost you."

"I have money." There was some bickering back and forth before Tina opened her purse and pulled out cash. The exchange was made – right in the open.

So it was true. His English friends were selling drugs. He suspected as much when he noticed neither of them had jobs now and yet they spent money like candy and had the newest fanciest cell phones and computers made. The huge flat screen television must have cost close to a thousand dollars, if not more. So now what?

76

"Josiah, I'm talking to you," Tina said, interrupting his thoughts. "I asked what you're drinking. Looks like vodka."

Wally and Jay glanced at each other and snickered.

"Ginger ale," Josiah answered.

"You're kidding, right?" Misty asked as she pulled her skimpy shirt closer to her waist. Her exposed skin drew his eyes briefly, but he turned back to his glass.

"I gotta go. You can have the burger when it comes," Josiah said quickly, looking for his wallet. He dropped a five dollar bill on the table and pushed his way past Tina and headed for the door. He could hear laughter coming from the group, but he didn't care one bit. He just knew he needed fresh air and distance from this bunch of losers. They may think he's weird, but he knew better. It was time to move on, money or not. He'd skip writing home and just take a bus. He didn't like to leave without giving his employer notice, but his boss had just laid off three good workers due to a slump in business, so Josiah suspected he was next on the list anyway.

When he got back to the apartment he sat on the edge of the bed. Maybe he should contact the police. But they were friends, well, sort of. They started out that way.

Josiah opened the drawer next to the bed and took out his money. It was neatly folded by value of the bills and he kept it in an envelope. He counted it out. Only a little over four thousand dollars. He needed more than that to purchase enough land to support a family. With the building contractors offering big bucks for land, the price of acreage had gone as high as the moon.

But this wasn't good. He had just wanted a roof over his head and the chance to make enough money. He had hoped he could leave at the end of the summer. But there was no way he could stay on now that he knew the truth about them.

It was already May and his mind drifted back to his farmhouse in Lancaster County. He missed the scent of the fresh turned soil—even the animal odors of the barn were part of who he was. Part of his heritage. He would always farm, even if it was only one acre and he had to work full-time in Lancaster to meet expenses. He needed land to survive. His dream was to one day marry a good Amish girl and raise a flock of children in the way of the People. Honest, hard-working, family people. The Zook girls had held his heart for a while. Jah, Ruthie and Emma were every man's dream of the perfect women. But they were both married now and he was happy for them. In truth, while attracted to each of them, he had never really been in love with either of them. The sad fact was, he'd never experienced love with any girl. Not yet, anyway. Then there was Katie. A sweet girl, really. A little over-weight, but that didn't trouble him. She had an adorable smile and lovely skin. He could hear her laughter and it pleased him. He smiled at the memory. He should have written to her. He missed her.

Josiah pulled out his duffle bag and stuffed it with his belongings. Then he left a note for Wally and Jay along with a fifty dollar bill to cover expenses and headed to the bus depot. With a little luck, he'd find a bus still headed for Lancaster tonight, and if not, well, he'd sleep at the depot.

Once he got outside, he took a long deep breath. Yeah, the stink of the city would remain in his memory forever, but he knew where he belonged and it wasn't here. Nee, he was an Amish man and would be so until his last day on earth.

"Katie!" Emma's voice penetrated Katie's consciousness and she looked up. The students looked up when they heard Emma's voice elevated and turned their attention to their teachers.

"Sorry, you said something?"

"Jah, I did. Two times! The little ones are waiting for their story time. It's your turn, remember?"

"Oh, jah. I was day-dreaming." Katie forced a smile and turned to her students who were studying her with quizzical expressions. "So we shall go on with our book."

Katie reached for Winnie the Pooh and turned to the page where they had left off the day before.

Lizzy's hand went in the air fervently. "Do you want help reading it, Aunt Katie?"

"No fair," her friend, Esse, in the next seat proclaimed. "I like to read, too."

"Kinder, I'll do the reading, but danki for the offer. You will all have your chance later to read for the group." Katie blinked several times at the dancing words and she felt light-headed. Then she noticed everything was becoming dark.

"Katie," Emma's voice was closer now. "Are you okay?"

"I...I don't know."

The children were silent as they watched.

"Lizzy, go get water for Aunt Katie. Hurry." Emma moved her sister to a chair and told her to place her head down between her knees. Katie complied, but her complexion was ghost-like and her breathing shallow.

"Now take slow, but deep breaths."

Lizzy returned with a glass of water, which Katie sipped between breaths. The black dots began to dissipate and she felt more confident she would not pass out.

"Any better?" Emma asked, concern written on her face.

"A little bit."

"Did you eat this morning?" Emma whispered in her sister's ear.

Katie shook her head. "I had a little juice is all."

"No wonder you nearly fainted." Emma turned to the class. "Don't stare. Open your books and do your next lesson. Miss Katie will be just fine." The children obeyed and Katie could hear the turning of pages and scraping of chair legs as normality returned to the classroom.

Emma handed her a banana she had brought for her own lunch and filled the water glass again. As Katie took small bites of the fruit, Emma leaned in and whispered again. "You are going to the doctor's. After the service Sunday, Ruth told me what happened. You have everyone concerned, Katie. You must take better care of yourself."

"I just want to be pretty and thin like you and Ruthie. I want what you have—a husband and a family. Is that so wrong?"

"Come outside with me. We need to talk." Emma turned back to the class. "Miss Katie needs some fresh air. We're going outside for a couple minutes, but we will hear everything that goes on here, so we expect gut behavior. Okay?"

"Jah, Miss Emma," a chorus of voices said together.

Once outside, the girls sat on the steps. Emma took her sister's hand. "Katie, you will have what we have some day. You are younger. You know that. Why are you so worried it won't happen to you? Look how Willis—"

"Don't talk about Willis." Katie put her head down and tears began to flow profusely. "He thinks I'm a fat pig and he only took me to the Sings as a joke."

"Katie! Don't be silly! He wouldn't do that. You're not a joke."

"Oh no? Did you know I had a nickname? 'Weighty Katie'? How would you like to be called that?"

Emma's brows shot up. "I don't believe it!"

"I heard it with my own ears. Now you see why I don't want to eat much. I have to get thin. I can't go on being laughed at."

"This is too much. Does Wayne know about your nickname?"

"Probably. He always makes fun of me."

"Mamm said Daed was making him do extra work and he's not allowed to ride his bike for a week. He's not been a gut bruder to you and I'm going to have a talk with him, too."

"That's not the point, Emma. Maybe he was trying to do me a favor. I need to face the truth."

"The truth, whether you believe it or not, is that you are perfectly fine just the way you are. Everyone is different. We are given different skills and looks and God knew what he was doing when he made each of us. Jah, you gain easy, but you look nice, Katie, not too skinny like some girls. Not all guys want broomsticks for wives. So maybe Willis isn't the right one for you and if he did see you as a joke, then you are way better off with him out of your life. Here blow your nose. I brought tissues out." Emma passed several fresh tissues over to Katie, who wiped her eyes and then blew her nose several times.

"One thing else, Emma. I'm nearly three weeks late with my monthly."

Emma's jaw dropped open. "Oh, Katie, you're not—"

Katie laughed through her tears. "In a family way? Goodness, no."

"I didn't think so. Not my Katie, but I had to ask."

"It's okay. I don't know what's wrong, but I am a little worried. I want boppli so bad some day."

"Does Mamm know?"

Katie shook her head. "She wants me to see the doctor. I told her I had problems."

"Today, Katie. You need to go *today*. I will stop at the house on the way home with you and make sure Mamm knows what's happened."

"I guess you're right. I feel so weak and dizzy so much now and I cry a lot."

"That's not like our Katie. You've always been so happy and fun-like."

"I want to feel happy again, Emma. I'm tired of...of being *tired*."

"Jah, well. I'd be tired, too, if I didn't eat. That has to stop. Look your skin is loose on your arm." Emma added as she pushed Katie's sleeve up. "You're losing too fast and your skin doesn't have time to catch up."

"Oh no. That's even worse." The tears flowed again and Emma passed over more tissues.

"It's not ever so bad as that, Katie. I'm kinda teasing you, but I just want you to be normal again and eat, even if it means plumping up a tiny, tiny bit."

Katie nodded in agreement. "I sure could use a piece of Mamm's peach cobbler she made yesterday."

"When we get back to the house, I'll cut you a piece myself and pour you some fresh milk. We have to get you back to being Katie—a smaller Katie, but still Katie."

Laughter and loud talk reached their ears from the classroom. "You stay here till you feel gut again and I'll go handle the class. Soon it will be recess and you can rest more."

"Danki for caring so much, Emma." Katie smiled weakly at her sister.

"Oh, you have no idea how many people love you, little schwester."

After school was dismissed, Emma and Katie headed home. Daed waved to them from the field where he and Wayne were working, and they walked into the kitchen where their mother was cutting up beef for stew. She looked over at them. "So what do we owe the honor of having our Emma come by today?"

"Hi, Mamm. Can we have tea together first?"

"Jah, of course. You look serious. Is anything wrong?"

"We'll talk over tea," Emma said as she gave her mother a kiss on the cheek.

Katie went to the sink and took a fresh cloth, soaked it in water, and held it to her forehead. Emma and her mother exchanged glances. Then Emma asked about the peach cobbler and Mary got out three plates. She cut two regular size pieces and a small one, preparing to hand it to Katie.

"I'll take that one, Mamm," Emma said reaching for it. "Katie hasn't eaten all day and she needs a bigger piece."

"Katie, you should eat something nourishing first. I have fresh rye bread and some ham. I'll make you a sandwich. Then you can have the sugary stuff."

"I don't think I could eat a whole sandwich. Maybe just one piece of bread and one slice of ham. Thin."

"That's gut. Better than nothing." Mary cut a slice of fresh bread and reached in the refrigerator for the ham. She put a plate with the slice of ham and piece of bread in front of her daughter as Emma placed three teacups on the table and added spoons.

After a few moments of silence while they ate, Mary turned to her daughters. "So what is this all about that you'd keep your Gabe waiting for your homecoming?"

"It's about Katie. She nearly fainted again today at school. Mamm she has mixed up problems with her monthlies, and look at her. She's so pale and she cries a lot."

Katie nodded as a tear trickled down her cheek.

"Jah, jah. I know. We have to take her to the doctor. Right, Katie?"

"I guess. I don't want to go, but I know I can't go on like this."

"Then tomorrow, Emma will handle things alone at school and Daed and I will take you to the clinic. Okay?"

Katie agreed. "This cobbler sure tastes gut, Mamm. I've really missed your cooking."

Mary laughed and pushed her chair next to Katie's. Then she reached over and Katie shifted into her arms and got her well-needed Mamma hug. Emma smiled and wiped her eyes.

At supper, Katie took slightly larger portions than she had in the past and savored every mouthful as the tender carrots and potatoes met her taste buds. Tomorrow she'd find out what was wrong and if it meant having surgery, so be it. All she wanted was to feel gut again.

Chapter Fourteen

Dr. Nichols had taken care of Katie before when her knee became infected after falling down the stairs, but that had been five years ago. He looked just the same to her. He was a stocky man in his late fifties with a wart on his chin. It used to fascinate her when she was real young as she'd watch it move when he talked. His untidy brown hair met his white coat on the collar, but he used a pleasant after-shave lotion and she liked his personality. Always sunny and friendly. The way she used to feel.

"So this has been going on how long?" He peered over his glasses as he went over her chart.

"I guess a few months, but I feel worse all the time."

"Hmm."

Katie watched as he read over the notes the nurse had taken. "Your height is good at five feet plus four and half inches. You've lost a lot of weight I see. Nearly thirty pounds."

"Jah." Katie looked down at her hands.

"Was that through choice?"

She nodded. Mary looked over at the doctor. "She did it too fast, Dr. Nichols. Much too fast."

He looked at Katie. "So you went on an approved diet?"

"I just stopped eating so much. I used to pig out."

He let out a chuckle. "Sometimes I do, too, Katie, but you're young and still maturing. I see here that you missed a period, had a light one, and now you're more than three weeks late. Is that correct?"

"Jah." Katie's eyes filled up and she nudged her mother for tissues.

"And this started about the same time as your diet?"

"I'm not sure. I've been eating weird-like for a while."

"Okay. Hop up on the examining table and we'll take a look."

Katie was dressed in a gown for the exam, but it was made to fit any size, so she wrapped it tightly around herself and followed his orders. Her heart beat wildly as he used the stethoscope and checked her breathing and her heart. After looking at her eyes, ears, mouth, everything visible, he asked her to lie down. When he pressed her lower abdomen, she let out a moan. He looked over at her. "Hurts?"

"Jah."

He found a few other sensitive areas and then left the room while she dressed. Mary's mouth twitched and she twisted her kapp ribbon till it nearly snapped off.

Katie sat down next to her mother after dressing. The doctor knocked and came back into the room with her chart.

"Well, young lady, I think I know what's causing your problems, but to be certain, we need to run some tests. I'm going to set up lab work. We'll check your electrolytes and protein and also your thyroid function. We'll get you back to normal as quickly as possible."

"Then you don't think I'm dying from cancer?" Katie asked wide-eyed.

"Oh, merciful day," Mary said under her breath.

Dr. Nichols stopped writing and looked at Katie. "No, honey, I don't think anything like that is going on, but if it is, we'll find out and take care of it, okay?"

"What do you think, Doctor?" Mary asked.

"I'm pretty sure your daughter has an eating disorder, but I can't assume something like this. After I get the results of the tests, I'll have you back in my office and we'll go over everything. In the meantime," he turned to look at Katie, "I want you to eat as normally as you can. Don't start eating in bulk. Your stomach won't handle that. Just increase the amount of intake slowly. Take your time eating and if you're stressed out, wait until you calm down before you eat a meal. You can eat several small meals a day. Drink lots of water. Easy on desserts. Let's see. Oh, keep a journal and if you have any unusual pain or vomiting, write it down. Also stay away from weighing yourself. I don't want you concerned about your weight right now. Understand?"

"Jah. Will I be able to have babies?"

"Well, I don't see why not. I'll set up an appointment with our female gynecologist if we need to check it out, Katie. Your problems could be linked to your eating disorder, if that's what we have here, so I'll hold off for now." He turned his head to Mary.

"Any questions, Mrs. Zook?"

She shook her head. "I guess not. How soon will you have the results?"

"We'll know in a couple days. Make an appointment as you leave for Friday afternoon."

"Oh, that's the last day of school and I'm a teacher. Can I wait?"

"A couple more days won't matter. Sure, come in the following Monday then. If you start fainting frequently or vomit more than once a day, please call the office and ask to speak to my nurse. If necessary, I can admit you to the hospital and start IV's. We don't want you dehydrated and right now your dry skin shows me you need to drink more water. Get down eight glasses a day, Katie. It's important."

"Jah, I will." Katie forced a smile and then stood and headed for the door.

"Go to the lab at the end of the hall and they'll take care of you. Nice to see you, Mrs. Zook. How's that hard working husband of yours?" They started walking together down the hall. "He hasn't been in for a check-up in years."

"Oh, he's another one, Doctor. But it was hard enough getting my Katie here. Leroy would be impossible."

"Is he having problems?"

"Jah, talk about fainting, he passed out in the field and wouldn't come to see you. He's ever so stubborn."

"Keep trying to get him in. Problems are much easier to solve if you catch them early."

"That's what I told him, right Katie?"

"She did, Dr. Nichols. He seems awful tired a lot too."

"Well, I'm afraid I can't diagnose Leroy from our conversation. Please work on him. He should be checked out." Then he handed Katie's chart to the nurse and entered another examination room.

After the lab work was completed, Katie and her mother headed home. "Looks like it's gonna make wet," Mary remarked as dark clouds formed overhead.

"Daed said he thought it would. Mamm, I'm so glad he doesn't think I'll die yet."

"Dochder, why would you keep that thought to yourself?"

86

"I didn't want you to worry about me, I guess."

Mary shook her head. "I am worried about you, but I never thought you had cancer."

"The pain gets real bad sometimes and when he pushed on my tummy, I thought I'd scream."

"Poor Katie. I had no idea. You have to tell me when things are so bad."

"From now on I will. I promise. I just hope I don't gain all my weight back now that I have to eat more."

"It's what you eat, Katie, as well as how much."

"I just have to stay away from a lot of bread."

"And desserts."

"And potatoes."

"Oh, my, that doesn't leave much for my little girl."

Katie grinned at her mother. "To feel gut again, I'd eat cotton balls."

They laughed as they turned the horse toward their drive. As they got to the farmhouse, a clap of thunder sounded and the rains began, but Katie felt encouraged in her heart. She might just live to have her dozen little boppli.

Chapter Fifteen

On the last day of school, knowing the children would be too excited to do any work, Emma and Katie decided to have a party instead. They brought balloons and party games including "Pin the Tail on the Donkey" and Mary made strawberry ice cream with fresh berries from the garden. It was a wonderful day and Ruth came by to help out with the games. Katie felt stronger already from eating more appropriately, but she stayed in the shade as much as she could, fearing too much sun might make her faint again. She had not vomited since her appointment with the doctor, though she had felt faint several times.

Emma and Ruth were relieved to hear the doctor thought it was something that would not require surgery or even long-term treatment. While some of the younger children played hide-and-seek, the older students sat under a tree playing checkers and chess.

The Zook girls spread an old quilt on the ground and luxuriated in the perfect May day, warm yet tempered with a gentle breeze. Ruth propped herself against a large maple and hummed a song from the *Ausbund*. Her sisters joined in. When they finished, Ruth pushed her kapp slightly off her head. "I wish I could let my hair loose."

"I bet you looked pretty with it down," Katie said.

"Jeremiah likes to brush it for me at night. It's not as long as it used to be, you know."

"Jah, you cut it in Philadelphia, right?" Emma asked.

"Not a terrible amount, but it's easier to wash when it's not to your waist."

"Did that Darrel guy like your hair?" Katie asked.

Ruth laughed. "I guess he did."

"Did he tell you he loved you?" Katie pursued.

"Nee. We never got that far, but he hinted he liked me a whole lot."

"And you let him kiss you." Katie cocked her head to the side, waiting for an answer.

"Katie," Emma said sternly, "you know better than to ask Ruthie a question like that."

"Well, I know she did. She almost admitted it."

"It's okay. Jah, I let him kiss me, Katie, but I discouraged it, too."

"How?"

"The first time he kissed me, it was New Year's Eve and it was much too much of a kiss."

"Like a marriage kiss?"

"Close enough that I was not happy. I made it clear to him I wasn't an English girl who could just be taken advantage of."

Emma looked up from the clover she'd been stroking. "Did he listen?"

"He had no choice. I can be tough when I want to be."

The girls laughed, but Katie continued her interrogation. "Did you like it, Ruthie? Tell us the truth."

"I don't lie, Katie. You know that. Jah, I liked it. Maybe a little too much. Sometimes it scared me to think about it, but in my heart I never stopped loving Jeremiah."

Emma looked down at the clover and added softly, "You might have ended up with Darrel and become fancy if I'd gotten Jeremiah instead of you. Do you ever wish that had happened?"

"No. Never. I like Darrel, but I would not have been happy in his world. It seems kind of phony next to the plain life. Emma, you don't still think about Jeremiah, do you?"

"Mercy, no. I love Gabe with all my heart. He's a wonderful-gut husband."

"Are you trying to have a family yet?" Katie asked.

"If it happens, it happens. We would be ever so happy if it did, of course."

"And Lizzy and Mervin? Would they be happy?" Katie continued.

"Jah, but we've been given orders by Lizzy to produce only sisters for her."

Ruth laughed. "That is not easy to do."

Lizzy came running over with a burst balloon. "Mamm, look what Merv did to my balloon! He broke it on purpose."

"Oh, Lizzy, that was naughty. Get yourself another and send him over to me."

She ran off and did as she was told. Mervin came over for his lecture. Then he ran off to play softball with the other older boys.

"He's usually so gut with her, but sometimes he can't help himself," Emma said with a smile.

"Boys will be boys." Ruth turned to her side and tried to get up. Now that she was in her last trimester, it was sometimes difficult to manage.

"Oh, I bet you'll be happy to have your baby," Katie said. "Still think it's gonna be a girl?"

"I think I'm having triplets," Ruth said as she finally stood up and straightened her apron.

"Maybe just a twenty-pounder," Emma said, grinning at her sister.

"We should check the clock and see if it's time to start clean-up. Some of the parents will be coming along soon to collect the children," Katie said.

"I have my watch on," Ruth said as she checked her wrist. "Jah, almost time. Did they finish up the punch we made?"

"I think all the food is gone," Katie remarked.

"I know they finished up the ice cream. That went so fast, it was like the speed of a hummingbird wing," Emma said. Then she stood and called her students for clean-up.

They heard the wheels of several buggies heading down the lane and the kids began cheering. Summer was beginning and hearts were light at the thought of warm days and some time to themselves. Of course, there was always work to be done, but once chores were out of the way, the fun began. Tree climbing, fishing in the streams, swimming in the water hole, and picnics. Lots of picnics.

Hugs and kisses were exchanged between teachers and students. Spirits were high.

After the last student was picked up and only Lizzy and Merv were left, Ruth departed and Emma and Katie finished packing up the materials until the following session.

"It seems strange I'm done teaching now," Emma said, a hint of sorrow in her voice.

"You'll miss it a little, won't you?" Katie asked.

"I think so, but maybe by then…"

90

"Jah, I hope so." Katie grinned at her sister.

As they left in separate buggies, Katie watched Emma make the turn toward her new home.

Monday, once the test results were in, Katie would know if that could be her some day. Would she know the love of a gut Amish man and be able to have a baby by him and live in their own home together? In her heart she believed it would happen, though in her mind, she still worried. She said a prayer to God.

For her appointment on Monday, Katie wore a new dress—one that didn't hang on her the way the others did. Even though the last time she weighed herself she weighed only one hundred and fifteen pounds, she still believed she was fat. No, she *knew* she was fat. As soon as she felt normal again, she'd cut way back on her food portions. If she took it slower, she'd be just fine. Maybe she had done things too drastically, but now she was more educated.

Mary and Katie sat in the same seats in the doctor's office, but this time it was not necessary for Katie to get into an ugly hospital gown. They waited about ten minutes before Dr. Nichols appeared. He shook their hands and went around to his desk, Katie's file in hand. He smiled and looked over at Katie. "So young lady, how are you feeling today? You actually look better already."

"I feel gut. Better than last week."

"Jah, cause I made her eat," Mary added.

"And that's going better? No more vomiting?"

"No. I still get a wee faint sometimes, but I sit right down and drink water."

"Good. I've gone over your results and they were as I expected. How is the abdominal pain, Katie?"

"That's getting ever so much better."

He smiled at her choice of words and nodded. "I'm going to give you some literature about eating disorders and a nutritionist will talk to you when I'm done and help you plan your meals. I'm glad your mother came along so she can help you stay on track."

Mary nodded. "Jah, I'll keep a close eye on her, you can believe that."

"Do you still think you need to lose weight?" he asked Katie, studying her expression.

"Uh, maybe just a little."

"Well, I have good news for you. You do not need to lose even an ounce more. You actually weigh under the desired weight for your height and bone mass. Sometimes what happens with young ladies like yourself, you're pressured by society—"

"Oh, but we aren't like the English. We don't—"

"I realize that, Katie, but even in your society, I'm sure some of your people put too much emphasis on the outward appearance and cause young women to diet when it isn't at all necessary. Granted, when you started your dieting, it was a good thing. It should have been done under my supervision however, but you were too heavy for your size. That's behind you, though. You need to re-think your situation."

"Doctor, is this a serious problem?" Mary asked, her brows creased.

"It can be. I believe we've caught this in time, but I may suggest counseling for Katie if she is unable to overcome her distorted self-image."

"Distorted? What do you mean?" Katie's heart beat faster. Maybe this was serious.

"Katie, some girls become so concerned with their weight, they only see themselves in a negative light. Do I make myself clear?"

"Um. I think so. But I know I'm still too fat."

"That simply isn't factual." The doctor tented his hands together. "Katie, would you like to talk to someone about all your feelings? There is a young woman connected with the clinic who has treated girls with your problem and she's been very successful."

Katie's mouth dropped open and she turned to her mother. "Mamm, what do you think? Am I a little *ab im kopp?"*

Dr. Nichols looked from Katie to her mother.

"She means a little off in the head—crazy-like," she explained. The doctor laughed.

"No, Katie, you're not in the least bit 'crazy,' but sometimes we need to talk things out with a third party to find out what causes our behavior—especially negative behavior."

"I think I want to wait before I talk to a stranger," Katie said, looking down as she twisted her hands in her skirt. "I don't like talking to Englishers about my secrets."

"I understand. Maybe you can find someone in your family, like an aunt or even a grandmother, whom you would feel free to discuss this with. The only problem I see, is that perhaps your People, the Plain People, aren't aware of this disorder."

"Oh, jah, I bet they know. They can be pretty smart, that's for sure and for certain."

The doctor smiled tenderly at Katie. "I'm always here for you, Katie, if you want to discuss things with me."

Katie looked up and smiled back. "Dank…Thank you. I know."

After the doctor left the room, he sent in the nutritionist and they went through food choices and discussed a balanced approach to eating. She left them with several pamphlets which gave more information.

As they returned home, Mary looked over at her daughter. "So, what do you think? You feel better after you heard everything?"

"In a way."

"Jah? Just in a way?"

"Well, I still think I need to lose—"

"Katie! Didn't you hear a word the doctor said? You think he lied to you?"

"Nee. Not lied exactly…"

"Well, what, exactly?"

"I don't know, Mamm. I just *feel* fat."

"Katie, Katie. Maybe you should see the counselor. You are too thin, my dear dochder. I'm going to keep a close eye on you and if I see you cutting back anymore, I will make the appointment for you myself. Do you understand?"

Katie glanced at her mother's expression, and she looked ever so serious.

"Okay, I'll do what you all want me to do, but if I start gaining weight, well…"

"You are *sehr* stubborn. Took after your daed, you did."

They pulled up to the drive and Mary let out a long sigh. "Oh, I heard from my friend, Maizy, that Josiah has returned home."

Katie's ears perked up. "Ach, I hoped he might."

"Oh jah? You like him?"

"As a friend, Mamm, as a friend."

Katie let her mother off at the front of the house and took the buggy to the back. Inside she was glowing! *Jah, more than a friend, Mamm, Much more.*

Chapter Sixteen

The Sunday preaching service was scheduled to be held at the Zook's barn. Their house was too small to handle everyone comfortably, but in July it was safe to set-up in the barn. If it rained, they were protected. For the last several days, Leroy, Wayne, and his older brothers, Mark and Abram, had spent time sweeping the loose hay into piles and neatening up the large open area for benches and tables. It was a lot of extra work, but it didn't happen often, so no one complained. Wayne started to once, but the look on his father settled him down before he actually expressed his thoughts on the subject.

Katie was in the herb garden on the Saturday before the big event when she heard a horse trotting down the lane toward the farm. Looking up, she realized it was Josiah. Oh, mercy, she had on her oldest dress and kapp. Her hair was spilling out and her apron had a rip. Of all times.

Josiah stopped his mare several feet from the herb garden and called out to her. "Hallo, Miss Katie. What are you up to?"

She stood as tall as she could and sucked in her dwindling stomach. Her hand went automatically to her hair and she tried futilely to push her wandering tresses under her kapp.

"Just picking some parsley to dry. It's gut to see you again. How was your time away?"

Josiah ambled over and stood with his arms folded. "Ach. How should I say it? Interesting, I guess. Jah, I learned a lot about the other world. Too much, maybe. Goodness, you've changed something fierce. I guess you're all grown up now."

"I just turned eighteen," she said with a smile forming on her lips. "I'm thinner, too."

"Oh, jah. That's probably it. You look real gut, Katie. Pretty."

Goodness, her heart must have done a somersault the way she felt.

"Are you living at home?" she asked.

"For now, but we're real crowded. There are twelve of us in the house now, so I'm thinking about buying a small place myself."

"You made a lot of money then," she said, questioning with her eyes.

"Nee. Not as much as I wanted, but I had to leave."

"Jah?" She grinned coyly. "Police trying to take you away?"

Josiah laughed and she listened to his wonderful deep happy sound and felt so glad to be near him again.

"I can tell you a lot of stories, Katie, but now I came to give a hand to your daed. I heard you're having the service here Sunday and right now I have no job."

"What will you do for money?" she asked as they both started walking toward the barn. Katie held her basket filled with parsley on her arm. She hoped he wouldn't notice the stain on her apron.

"I saved some, but I want to use that for a down payment on land or a small farm. I can get a job in construction for a while. I heard about the Kapp group needing an extra man for the summer. By fall, I hope to have my own place, even if I have only a couple acres to farm and no house on it. Daed offered to help me and he'll supply me with some livestock to get started."

"Jah. I bet you missed your cows," Katie said. They stopped by the entranceway to the barn. She could hear her brothers speaking in the old dialect and she could smell the scent of the hay.

"I missed Miss Katie even more than my cows," he said with a crooked grin.

"Oh, jah? Then how come you never wrote?"

"I was gonna write, but then I came home instead. I'm ever so sorry I didn't Katie. Would you have written back, if I had?"

Katie cocked her head to the side. "Maybe. You'll never know now."

Wayne came through the open barn doors with a wheelbarrow full of manure for the fields. "Hey, Josiah, I heard you were back." He stopped, dropped the handles, and reached for Josiah's outstretched hand. "Wilkum back."

"Danki. I sure missed the smell of a barn."

"Jah, I know what you mean," Wayne said with a grin.

"I'm here to lend a hand. Is your daed inside?"

"Jah, we can use the help. When's dinner, Katie. I'm starving."

"Mamm's almost finished. Pot pie. I'm sure you could use a gut meal, Josiah."

"Jah, always ready to help out there."

"Ring the bell when it's ready," Wayne reminded Katie.

"I will. I have to get this parsley in for Mamm. See everyone soon."

She had a spring to her step as she headed back to the kitchen. *So, he was gonna write and he thinks I'm pretty. Willis is done. Yah, he lost out, that's for sure.*

Dinner went quickly. Josiah stayed to join the family and was very polite, but it seemed to Katie that he avoided looking at her. She felt slightly let down, but as she helped her mother clean up the kitchen, he and Wayne sat in the parlor and played checkers. When clean-up was done, Katie laid aside the dishtowel, removed her work apron, and went over to the card table where the men were just finishing up a game. Josiah looked up and smiled.

"Your bruder is too gut. He wins me every time. Any hints, Katie?"

"Not really. He always beats me too."

"You won once, Katie, when you were five."

"Ha. Ha."

"Lost again," Josiah said with false exasperation. "So I go for a walk instead. How 'bout you, Katie? Want to check out the barn and see what you think?"

"I could use some cool air. It's mighty hot in the kitchen tonight. Summer days can be draining, I'm thinking."

"Jah. There's a breeze stirring up. Let's walk."

"Next time, I'll play with my eyes closed," Wayne said as he grinned, setting up for a new game.

"You may have to, for me to stand a chance," Josiah said.

As they headed toward the door Leroy came in to refill his water glass. "Don't be a stranger, Josiah."

"No, Preacher Zook, I hope to see you often."

When they got outside, Katie looked up into the sky. It was still sunny, but the temperature was falling as the winds shifted.

"We need rain," Josiah remarked as he shifted his gaze to the fast moving formation of storm clouds coming in from the west. "Looks like we may be in for some tonight."

"It might cool things off," Katie said. "Ach, I love it when it makes wet in the summer. Smells so gut."

"Jah, me too." They walked over to a bench and sat down.

"So tell me why you left so soon," Katie suggested.

"It was the way people live. The Englishers. I don't like it." He broke a piece of hay that had fallen on the ground when they were cleaning up, and put it between his teeth.

"Ruthie said she met nice fancy people while she was in Philadelphia."

"You can be sure she did, but I was staying with some guys I met who were into all kinds of stuff."

"Stuff? Like what?"

"You don't even want to know Katie. Like drugs." He tossed the stalk of hay to the ground and meshed his fingers together as he leaned forward.

"That's stupid."

"Jah, it is. They were gettin' involved in selling it."

"Did you work with them in the factory?"

Josiah leaned back on the bench and stuck his thumbs under his suspenders. "At first we worked together, but I guess, once they got into drugs, they quit their jobs at the factory. Actually, I think they were fired, but they wouldn't talk about it. I knew the one guy pretty well. He used to live in Lancaster and I worked one winter on a construction job with him. He changed though. Once, I thought he was a pretty nice guy, but not anymore. I don't like his life-style."

"They could go to jail for selling drugs, couldn't they?" Katie asked, wide-eyed.

"Oh jah. For sure, but so far they haven't been caught."

"I'm glad you didn't stay, Josiah. You might have taken some and gotten into trouble."

"Katie, I never touched drugs, but I admit, I did drink some beer. I didn't like the taste though or the way it made me feel, so I only did it once."

"That's gut." Katie tapped him on the hand. "You are a gut Amish man."

"I try. Can I put my arm around you Katie? I think I saw you shiver before."

"Uh, I can't remember if I shivered, but it would be okay if you don't leave it there too long."

Josiah moved closer and placed his arm loosely around her shoulders. She could smell his peppermint breath. She was glad her mother always kept mints around. She had a couple stored in her pocket and offered one to Josiah as she popped the other in her own mouth. Goodness, she certainly didn't want to offend him with the onions she ate in her salad. That would be ever so bad.

"Are you jealous that Emma is married to Gabe?"

Josiah moved his arm away and let out a laugh. "Katie, we were never so serious, you know. Jah, I wanted to have me a nice Amish bride—still do—but we were never in love, like a man and woman should be before they marry. I don't know what I was thinkin'. Gabe is a nice guy and I hear they're real happy."

"Okay. Just checking, is all. You can put your arm around me again, if you want."

He chuckled and held her a little closer than before. Katie took quick breaths and wondered what it would be like to be kissed, but of course she knew it *wouldn't* and *shouldn't* happen. Not yet, anyway.

"Tell me about you, Katie. What have you been doing these last few months?"

"Teach—diet—clean—diet..."

"Stop! Why so much diet stuff?"

"Why? Because I was humongous! Fatty-two by four! Weighty Katie!"

"Katie, you are so beautiful anyway. Look at your eyes. Your two sisters look plain next to you."

"We're supposed to look plain."

"Oh, jah, I forgot," he said. Then he laughed heartier than before.

"Okay, if you want, I'll say it different. Katie, even though you're plain, I find you prettier than all the fancy girls I saw in Philadelphia. Is that better?"

"Mmm. I think so. You don't think I should lose more weight?"

"Not one little ounce. I'll be mad if you do. Girls should look like girls."

"Jah, that's what my daed said."

"It's true. God made you different and you should not try to hide it so much."

"Josiah, that's a strange thing to tell an Amish girl. We always try to hide our...hide ah... I guess we should talk about something else. How did your cows act when you came home?"

"Like cows. They said 'moo' and chewed their cud."

"I guess they didn't realize you were gone."

"Cows don't seem to care about anyone as long as they get fed and milked on time." He moved over a couple inches closer to Katie.

"How many will you have when you get your land?" she asked, pretending not to notice.

"Probably a dozen. We got four new calves this spring."

"That's gut."

"Katie, you're the first girl who ever asked me about my cows. I like that."

Katie turned and looked into his eyes. "I like to hear about them. I really do."

He squeezed her arm and for a brief moment leaned his head over to touch her forehead with his. Katie thought she'd faint. Oh my, she never felt this way with Willis. Never!

"Well, I guess I'd better head for home. I have to take my mamm over to my *aenti's* house. She just had boppli and now she's feelin' poorly so Mamm's gonna stay a couple days to help out."

Katie stood up, ever conscious of her posture now. She felt slimmer when she stood erect.

"I'm glad to see you again," she said as she watched him adjust his straw hat.

"Jah, I'm glad to be home. Do you want to go to the Sing with me tomorrow night?"

"I'd like that ever so much."

"I'll see you at service tomorrow, Katie. I'll come a little early to see if your daed needs me."

"That's nice of you, Josiah."

100

She watched as he headed down the drive on his horse. He sat tall in his saddle like a cowboy she saw once on the cover of a book. Emma was crazy not to marry him. But then, there was no love—on either part. That new information was a comfort. She hadn't realized before how much she feared he had gone to Philadelphia to get over a broken heart. Thank goodness Emma realized he wasn't the one for her. Gabe was perfect. Jah, God had brought them together, that was for sure and for certain.

The service went quickly for once. Katie loved the singing, but sometimes found the preaching dragged on. Her daed gave the main sermon today, speaking without any notes. She was impressed with his knowledge and fought the sin of pride that she was his daughter.

After the meal was served, Katie and her sisters, as well as friends and her sisters-in-law, cleaned up. They insisted Mary had to leave the work to them as her limp was quite noticeable. She fussed with her grandchildren instead. Mark and Hannah's little Joseph was nearly able to sit on his own. He was cutting teeth and Mary cooed to him as she rocked in order to soothe him. He was sleeping poorly at night and with three other children, six and under, Hannah was delighted to have her mother-in-law take over the fussy child and give her a break.

Katie saw Josiah watching her every single time she sneaked a peek over at him. It made her heart thump each time their eyes connected. Their exchanged smiles were reassuring. Willis barely said hallo and she saw him talking with Ida Mae, who returned his attention with high pitched gales of laughter. Katie avoided him as much as possible without being rude.

After most of the people left, Josiah remained to help clean up the barn, stacking the benches with Wayne in an unused section of the barn. He reminded Katie about the Sing and told her he'd pick her up at six. The bishop was holding it in his barn as he so often did. He got along with the youth and didn't seem as intimidating as the previous bishop had been. Katie was pleased he bent a few of the rules, ever so slightly.

The afternoon dragged and she decided to make brownies for the refreshment table. As they came out of the oven, Wayne came over to snitch one. "Not yet, Wayne, they're too hot."

"That's the way I like them. You're a gut cook, Katie."

"Glad you think so." Katie still had a pain in her heart from his earlier comments about her weight, but she had prayed a lot about forgiving him and it was getting easier.

"Look, Katie," he started speaking softly, with his eyes averted. His hands went under his suspenders and he snapped them a couple times.

"Jah?" She stopped and waited.

"It's just that…well, I'm sorry…you know about calling you fat and all. You really ain't, you know. I just like teasing you, but I won't do it anymore." Then he looked up and grinned. "Not about that, anyway."

"It's okay. I've already forgiven you. Now that I'm eating a little more, I feel better and not so close to tears all the time. I'm trying to convince myself I'm not fat. Even if I am still chubby, Josiah said he likes me the way I am."

"Oh! Wow! So you left Willis in the lurch for Josiah! Gut move, Katie. Josiah is a cool dude."

"You sure talk fancy-like, Wayne. Don't let Daed hear you."

Wayne laughed. "Sometimes he looks the other way."

"Jah, but a preacher's son has to be more careful."

"Katie, you sound like Mamm. Anyway, hope it works out for you two. I'm gettin' serious about Sadie."

"Like I didn't know that. Everybody knows it."

"Everybody? We try to be quiet about it."

"You're together every chance you get and people see you hold hands sometimes. It's not much of a secret."

Mary swung open the kitchen screen door and called out to them. "Where's Daed? He was supposed to come in and relax when everyone left."

"I'll check the barn." Katie went with her brother and they found Leroy sitting on a bale of hay, smoking a pipe.

"Mamm's worried about you, Daed," Katie said.

"Your mamm worries too much about everybody. I'll be right in. Just wanted to relax without noise for a bit."

"Want me to keep you company?" Wayne asked his father.

"Nee. Leave me be. I'll come in shortly. Tell your mamm to put coffee on. I Like to sit and meditate."

"You meditate, Daed?" Katie asked in surprise.

"Well maybe the word is cogitate. Some kind of 'tate.' I kinda forget which."

Katie smiled and she and her brother returned to the kitchen and arranged the brownies on a serving dish. Katie allowed herself one half a piece and Wayne took the other half plus three more full pieces. Weight was not a concern for her brother.

Chapter Seventeen

Sunday night Katie and Josiah spent every minute together. Before and after the singing took place, they walked around the outside of the Bishop's barn. At one point, Josiah took Katie's hand in his and it felt so right. He was strong, yet gentle. He joked with her and told stories about his short stay in Philadelphia, but he seemed to steer away from mentioning his friends again.

One of the young Amish carpenters with the Kapp group was at the Sing and he talked to Josiah about working for them. Josiah was enthusiastic and told Katie he would start the next day. "I'll work from dawn to dusk to make as much money as I can. I'm real anxious to get on my own."

"They pay gut?"

"Pretty gut, I guess. I have to talk to the boss tomorrow, but Johnny just told me he makes enough to put a couple hundred away every week. Course he's not married yet and lives at home like me, accept I need to give money to my folks for food and all."

"Sounds like a lot of money, Josiah, but don't kill yourself by working so many hours. You need to have fun, too."

"I guess you're right. Now that I've met someone nice like you."

"Goodness you've known me for years."

"But I didn't pay much attention to you, I'm afraid. My brain must have been missing."

Katie laughed. They walked around and then came back to the refreshment table. Josiah reached for one of her brownies. "These are wonderful-gut. Do you like to cook, Katie?"

She nodded. "And clean, too, except tubs. They're hard. Actually, now that I'm thinner, it isn't that tough to do."

"I guess you're right. You can jump right in and scrub away."

The rest of July and the first week in August, there was a major draught over the whole northeast. All the crops had drooped and there was definitely going to be a loss for the farmers. Mary watered their personal vegetable garden, but to irrigate the fields was futile and the men sometimes got together to exchange thoughts and complaints.

The temperatures rose mid-August and for ten straight days, Pennsylvanians throughout the county dealt with three digit degree weather.

Ruth was due anytime now and Jeremiah left her off each morning at her parents' farm on his way to the buggy shop so she would not be alone if labor began. She looked drained from the heat and Mary encouraged her to drink water, sipping frequently to avoid dehydration.

Katie sometimes sat and cooled her sister off with a fan she made from construction paper left over from school projects. "It feels gut, Katie. I can't wait till this is over with. I feel so bloated."

"Now you know how I felt all the time."

"Oh, what a shame for you. You feel gut now that you're eating a little better?"

"Mmm. I try to follow the dietitian's notes, but it's still hard sometimes."

Ruth's face changed from pleasant to fearful and she grabbed at her abdomen.

"Ruthie, what is it? Is it time?"

"I don't know, but it's tightening real strong. Just in case, write down the time. Do you have your watch with you?"

"On my wrist. Okay," she said as she put the fan down to grab a pen and a slip of paper from her mother's desk. "Let's see, it's 1:35. Did the pain go away?"

"It's starting to. Probably false alarm."

"Jah, though you're due in only a week."

"It would be nice if it came early. With all this heat…and all. The bishop gave us permission to use cell phones, so one of Jeremiah's English friends loaned us a couple until the baby's born."

"That was nice of him to think of it. Do you know how to use them?"

"It's not hard. Look, I'll teach you." Katie moved over to the sofa and sat next to Ruth while she showed her the basics.

Mary came in the room from the garden where she had picked zucchini for their meal. "Where did you get that phone, for

Heaven's sake?" she asked Ruth. After explaining, Mary reached for it and turned it over, pressing a few numbers.

"Careful, Mamm, you might be calling Germany," Ruth teased. "Oh, no. It's starting again. Check your watch, Katie."

"What's starting?" Mary's face blanched as she saw Ruth puffing small breaths as she held her protruding abdomen. "Oh, Ruthie, you're in labor, aren't you?"

Ruth said not a word, but moved her head slowly to show agreement about her mother's diagnosis.

"Katie," Mary looked over at her other daughter who was writing down the time. "How long has it been?"

"Oh, my. Only about four minutes and ten seconds."

"Was it strong, Ruthie. Did you have to grab hold of anything?"

"Just my belly, Mamm. It's not too bad yet—just fast."

"Call Jeremiah," Katie said. "He should know what's going on. Can I dial?"

"Oh listen to you, wanting to be all fancy with a phone," Ruth teased. "Jah, go ahead and dial, but I'll talk to him or he'll be upset."

Katie handed the phone over as it began to ring. Then they watched as Ruth told her husband about her contractions. They spoke a few more moments and then Ruth handed the phone back to Katie. "He's coming right home and he wants to stop at Mrs. Horner's on the way here. She'll think we're panicking to call her in so soon."

"Ruthie, it's a gut idea," Mary said. "No one knows how long you'll be. Some girls have them real quick like."

"Jah, and others like poor Abby have all kinds of problems."

"So much more reason to let her come by early," Mary said. "I changed the sheets and put padding down in your old room. I also got out some baby blankets I'd stored away—just in case."

"You think of everything, Mamm. Oh, here comes another. Ach, this is a nasty one. Ruth leaned over and grabbed the arm of the sofa as the contraction washed over her.

Katie felt queasy. She wasn't too keen about this part of becoming a mother. She wasn't even too sure she would be happy with the first part of becoming a mamm.

There was a knock on the front door and when Katie went to answer, there stood Josiah. "Hallo, Katie, I was just comin' by your place and thought I'd see if you wanted to go for a buggy ride."

"My goodness, Josiah. You couldn't have come at a worse time."

His mouth drooped and he took his straw hat off and held it in both hands. "What's wrong?"

"Not wrong exactly, but Ruthie is having her baby."

"Right now?" His eyes widened the size of goose eggs.

"Pretty soon. We just called Jeremiah to come home and he's stopping for the midwife."

"Wow! I'd better leave you be, then. Can I stop by in a couple days to see how things went?"

"That would be ever so nice."

He nodded, plopped his hat on and took off like a jack rabbit. Katie giggled as she returned to her sister. What kind of father would he make, she wondered as she noticed it was time to mark another contraction.

Ruth's contractions became closer and closer and Mary paced nervously back and forth from Ruthie's side to the kitchen window watching for Jeremiah and the midwife to arrive. Ruth relaxed between her pains and talked to Katie and her mother about unimportant matters, obviously trying to reassure them as well as herself, that she was not nervous. Soon though, she stopped talking as the contractions tumbled closer together and became more intense. She breathed as she had been taught by the midwife, though Katie noticed her hands were clenched into fists and her forehead had beads of perspiration.

Oh, where was Jeremiah?

Finally, they heard the wheels of the buggy grinding on the drive and Katie ran to the kitchen door to let them in. Mrs. Horner climbed down with Jeremiah's assistance and pulled her medical bag with her. Jeremiah looked terrified—his face blanched and his jaw set tightly. "How is she?" He asked as they both entered the house.

"See for yourself. She's still on the sofa, but we should get her to the bedroom now that you're here." Katie and Mrs. Horner exchanged greetings and the midwife went over to Ruth and placed her hand on her abdomen as the next contraction began.

Jeremiah knelt by the sofa and ran his fingers through Ruth's loose tresses spread on the cushion. "Rough, honey?"

"Jah, but I'm glad you're here. Ohhhh." She turned away and closed her eyes, then Jeremiah gripped her hand and held it close to his lips.

"We need to get her upstairs as soon as she's finished with this contraction. She may be delivering shortly," Mrs. Horner said.

Jeremiah nodded, but his gaze never left his wife's face. Eventually, the pain subsided and he lifted her off the couch and moved her swiftly up the stairs to her old bedroom. Mary followed behind with Mrs. Horner, and then Katie reached for a banana before going upstairs. It was the first food she'd had all day, and this was no time to black out.

Jeremiah stood in the hallway with Katie as the midwife examined Ruth. They heard Ruth moan several times and they stood silently waiting for the report. Mary came out and said that Ruth had dilated almost eight centimeters and it would not be long before she delivered. The baby appeared to be in the proper position for a normal delivery and the midwife was pleased with her progress.

"Can I see her?" Jeremiah asked, after licking his lips.

"Of course. Come with me. You, too, Katie."

"I don't know…"

"Just for a minute," Mary suggested.

They followed her into the small bedroom and Jeremiah lifted Ruth's hand and held it tightly in his. "You're doing real gut. Mrs. Horner says it won't be long."

"I hope not. This is work." Ruth forced a smile as she looked at the worried expressions of her loved ones. "Does Daed know what's going on? Oh, goodness, here comes another." Ruth squeezed her husband's hand until his fingers turned white. She let out only a thin moan, but her eyes exposed the difficult moment she was experiencing. It lasted longer and she turned her head to the midwife. "I feel like I have to push," she cried out weakly.

"Gut. Leave us now."

Jeremiah and Katie left the room and he went over to the rail in the hall and clutched it. His eyes were closed and Katie knew he was praying. She stood next to him and added her prayers. Ruth let out some cries that frightened them both, but no words were spoken. Katie started pacing in the hall while Jeremiah continued to cling to the rail, as if it was his life support.

And then they heard Ruth's voice pierce the air, followed by the wails of a newborn. Jeremiah turned abruptly, pushed open the door, and ran to his wife's side, with Katie right behind him. Mary's eyes glistened from unshed tears and the midwife held the infant briefly and then laid the little boy on his mother's abdomen. Ruth was weeping and turned to Jeremiah. "It's a boy, Jeremiah. Your first son and he's beautiful."

"Oh, jah, he is that." Jeremiah knelt beside the bed and touched his son's cheek with his finger. "He looks just perfect."

Katie went over to her mother's side and they embraced. "Ruthie did just wonderful-gut—and so fast."

Ruth smiled over at the two women. "I was hoping for a boy in my heart, but I thought it was a girl the whole time."

"So you're not disappointed it's a boy?" Mary asked.

"Nee. He's so cute."

The midwife tied off the umbilical chord and remained busy with the afterbirth while the infant settled down next to his mother. He had stopped crying though he moved his arms about, flailing like a new lamb. Jeremiah laughed and touched him again. "He's an active little one. What are we naming him, Ruthie? We hadn't made a final decision."

"Nathanael. He even looks like Nathanael."

"Jah. A gift of God. I like that," Jeremiah said.

"What do you think, Mamm?"

"It's a gut name. Jah. Your father has a great uncle by that name. He will be ever so pleased."

"Katie? Do you like it, too?"

"Whatever you like is fine with me. He is the cutest baby I've ever seen. I can't wait to hold him."

"Soon, Katie."

Mrs. Horner grinned at the new parents. "I clean him up a little first and weigh him, jah?"

"Don't take too long, Mrs. Horner," Ruth said. "I will miss him."

"Katie," Mary suggested, "while this is going on, go tell Daed and Wayne. They were in the field when she started and have no idea. Then Wayne can tell Matt and word can get around real quick. Emma was going to come by in a while anyway. Wait till she finds out what happened."

Katie looked over at her sister. Her smile was so beautiful—she looked like an angel. What a wonderful-gut mother she will be, Katie thought as she went to give the wonderful news.

Chapter Eighteen

Baby Nathanael weighed in at six pounds, five ounces. He was twenty inches long and had light blond hair—barely visible, as well as slate blue eyes. All in all, the family decided he was a very handsome infant. Jeremiah and Ruth beamed at all the attention he received and spent hours holding him and just enjoying the miracle of his life.

Ruth decided to stay a few days with her family before heading back home, since Jeremiah had to work at the shop. Orders were backed up.

Katie was thrilled to have them there at the farm and Jeremiah seemed most happy to have hot meals prepared for him when he arrived from his work day.

When she held the infant, Katie wondered what kind of mother she would make. She loved the scent of her nephew's hair and kissed his forehead. He looked so serene as he slept peacefully between feedings.

Three days after he was born, Josiah stopped by briefly on his way home from his construction job. He seemed embarrassed for Katie to see him covered in sawdust and sand from working on his project. He stood outside, refusing to enter the house, but waved to Ruth who was burping Nathanael in the background.

"He looks like a strong lad," he called over.

"Jah, he's a gut boy," she said with a smile. "He'll be just like his daed."

"Tell Jeremiah I stopped by to congratulate you both."

"I will. Danki."

Katie walked out to his horse with him. "It's a hot day."

"But there's a breeze. Makes it better."

"Jah. Will I see you later this week?" Katie asked, looking up into his clear rich brown eyes.

"I'm working extra hours all week, Katie. I'm going back this evening after I go home and eat. We have three houses that have to be completed by the 15th. Doesn't leave much time. If I'm not too dead tired from puttin' in so many hours, I'll be at the preaching service on Sunday. I can't go to the Sing though because

I have to watch my *dawdi* while everyone else is gone. I take turns with my brothers."

"What's wrong with him?"

"His mind is going. Real sad. Sometimes he wanders away, so we can't leave him alone."

"How old is he?"

"Only in his late sixties, but his daed was the same way at his age. Hope I don't get like that. He repeats everything he says a hundred times."

"My, that's so sad."

They reached his horse and Josiah mounted it and reached for the reins. "I'll be thinkin' of you though, Katie. The harder I work the sooner I can…you know…move on with my life."

Katie tried hard to look understanding and pleasant, but her heart was sinking. She wondered if he really was working hard, or if he had decided she was too fat and wanted to break it to her gently. He was a nice man and humble. He would be kind that way. As he rode off, she stood waiting for him to turn his head and wave, but he didn't. The pit in her stomach grew greater and she fought back tears unsuccessfully as she headed back to the house.

When she entered the parlor, Ruth looked up as she swaddled the infant to lay him down for his nap. "Katie, what's wrong?"

"What do you mean?"

"You're crying. Did something happen?"

"Nee. It's okay. Can I hold Nathanael before he naps?" Katie asked, trying to change the subject.

"If you tell me what's wrong first."

Katie let out a small smile. "That's called a 'bribe' isn't it?"

Ruth grinned back. "Jah, I think so."

"It's just that Josiah won't be around much. He says it's because he has to work long hours, but—"

"It's probably true. Naomi's husband works with the crew and she was complaining the other day when I saw her at market about not seeing much of him."

"Really?"

"Katie, I don't lie."

"I'm sorry. I know that. I just felt he had changed his mind about seeing me."

"Why would he do that? You can see he likes you."

"I know he did, but he may have changed his mind about me—since I'm still so fat."

"Katie! You have to stop thinking like that. You are not fat! I don't know what you see in your mirror, but the rest of us see a pretty, almost-thin girl."

"*Almost*—that's the part I hate!"

"I won't say 'almost' again then. Sure you're not a skinny person. You never will be because your bones are a little bigger than Emma's and mine, but that doesn't mean you're fat. Maybe you should see a counselor or nurse or someone who can put some sense into you."

"You think I'm *doppick?*" Katie's eyes burned into Ruth's.

"No. Not stupid, but very stubborn! You need to listen more and think less. What happened to the happy Katie I loved all these years? Maybe you think too much about yourself and not enough about others."

"That's not fair to say, Ruth. Look at you. Beautiful, thin, wonderful husband, even a perfect baby! I want that, too, but I may never have that. I may always be known as 'weighty Katie' and be laughed at behind my back."

"Ohhh," Ruth said, shaking her head. "I can't talk to you. Mamm will have to knock sense into you. Here, hold the baby till I'm ready to take him for his nap, but I'm tired of talking about all this."

Ruth handed over the sleeping infant and made her way to the bedroom to tidy the room. Katie felt tears roll down her cheeks and one landed on Nathanael's forehead. She gently removed it with the hem of her apron and sat on the rocker with him. Where was the Katie from before? Why was she so obsessed with her appearance? Maybe she did need help from the outside, but to admit all this to an Englisher went against her grain. Maybe Emma would have more compassion. Ruth just added to her pain and guilt. Why couldn't she understand how she felt? There was a saying she heard once about walking in another man's sandals. Jah, maybe no one would understand her feelings. Maybe she should forget the whole diet thing and just enjoy eating again. Not every woman has to get married. She enjoyed teaching, to a point, and if she stayed on as a teacher, she would be fulfilled that way. Wouldn't she?

When Sunday arrived, the family rode over to Pottsy Miller's place for services. Katie looked around for Josiah as she emerged from the buggy. He was no where in sight, but she spotted his family. Would he go so far as to miss service just to avoid seeing her? That seemed unrealistic, knowing how much he enjoyed the preaching.

Daed was always prepared to give the sermon but today the privilege was extended to one of the other preachers. He gave a lengthy, but interesting sermon based on Ephesians and it held Katie's interest most of the time. She glimpsed over once at the group of young potential suitors. Not one of them appealed to her. Willis caught her eye once, but looked down at his hands without a smile; confirmation in Katie's mind that she was undesirable.

The day went slowly after they ate and left for home. Her grandparents came in and stayed for awhile as well as Mark and Hannah with their four young children. Katie made an excuse to go to her room where she removed her kapp and took the pins out of her bun, allowing her hair to flow to her waist. Then she removed her dress and apron and laid on the top of her quilt, allowing the fresh air to pass over her flushed body. It seemed the heat spell lasted forever and it was at times like this, she wished they could have electricity to run an air conditioner. It felt satisfying to have a real meal in her stomach for once, though the third roll had caused that 'too full' feeling to leave her uncomfortable and discouraged.

Katie closed her eyes and fell into a shallow sleep, dreaming vividly of Josiah with her friend, Becky Hosteller. They were hammering nails into a wall, which looked like the side of a barn. Becky was obviously with child and Josiah was beaming. Then she saw herself carrying pails of water over to them. Josiah ignored her and laughed about fat girls he'd dated. Becky was nodding and then she put her finger to her lips as if hushing Josiah. In the dream, Katie found herself jumping into a pond with a blanket sewn around her huge waist. She was paddling as fast as she could, but the water was surrounding her and she felt herself being pulled under.

"Katie!" her mother's voice came to her and she awoke from her nightmare. "Honey, I could hear you from my bedroom. Mercy, you were yelling something fierce."

Mary came in and sat on the edge of the bed taking her daughter into her arms. "What has you so upset my little one?"

Katie broke into tears and held her mother so closely, she could feel her breathe.

"Now, now, nothing could be that bad. You were just dreaming, Katie." She rocked her back and forth as she had done so often when Katie was a child.

"I'm so unhappy, Mamm, and I'm not even sure why. Maybe I *should* talk to someone about it. Someone not in the family, I mean."

"Jah, that's fine, Katie. Sometimes we don't know why we think the way we do, but someone with fresh eyes can see the reason. I'll call on the doctor this week and see what he says. He's a gut man and cares about you. We all do, Katie, and we're all concerned about you."

"Ruthie got mad at me." Katie sniffed loudly as she remained in her mother's arms. She loved her mamm so much. Her mother always knew how to comfort her.

"Nee. Not mad, Katie, just frustrated. She told me about your talk. Don't forget her hormones are a bit crazy right now, too. She has her own issues."

Katie pulled back to look into Mary's eyes. "What issues?"

"Nothing serious. Just when a woman gives birth, sometimes things are confusing for awhile. She gets emotional, too."

"Oh, I've been so selfish. I didn't realize that. Were you that way after your babies, Mamm?"

"Oh, jah, I guess so. I kind of forget you know. It's been a long time since I had a boppli."

"What about Hannah?"

"Jah, she had her sad days, but things are gut now. Honey, have you gotten your monthly yet?"

Katie shook her head. "But I feel real crampy. I think maybe soon."

"Let me know when you do. The doctor wants us to stop by or call him when you do."

"Doesn't he know we don't have a phone?"

"I guess he does. I'll take the buggy when I need to. Now get dressed and come down and we'll have tea together. I have some left-over spice cake. I'll cut you a small piece."

"Make it regular size, Mamm. I'm so sick of this diet."

"Really, Katie? After all your work to get slim?"

"What does it matter?"

"Okay. I'll put the kettle on while you dress. Jeremiah is packing up their buggy with the baby items. They want to leave soon."

After Mary left the room, Katie washed up, put on a fresh dress, and twisted her hair into a bun, placing a fresh kapp on top. It felt good to be understood. It always helped to confide in her mamm. Poor Ruthie. Here Katie had been so concerned about herself she hadn't even noticed Ruth was struggling with her new roll as a mother. She knew Ruth had been having some trouble getting the baby to nurse correctly and she'd seen her tear up when he kept crying and turning his face in every which way unable to latch on. But this morning he seemed more content and her milk was coming in so certainly she should be relaxed about it now. Maybe motherhood wasn't so simple after all. Still, Ruth and Jeremiah were ecstatic about their new one, so sleepless nights and baby tears were just a part of parenting.

Several days later, Katie had her monthly. She was relieved that her cycle was finally straightening out. Tears still came too easily and her mood swings were not unnoticed by the other members of her family. Wayne complained to Leroy, Leroy complained to Mary, and Mary decided it was definitely time to seek a counselor. She took an open buggy and made her way over to the doctor's office to set up an appointment with a young woman counselor, whom the doctor recommended. In fact, Kelly Madison, came out to greet her between her appointments and Mary was shocked to see she wasn't much older than Katie herself. How on earth would she know how to help her daughter? Oh, well, if the doctor felt that highly of her, then she must be gut.

Katie helped around the farm, weeding in the early morning and evening, since it was still too hot in the middle of the day to be in the sun. She helped with the cooking and fluctuated between over-eating and starving herself—unsure of which way to go. She checked her waistline twice a day and went accordingly. Lose an inch? Eat dessert. Gain? Skip a meal. Mary was totally frustrated as she watched her daughter's erratic eating habits, and marked the days on the calendar until Katie's appointment.

The day arrived and Katie rode silently beside her mother as they made their way to Bird-in-Hand to see the counselor.

"Now be sure you don't forget to tell her everything."

"Jah, Mamm, you told me already." Katie listened to the rhythm of the horse's hooves as he trotted along the shoulder of the road.

"Tell her the truth, no matter how embarrassing the question. That's the only way she can help you."

"Mmm."

"Katie, are you listening?" Mary scowled as she turned briefly to see Katie's expression.

"Jah, but you told me all this already. I'll tell the truth, the whole truth, and nothing—"

"Katie! Don't make fun. It ain't proper."

Katie let out a sigh. "I hope she knows what she's doing."

"Dr. Nichols thinks she's real gut. He ought to know."

"I guess so."

The rest of the trip was made in silence. When they arrived, Katie got down first and tied the reins to a post. Mary shoed her on as she decided to let her be alone with the counselor. "That way, you can be freer to talk."

Katie wondered if she wanted to be freer. She was so nervous about the whole thing, she was tempted to turn around and go back home. It just seemed so un-Amish. She felt ashamed that she needed help like this, but there was no turning back now. She straightened her posture and walked in to the waiting room, eyes straight ahead, aware of stares from the other patients, but determined to get through this with her dignity intact. The receptionist smiled and checked the computer. "You can take a seat. It will only be a few minutes."

Katie nodded and shuffled through some old magazines on the table next to her chair. She found an old "Field and Stream" and leafed through it avoiding the eyes of the others.

"Katie Zook?" A voice resounded through the room.

Oh, mercy, that was her. What was she getting into!

Chapter Nineteen

Josiah trailed after his fellow workers to take a break under a large maple tree on the side of the property where they were constructing new homes. He drained his second water bottle and set his straw hat on the ground. His hair was matted against his scalp and he took a third bottle of water and poured some over his head. The cool liquid felt good on his forehead and scalp as it ran down his parched head. He laid back on his folded arms to catch a few moments of rest. One of the other Amish men followed suit next to him and let out a sigh.

"I'll be glad when we get this project over with. I haven't been home before nine once this week. My poor wife is stuck alone everyday with the six kids and no help."

"No family around?"

"Oh, plenty of family, but everyone has their own litters," he said with a grin. "What about you, Josiah? Anyone on the horizon?"

"I hope so. Jah, but I don't know if she feels the same about me yet."

"So ask her."

Josiah laughed. "Too soon. She's a nice girl, real pretty, too, but she can be kinda moody. Sometimes she looks happy to see me and other times she looks like she could cut the head off a canary."

"Take your time, then. You're a long time married."

"Jah, I know that. She's easy to talk to. I like that. Most girls are all silly-like."

"That's one thing about my Priscilla. She ain't silly. Sometimes I wish she was."

They stopped talking for a few minutes and relaxed in the shade.

"I'm trying to save money enough for my own place," Josiah said quietly to his friend. "I don't know how I'll earn money when winter comes. I'm asking around already, but work is scarce. I may have to go back to Philadelphia and work in a factory if I can't find work here."

"I'll keep my ears open, Stoltz. How 'bout the buggy shop?"

"I doubt it. My girl's bruder and her schwester's husband work there, but they rarely have an opening. Gut pay, though."

"Okay fellas, let's head back," the foreman said as he stood up from under another tree, picked up his tool belt, and walked toward the partially built homes.

"That was the shortest break on record," Josiah said under his breath to his friend.

The foreman stopped Josiah on his way back to the area where they were studding out the first floor of one of the houses. "Wait a second, Stoltz. I forgot to tell you. Some English guy came by yesterday when you went to get supplies with Cooper. He was looking for you, but I didn't like his looks so I avoided answering him."

"What was his name?"

"I think he said it was Jim or Jay. I forget. Something that started with a *J*."

"I stayed with a couple guys named Wally and Jay in Philadelphia. Maybe it was Jay. I don't know why he'd be looking for me though. I guess we didn't part on real good terms. They knew I wasn't happy about some of their ways."

"Well, anyway, I thought I'd better tell you. If he comes back and you're not here, do you want me to give him your home address?"

"That would be all right. Maybe I still owe them for the water bill or something."

"I felt uneasy. I swear the guy had a handgun on him. Something that shape was poking through his shirt."

"Yeah, they both owned guns. Not legal of course."

"Were they jailbirds or something?"

"I don't know. I hardly knew them. I worked with the one guy once and thought he was okay, but I found out they were both messed up with drugs, big time. Not just using them. I got out of there as soon as I had some money."

"Smart move. Don't want to hook up with people running from the law."

"That's what I figured, too. I don't know how people live like they do. Messed up, that's for sure. Makes me glad to be Amish."

As the men took up their posts, Josiah started using the nail gun again, while supporting the plywood sheets with his free hand. As he did the repetitive chore, his mind wandered back to his life in Philadelphia. Only once had he nearly slipped himself. The face of Tanya came to him—pretty blue-eyed Tanya—with her star-studded spiked shoes and spunky jeans, which looked glued on, they were so tight. Her beautiful full painted lips and friendly manner had enticed him and she had been obvious about her desire for him.

She had stopped by one evening and taken a fancy to him. She'd even gone so far as to sit on his lap, teasing him by kissing his ear. The memory made him uneasy when he realized how close he had come to giving into temptation.

"Stoltz!" the voice of his partner shook him up as it resonated through him.

"Jah, what?"

"You nearly nailed your hand, buddy. What's with you?"

"Sorry." He returned to his job at hand and kept his mind on his work. He was relieved that he hadn't spent more time with Tanya. After that night, he avoided her altogether, even leaving the apartment if she was headed over. She would have been nothing but trouble. No, he made the right move to get away before anything happened.

Around five the group sent out for pizza and took a half hour break. He hated being dirty, but it was unavoidable. His mother was too busy to keep up with the laundry and his sister-in-law spent half her time trying to keep her family in clean clothes. His three sets of work clothes were getting worn and never came really clean at this point. He'd break down and purchase some jeans for work if necessary, though he knew the bishop would frown upon his choice.

Around eight, the crew dispersed and he rode his horse home. Most of the family had retired for the night, but his mother was still mending the children's clothing by the light of the kerosene lamp. She looked up as he let himself in the back door.

"Ya look a sight, *Sohn.* They're working you to death out there."

"I'll be fine after a night's rest. It'll be worth it to finally have enough for my own place."

She nodded and took a few more stitches. "Some young man came by before. Englisher. He wanted to know where you were."

"What did you tell him?"

"I didn't like him, Josiah."

"No? So what did you say?"

"I told a little lie and said I didn't know where you were. I guess it wasn't really a lie though, since I wasn't sure *which* house you were workin' on." She looked up with a grin.

"He was probably the guy I lived with in the city. Jay."

"Well, I don't think he was up to good. He looked mean-like and he had a nasty scar on his chin. Looked like he'd been in a scrap. I don't want him around again."

"Hopefully, he'll take off. I'll write him a letter when I have a chance. Most likely I still owed the guys some money, and of course, they can't call me."

She nodded. "That's for certain. I washed a couple pairs of your work pants and they're on the line in the basement. Should be dry by now."

"Danki, Mamm." Josiah leaned down and kissed his mother on the cheek before heading for the storage room where he had set up a bunk for sleeping.

"Sohn?"

"Jah?"

"I'm real sorry we couldn't give you your own farmland. With all your bruders and—"

"I know, Mamm. It's fine. I'll have enough soon to make a down payment. I don't mind working for it. I just want to stay in the area."

"You got yourself a girl yet?"

"I don't know. There is one I like a lot, but I'm not sure she feels the same."

"God will bring the right one into your life, Josiah. Just be patient."

"I will, Mamm. I promise."

That night before falling asleep, his mind returned to Tanya. His English friends had teased him when he refused to spend the night with her. That was not his way. Sex was reserved for the marriage bed, but he had felt tempted. He had to pray for strength and God was true to his Holy word and gave him the ability to say no. Why did it pop into his head sometimes though, causing him to yearn for a woman by his side? Oh, it was time for him to find his mate. He needed to know the love of a good woman and begin his life as an Amish husband and father. Katie's sweet smile came to mind immediately. Pure sweet Katie. Yah, she would be such a wonderful-gut wife and mamm. Tomorrow he'd stop by, no matter how tired he was.

Chapter Twenty

Kelly Madison sat looking over Katie's charts with her test results while Katie sat twisting her kapp ribbons until she felt the tug on her neck. She released them and took a deep breath, longing for the silence to be broken. She felt uncomfortable sitting here with a stranger, and an Englisher at that, ready to bare her soul.

Kelly finally looked up and smiled at Katie. She was a beautiful woman, not much older than Katie herself. "Have you kept the journal Dr. Nichols suggested?"

Katie nodded and took a folded paper from her pocket and handed it across the desk. "I might have forgotten some things, but most of it is down."

Unfolding the lined yellow paper, Kelly scanned both sides. "It looks like you're doing a good job of getting your nutritional requirements met. You could use more protein at breakfast, however."

"It's hard to eat much that early."

"You could stop mid-morning and have some peanut butter on a piece of wheat bread maybe."

"But then I'll have too many calories."

"Right now you're getting only about 1300 calories a day. You have room to move on that. We don't want you losing any more weight. Let's see," she said as she turned back to the chart, "you lost another pound just since you were here last. We don't want you losing any more weight, Katie."

"But I'm still way too fat." Her voice started to quiver as she fought back tears.

"You really believe you're fat?"

"Of course. Look at me."

Kelly leaned across the desk, tenting her fingers. "You won't believe me, Katie. You won't believe anyone right now, but I'm not lying to you. You have a very slim body. I know it hasn't always been that way, but it is now. You have just gotten used to seeing yourself as overweight and we're going to work on your self-image. We need to talk about when you first thought you needed to diet."

"When people made fun of me, I guess. My brother was the worst, although even my father called me his little Wootzer."

"Sorry?"

"Pig."

"Oh. I'm sure he meant it affectionately."

"But it hurt ever so much."

Kelly nodded. "And how old were you when you felt offended by remarks like that?"

"I guess not until a couple years ago."

"I see." Kelly stopped to take notes.

"Then this guy seemed interested in me. At least I thought he was, but then I heard his friend ask if he was still taking out 'weighty Katie' and so I think he only took me out so he could tell his friends jokes about me. It was so awful." Katie began to cry and Kelly handed her a box of tissues.

"You're assuming a lot, Katie. It's more than possible that he liked you."

Katie looked up through her tears. "Then why hasn't he been back?"

"Well, I can't answer that."

"Then there's Josiah."

"Another young man you know?"

Katie nodded. "He's more of a friend. We talk a lot and he seems interested in what I say."

"That should be encouraging. Friendship is important, too, Katie. We learn a lot about ourselves as we relate to others. Caring for someone else is healthy. Do you have other friends?"

"Jah, but not so many now. A couple of my friends are engaged to marry and one girl is dating the first guy I told you about."

"It says on your chart you have been having serious mood swings. Has that improved since you're eating better?"

"I guess so, but I still get mad easy. I don't like it. I even get mad at my mamm sometimes. It ain't right."

"Perhaps now that your body is stabilizing, you'll notice a difference. Your chemistry has been out of order, which can make a huge difference. And your cycle? Any change?"

"I finally got my monthly. I guess it's better."

"Was it normal?"

"Pretty much."

"Make sure you keep a record of that also, Katie. Some girls need hormone therapy if things get too messed up, but we'll watch it for a while. The doctor would have to determine that anyway. I see Dr. Nichols has made a note to call in a gynecologist if we need to."

They discussed her teaching position and her relationships with family members. Katie found herself opening up and recalled incidents when she was a student, which had caused her to think poorly of herself. She remembered one girl teasing her because she couldn't touch her toes without bending her knees. The child had remarked that it was because her stomach was too big. It was revealing to connect the events of her past to her present day feelings. After about half an hour, Kelly went back to the present.

"Now I don't want you weighing yourself before seeing me again. It's far more important to get your nutritional values straightened out. It should be a maintenance diet now, not for weight loss. Also continue your journal. That's helpful." She stood up and Katie rose.

"You're doing well, Katie. It won't take long to get your thinking straight again. You've been through a lot and one's self-image can be distorted very easily. Don't worry about attracting young men your age. When the time is right..."

"You sound like my sisters. The hardest part will be staying off the scale. I usually weigh myself three times a day."

"Think of all that extra time you'll have to read a good book," Kelly said with a wink. "Here's my card if you need to talk to me between appointments. I'm always available. Oh, and don't forget to exercise." They walked down the hallway toward the receptionist's desk.

"I get plenty on the farm."

"That's true, I'm sure, but take time to take fast walks— about twenty minutes a day, if possible. It will help with the depression and also firm up your body."

"I'll try." Katie reached the receptionist's desk and held out her hand. "Dank...Thank you."

Kelly smiled as she shook Katie's hand. "See you soon."

Katie made an appointment for the following week and she and Mary stopped for orange juice at the store before heading home. Katie caught sight of herself in a storefront mirror and actually realized she wasn't as bulky as she had thought. She smiled and took the package from her mother as she stood a little straighter and walked with confidence.

After cleaning up from supper, the family sat to read their devotions. Before Leroy had a chance to begin reading a Psalm he'd picked out, Katie heard the grinding of wheels on the gravel drive. Mary turned to Leroy and asked if he expected anyone. He shook his head and nodded to Wayne to go to the door.

"It's Josiah," Wayne called over as the buggy came to a stop. Katie's heart skipped a beat as she realized he was probably here to see her. A moment later, Wayne and Josiah came into the parlor to join them.

"Sit yourself down, young man," Leroy said. "You're just in time to hear the Word of God."

"Danki." Josiah looked at each of them and nodded, adding a bright smile as his eyes reached Katie's. He laid his straw hat on the floor and folded his arms. Katie noticed how fresh his clothes looked. She wondered if he had left work early in order to visit. After reading three Psalms, the group bowed their heads and prayed silently. Then Leroy cleared his throat and that called an end to their shared time.

"So what brings you here tonight, Josiah?" Leroy asked with a twinkle in his eye.

"I just wondered if Katie might like to take a ride in my buggy. The sky is cloudless this evening and it's a nice cool night for a ride. I'd have her back whenever you say, Preacher."

"I guess we'll leave it up to Miss Katie. Do you want to take a turn in Josiah's buggy?"

Oh my yes. "Jah, that would be fine." Katie felt dampness under her arms and her mouth was dry.

"So go," Leroy said, grinning. "Just be back before nine," he added.

Katie grabbed three peppermints before heading out.

"Do you need a shawl, Katie?" Josiah asked as they proceeded to the screen door off the kitchen.

"I'll take one just in case it gets nippy," she answered, reaching for the shawl on the knob by the door.

Once they started down the lane, Katie sat back in the open buggy and looked to her right at the fields ripe for harvest. It was late August and since the rains had fallen, the crops were thriving. Her father's field of corn was perfectly laid out reminding her of the corduroy material she used for her brother's good trousers.

"So how's Ruthie's new boppli?"

"Ever so sweet. He has strong lungs though." Katie grinned just thinking of her new nephew.

"You like babies, Katie?"

"Oh, jah. They're wonderful-gut. I want a whole bunch some day." Katie felt her heart flutter wildly. She needed to catch her breath. "So how's the job going? I was surprised to see you tonight."

"It's moving quick. I just decided to take off one evening. Wanted to see you."

"Oh, that's ever so nice."

"You look real gut."

"Danki."

They rode silently for a few minutes and then he pulled the buggy off to the side. "Look, the moon is almost full. You can see it clear now even though it's dusk."

"It's beautiful."

"You know men went to the moon."

"Of course I knew that, Josiah. Everyone knows that."

He let out a laugh. "I guess you're right. I'd like to go someday."

"Really?"

"Of course, you need to get a lot of schooling and give up everything else to become an astronaut. Besides, the space program is nil. It was just a dream I had as a kid. Do you ever have a dream, Katie?"

"Just to be a gut wife and mother some day. And be a gut cook, too. Oh, and be thin like my sisters."

"So that one you already got. That and the cook one. Just the first two, not yet."

"I talked to a counselor today."

Josiah turned his body to face her. "Jah? What's wrong?"

"Just that everyone seems to think I have to stop dieting so much. I was feeling pretty bad for a while, I'll admit."

"But you're not still on a diet, are you?"

"I want to be. I'd like to lose more weight, but—"

"Katie, you'll blow away if you lose any more. Don't be foolish."

"You mean that?"

"I do. You are just perfect right now. Don't change one ounce."

Katie felt her neck heating up and knew her cheeks were flushed.

"I guess I'll just try to stay the same then. If that's the way you like me."

"Jah, it is. Do you want to walk over to the stream? With the light of the moon, we should be okay."

"That would be special."

He took her hand and they made their way down a worn dirt path to the edge of an active stream, known for its trout. "Do you come here often?" Katie asked as they stood quietly watching the rippling water as it cascaded over the rocks.

"I did when I was younger. Great fishing. But I'm too busy now."

"When will you be able to slow down?"

Josiah dropped her hand and folded his arms as he looked out across the water. "Soon, I hope. I'm saving everything I can and I talked to Ferd Hanson about the land next to his place. Apparently it belonged to the Brewsters. Old Bucky Brewster, who lived there alone, passed on. His family lives out of state and they want to sell it. It's with a realtor now and they're not asking that much for the parcel with the house, but I guess it needs some work."

"Think you'll have enough to buy it?"

"Since they're dividing up the land, I could manage the parcel with the house. It comes with fifty acres. It's enough to get started. My parents will help out where they can. Even my bruders offered to add some to the kitty."

"That's real nice of them. I know the land you're talking about. I think I was there once with my mamm. I remember the family was Mennonite and they even had a car. I never rode in it, but it was real shiny and black and I was fascinated when the woman let me climb in once. I pretended I was fancy."

"I guess you don't remember the inside of the house, do you?"

"Nee. I was pretty young. Things like that didn't mean much to me."

"I'm real anxious to check it out. I don't think it will be on the market long."

"How's your job going, Josiah? Think you'll work with them for a while yet?"

"Hopefully. Once the houses are complete, I expect another project will come up, but no one has said anything yet. I could always go back to the factory I guess, but that's my last option."

"You really didn't like it there, did you?"

"Philadelphia is okay—for a city, anyway; but the area I was in was filled with drugs and crime. I never felt real safe. My friends even carried guns."

"Oh, mercy. That's scary."

"Remember I told you they were involved in drugs? I heard one of the guys was around here looking for me."

"Why? Are they mad at you for something?"

Josiah shrugged. "I don't know. I may owe them money, but I left some behind and thought it would cover any expenses. Maybe they just want to say hallo."

"Do you believe that?"

"Probably not."

"You'd better be careful, Josiah. It's not like you can protect yourself. It's not the Amish way to be violent."

"I've thought of that. Hopefully, they'll just return to the city and leave me alone. I'm gonna write to Jay next week, if I don't see him first."

They turned back toward the road and walked slowly, her hand in his. She wondered what it would be like to be kissed, but reminded herself that it should be only a husband who kisses his wife. Not before. Of course, she knew plenty of girls who didn't wait, but they at least made sure it was the man they would one day marry.

"Maybe we can see each other this Sunday," Josiah suggested as he helped her into the buggy. "There's no preaching service, but maybe we could have a picnic or something."

"How about right here at the stream?" Katie asked, thrilled at the thought.

"I think that's a gut idea, Katie."

"I'll make my famous brownies and bring sandwiches."

"And I'll bring an old blanket to sit on."

Katie started running a list through her mind of all the things she'd bring. "I'll have to ask my parents if anything was planned. I think Ruthie and Jeremiah were coming by for dinner with the baby."

"Oh, well, I don't want you to miss seeing—"

"It's okay, really. I see them a lot. I just like to get their permission, is all."

"Katie, have you taken the kneeling vow yet?"

"No, but I plan to next year. I just wanted to wait until I was absolutely sure. You haven't either, have you?"

"Nee, but maybe next summer you and I can take class together. Would you like that?"

"Jah, that would be gut."

"Who knows, maybe after that…"

His words hung in the air and Katie filled in with her own silent words—*we'll get married.* It seemed to fit real well. Oh, my, was she letting her imagination run away with her? But what else could he mean?

It was five minutes before nine when they made their way down the drive to Katie's home. Katie was alarmed to see several buggies parked in the drive. Three men were standing on the porch as Josiah added his buggy to the crowd. Their faces were somber and she noticed the bishop was among the group. What could be wrong?

Chapter Twenty-One

Katie ran onto the porch intending to enter her home, but the bishop stopped her and held her shoulders with his hands. "Katie, slow down. It's your daed, but he's going to be all right."

"What happened?"

"We were having a meeting of the brethren when he fainted. We brought him here but—"

"He should be in a hospital! What's wrong with him?"

Josiah stepped up onto the porch to listen to the answer.

"We don't rightly know, but he's breathing okay and he's talking. Your Mamm is in there with him."

"I just saw him a couple hours ago. How could this be?"

"Katie, things can happen fast. Go see him. You'll feel better knowing he's okay now. I just wanted to tell you he was all right so you wouldn't act too scared."

Josiah steered her past the others standing on the porch and into the parlor where her father lay on the sofa. The bishop followed. Mary looked up. Her face was tear-stained, but otherwise she looked calm. "Katie, he's gonna be okay, but he agreed to see the doctor tomorrow."

"Tomorrow! Why not now?"

Leroy turned his head toward his daughter's voice. "Because I'm fine now, Katie. Too much fuss over me. Everyone thinks I'm ready to croak."

"Nee, Leroy," one of his friends said to him. "We was scared when you didn't talk, but once you started complainin' we knew everything would be just fine."

Leroy grinned. "Then tell everyone to go along home and let me get some rest."

The bishop nodded to the others and they looked over at Mary who shrugged. "What can I do?" she asked. "He's a stubborn man, for sure and for certain."

After the brethren left, Mark suggested his father remain on the sofa rather than climb the flight of stairs. Katie was surprised to hear her father agree to his plan. Mark planned to spend the night on the floor nearby in case his father needed anything. At first Leroy objected, but then he sighed and gave his permission. "I still think this is all needless, but if it will make everyone else happy, I'll go along with it." Mark rode his horse over to tell Hannah and to grab some items he'd need for the night.

"Stop worrying, Katie. You look like you saw a ghost. Josiah, tell her to relax," her father added, looking over at Josiah, whose expression was somber as well.

"Katie, listen to your daed. He says he's gonna be fine," said Josiah.

Katie looked over at her father and then nodded. "Jah, I'm sure he will be." Then she and Josiah walked out to his buggy.

"You okay?" he asked as he removed the reins from the post.

"I guess so. Daed is so stubborn. I'm so worried about him." Katie put her hands to her face and began to weep.

"Oh, Katie." Josiah put his arms around her and held her to him while she allowed herself to cry.

"I don't know what we'd do without Daed," she said between sobs.

"They have medication for all kinds of illnesses, Katie. I'm sure your daed will be just fine once they figure out what's causing his problems."

"You think so? Really?"

"Jah, I do. He seemed pretty gut just now. If it was super serious, he would still be unconscious. At least, that's what I think."

"You're probably right." Katie removed her hankie from her apron pocket and blew her nose. She sniffed a few times and then Josiah wiped a lone tear with his finger.

"I hate to see my Katie so upset."

Her voice trembled slightly. "Am I your Katie?" She looked into his eyes, waiting for his answer.

"You're the only Katie I know," he answered with a tender smile. "I'd better let you get back with your family now. We'll have to skip the picnic idea, but I'll come by tomorrow, even if it's late, just to see how things are going. Okay?"

Katie nodded and did her best to smile. She watched him leave, before returning to the house. When she entered the parlor, her mother was sitting next to her father. When she saw Katie, she nodded toward the kitchen and stood up. "I'll be right back, Leroy."

"I ain't going anywhere, Mary. Take your time."

Katie and her mother went to the back end of the kitchen so they could discuss their plans for getting Leroy to the clinic the next day. "Mark is going to stop by Abram's to tell him what happened. I'm sure Abram will be able to take Daed in the morning. Mark will also go over with us, but he's so busy at the shop, he'll have to leave and we think it would be easier for Abram to stay. We'll borrow phones tomorrow to keep in touch with the family."

Katie nodded and then she let her tears escape again. "Mamm, I was so upset when I saw all the men standing around. I knew something had happened to Daed. I just knew."

"Oh, Katie," Mary said as she reached out to put her arms around her daughter. "I know. I was so scared when I saw your daed. Even though he was conscious, he looked so awful bad. His color was like a sheet. What could be wrong with him?"

"I wish I knew, but we can't think the worst. I'm gonna pray and ask God to heal him ever so fast." Katie tried her best to stop crying, but the tears continued to flow. She reached in her pocket for more tissue, but they were already damp from earlier.

"Jah, I'll do the same. Maybe I should sleep on the floor, too—to be nearby."

"You'll need your strength, Mamm. Mark will call you if it's necessary. If Daed needs surgery or anything, a lot will be on your shoulders, so you need to take care of yourself," Katie reminded her.

"Jah, you're right. He's so young, Katie. Only forty-seven."

"He seems even younger. He's a strong man, Mamm, and I know he'll be just fine."

"Let me go back to him now. He may need more cool cloths on his head. It seems to help."

Leroy was sitting up on the sofa when they got back in the room. He was fanning himself with his farm journal as Mary and Katie went to his side. Wayne sat across from him, resting his chin on his hands. His brows were creased as he watched his father attempt to cool himself off. "I can do that for you, Daed."

"Nee. It gives me something to do, is all."

134

"Here, Leroy, hold this on your head," Mary said after squeezing out a fresh washcloth. "That'll keep you busy."

"I don't need it anymore, Mary. I feel ever so gut now."

After returning the cloth to the pan of cool water, she looked at Leroy. "Do you want me to sleep next to you on a chair tonight to keep you company?"

"Goodness' sake. Pretty soon I'll have the whole family sittin' here waiting for me to—"

"Leroy! Don't say another word! All right, I'll sleep upstairs, but I don't want to hear you talk like that again!"

"My Mary is a spunky Amish woman," Leroy said with a crooked grin. "So, Katie, are you learnin' how to talk to your husband from your Mamm?" He let out a solid laugh, which was music to Katie's ears.

"If my husband was as stubborn as you, Daed, I'd be in real trouble." Everyone smiled, relieved to hear their banter.

Eventually, after everyone was settled down, Mark and Abram piled quilts on the floor to be near their father. Wayne insisted on staying downstairs with the men, so Mary added three more quilts and extra pillows and then left reluctantly for her own bedroom. Katie climbed the stairs behind her. They stopped in the hallway to say good night and encircled their arms around each other briefly for moral support.

After a restless night, morning finally arrived. Katie tiptoed downstairs. Her father was still asleep on the sofa, but Wayne and Mark were no where to be seen. Katie figured they were tending to their chores. Abram was making coffee in the kitchen while her mother was busy frying up bacon.

"How did you sleep, Mamm?" Katie asked as she helped herself to juice.

"Not real gut. How about you, Katie?"

"I've had better nights, that's for sure. Have you talked to Daed yet this morning?"

"Nee. He's been asleep the whole time, but he was restless all night according to your brothers."

"Jah, he tossed about and must have had nightmares, 'cause he called out a few times." Abram buttered a slice of toast for himself, laid it on a paper napkin, and leaned against the counter.

"We'll take him in a few minutes. We're waiting for Wayne. Mark's going too, until he has to be at work. Glad it's close by the clinic."

"I want to go, too, Mamm," Katie said, her voice cracking as she held back her tears.

"Jah, but we'll have to let Emma and Ruthie know," Mary said.

"Fanny's going to make the rounds, Mamm," Abram said. "Oma will watch the children, I'm sure. we'll stop by on our way. We go right by their farmhouse."

"Oh, my, I'm so concerned," Mary said as she smoothed the front of her apron. "I should go change. This dress is soiled."

"You look fine, Mamm, but you have time if you want to," Abram said. He took a bite of his toast and checked the coffee, which was still brewing.

It was another hour before they finally headed out the door. Mark helped his parents into the back of the closed buggy while Wayne took the driver's seat in the front. Katie climbed next to him.

Mark rode his horse and Abram followed in his own buggy, first stopping at his farm to give an update to Fannie. He left a cell phone with her, which belonged to the buggy shop where he worked, while holding on to a second one in order to give updates.

There were advantages to having the newer technology, as Katie watched her brother place the phone in his pocket. It still didn't outweigh the disadvantages in Katie's opinion.

The waiting room was crowded. The triage nurse took Leroy back to be examined almost immediately upon his arrival. Mary went in with him, while the rest of the family remained in the waiting room. Katie's three brothers stood in a corner discussing their father's condition as she tried to distract her thoughts by reading an old magazine. It was about housekeeping, and normally she'd enjoy reading the recipes, but today the words danced before her eyes. What could be wrong with her father? How serious was it? What if? *Nein! I won't go there!* She berated herself for even having the thought.

Mary came out to the waiting group. "They're putting him in an examination room now. I'll go with him, but it's crowded in there so I'll just have to give you updates."

"Mamm, what can we do?" Katie asked with furrowed brows.

"Pray, Katie."

Katie nodded, then her mother returned through the double swinging doors while Katie and her brothers sat in a corner and bowed their heads in silent prayer. They were oblivious to the stares of the others. Even in Lancaster County, they were considered "quaint" and "different." They were quite used to it and had learned to ignore it.

An hour passed before Mary returned. "They took blood for the lab already and now they're doing an electro—something. Wait, they wrote it down for me." Mary handed a card with the information over to Abram.

He read it aloud. "electrocardiogram."

"Jah and read the other side."

Abram turned the card over. "Echocardiogram."

Mary nodded. "The doctor said it's an ultrasound."

"Sounds like they're checking his heart," Katie said.

"Jah, and then they may do a stress test, depending on what they find. Your Daed is having a fit and keeps asking how much it costs."

"It doesn't matter. We'll all help out. He knows that." Mark placed his thumbs under his suspenders. "Amish take care of their own."

"Jah, but he has to complain about something."

"Do you like his doctor?" Katie asked her mother.

"He's nice. He was gone quick-like. I didn't have time to ask him much, but I think he's ever so smart. That's what one of the nurses told me. She said not to worry with Dr. Levin on the case."

"So what now, Mamm?" Mark asked.

"It will be a while, Sohn. You go on to work and we'll call you on your phone when we know something."

"Okay, if you think he'll be all right."

"He's getting the care he needs. He should have been here months ago."

"You're right," Mark agreed.

Wayne went over to a seat and slouched down. He had barely spoken and Katie went to sit beside him. "You look worried, Wayne. I think Daed will be just fine."

"How do you know, Katie? You're no doctor."

"I know, but he's getting care now."

"Maybe it's too late."

"Don't, Wayne. We have to have faith."

"Gut people die, Katie. It ain't a matter of faith sometimes."

"Well, I just have a gut feeling about it, is all."

"I hope you're right. I can't lose my daed." Wayne put his head in his hands and Katie saw him swallow several times. It was not like her brother to show emotion. She wanted to reach over and hug him, but she knew it would only embarrass him, so she merely patted his shoulder.

Mary slipped back through the doors to be near her husband, while Katie stood and paced the floor. After a few minutes spent wearing out her soles, Wayne looked up. "Katie, sit down. You're making me nuts."

"Leave her alone, Wayne," Abram said. "Everyone deals with stress different."

"Here comes Ruthie with Emma," Wayne said, looking over at the elevator as the doors closed behind them. Ruth had the baby in her arms and looked upset as she headed toward the group.

"How's Daed?" Emma asked first.

"They're doing testing now. Mamm's in the room with him."

"Can't we go in?" Ruth asked.

"Mamm said it was real crowded and they don't encourage too many people in there at one time. Besides Daed is complaining a lot. We should just wait here." Abram smiled at his new nephew as he peered over the blanket. "How's Nathanael? Does he sleep gut?"

"He sleeps a lot during the day, but he still wakes up several times during the night. I catch naps sometimes; but he's so sweet, I don't mind being with him at any hour." Ruthie smiled at Abram as she moved the blanket slightly to show her son's fine blond hair.

138

"Jah, he's cute, that's for certain."

An hour passed and then another. Ruth found a vacant waiting room and nursed Nathanael. Katie and Emma sat with her. "How's Mamm doing?" Ruth asked.

"Pretty gut, considering."

After a few minutes, the baby stopped nursing and Ruth rested him against her shoulder to burp him. "Nathanael's fallen asleep. Do you want to hold him, Katie?"

"Oh, jah." She took the little bundle in her arms and watched as his tiny mouth gave sucking motions. His eyes remained shut, but she could make out the faintest of lashes. How sweet.

"Here comes Wayne." Emma got up and walked over to him. "Any news?"

"Jah. They're releasing him soon, but he needs to see Dr. Nichols tomorrow. The nurse is calling to make the appointment."

"That's probably gut news, don't you think?" asked Katie to the group.

They all nodded and Abram answered for them. "They wouldn't let him go if they thought it was dangerous. What could it be to make him pass out like that though?"

"Hopefully, Dr. Nichols will have some answers tomorrow," Emma said.

When Leroy came into the waiting room with Mary, Katie noticed his strained expression. She knew he was worried himself and the way he always handled stress was to snap at her mother or get annoyed with other people, but she was ever so glad he would be spending the night at home.

As they all headed toward the parking area reserved for the Amish buggies, Katie spotted Josiah dismounting his horse. When he spotted her, he came right over to ask about her father. After explaining what had happened, he told her he'd keep in touch, but he needed to return to his workplace. She watched as he took off. Jah, he was a very considerate man. He had a lot of fine qualities. Just maybe God had sent him to her at this time of her life.

She took hold of Emma's arm and walked her to her buggy. "We'll see you tomorrow at the house. Ruthie said she'll stop over in the afternoon since we won't know much till then. Daed's appointment is at nine."

Emma leaned over and kissed her sister on the cheek. "We'll be by tomorrow. Tonight we all need to pray."

Wayne looked brighter than he had, but she read lines of worry on his young face. What indeed would they do without their daed?

Chapter Twenty-Two

Leroy ate very little supper, though Mary made one of his favorite casserole dishes—noodles with vegetables and chicken. Afterwards, he sat in his favorite arm chair and caught up on the farming news. Wayne insisted on handling the animals himself and Leroy didn't put up a fuss for once. He was unusually quiet all evening and Katie knew her mother was concerned.

She decided to work on a quilt with her mother, though her heart wasn't in it and she noticed her mother's stitches were longer than normal. She'd probably end up pulling them out and redoing them, but at least it was activity and helped with the passage of time.

Leroy went to bed around seven and Mary immediately set her work aside and followed him up the stairs. "Leroy, you've barely said a word all evening," she remarked as she removed her kapp. She released her bun and began brushing out her long tresses, now sprinkled with gray.

"Jah, well, I didn't have much to say." He sat on the edge of the bed to remove his shoes and socks.

Mary set her brush down and came to sit next to him. She took his hand in hers. "You're still worried, aren't you?"

He avoided looking at her. "Maybe a little."

"But you're feeling a little better, aren't you?"

"Not like my old self." He pushed his shoes under the bed and turned to his wife. "Honey, if it's serious, I want to know."

"They'll tell you, I'm sure of that." Her chin began to tremble slightly.

"Mary, if it's my time, you'll have to be strong. For everyone."

Mary buried her head in his chest and allowed the pent up tears to flow. Leroy held her close and rubbed her back gently. "Now, now, sweetheart, please don't cry."

"I can't imagine my life without you."

"I know. I'd be the same. But if God is ready to call me home, we must accept it."

Mary tried to control her tears, but they kept flowing. She held on to Leroy with all her strength as if by doing so, she could keep her with him forever.

"You're strong, Mary," Leroy whispered in her ear and she felt a tear from his eye rest against her own cheek.

"I try to be. If it was serious, though, wouldn't they have kept you in the hospital?"

"Maybe not. Especially if there's nothing they can do."

"Oh, Leroy, we must continue to pray for God to heal you."

"Jah. I pray a lot, but I also know when your time is up, there ain't much a person can do. Death doesn't scare me, Mary, but leaving you alone—does."

Mary reached for the tissues by the side of the bed and wiped her eyes. She tried to control her own tears now, knowing she needed to reassure Leroy. It wouldn't be fair to let him leave this earth, fearing for her future—if indeed that was God's plan.

"Leroy, you know I love you with all my heart. There has never been another man in my life and never will be, but if the Lord takes you home, I will accept it as his will and somehow, I'll manage. Our children and grandchildren would be my main concern. I would have to show them how God gives us strength— in all circumstances."

"Jah, Mary, and he does. And if necessary, he'll help you through. You know there's enough money in the safe in the basement to get you through."

She nodded.

"Mary, you are the most wonderful-gut wife a man could ever ask for. I've been ever so happy with you."

Mary smiled through her puffy eyes at this man she loved so much. "I'm so glad I've made you happy."

"God has been so gut to me."

"Jah. Now let's not talk any more. We may be laughing tomorrow night at how concerned we were."

"I hope that's true, honey. I want to be with you for many more years." Leroy lifted her chin and rested his lips on hers. It was a kiss of love so deep and so pure, Mary felt renewed strength.

Once they got in bed, Leroy pulled her over to him and they laid in each other's arms all night. Nothing more was said. It wasn't necessary for more words.

The next morning, the four of them set out in time to make the trip to the clinic by nine. No one spoke during the buggy ride and Katie felt her throat close up a few times when she allowed her thoughts to run away with her. She usually was optimistic, but this morning the cup looked half empty.

The four of them squeezed into the small office after the nurse called Leroy in for his appointment.

Dr. Nichols came through the door and smiled at everyone. He reached out and shook Leroy's hand and gave him a hearty greeting. "So my friend, looks like you're having some problems. Let me check out the results they sent over." He sat down on the chair behind his desk as Leroy and Mary took seats in front of him. Katie and Wayne stood silently waiting for his review. Katie noticed her mother fan herself with an old magazine she picked up off a table between the chairs. Wayne leaned against the wall with his head turned down.

Finally the doctor looked up. "Well, I'm pleased with some of the results, but we need to run a stress test. We've ruled out anemia, which can often lead to fainting spells. So that's good. I'm concerned about your high blood pressure, though. If we're not dealing with anything more serious, we can try a beta blocker to treat you."

Mary looked stunned. "Isn't that serious?"

"It's something we can treat, Mary. If medication is warranted and he can be normalized with it, then that's the route we'll take."

Wayne took a step forward and cleared his throat. "Can I ask something?"

Dr. Nichols looked over at him. "Of course, son, what is it?"

"Well, if you're right and then he takes the medicine and it doesn't help...then what?"

"We can always put a pacemaker in if that is what is needed, but we have to rule out other conditions first. So if you can hang around awhile, I'll see if we can perform the stress test today and also the tilt table test, which shows us how postural changes affect your father."

"Wow, you guys have a lot of tricks up your sleeves," Leroy said, trying to smile.

The doctor smiled back. "We do, Leroy. And of course we also have MRI's and scans we can utilize if necessary. I'd like to save you folks a trip back, so you can stay in our family waiting room if you'd like while I get things set up. I'll be here all afternoon, so I can report back as soon as I get the results."

"Dank...Thank you, Doctor," Mary said.

"I'll get my nurse to make all the arrangements, Leroy. Go back to the waiting room with your family for now and we'll find you when we're ready."

"Jah. That sounds gut."

After waiting a few minutes, the nurse came over with a wheelchair for Leroy, who balked at using it. Finally they convinced him it was just precautionary. Not wanting the staff to get into trouble, he eventually sat down in it and an aid took him back for his tests.

Time dragged, but Mary, Wayne, and Katie took walks around the building and managed to eat some lunch at a nearby diner. Leroy had not been given anything to eat due to the Tilt Table test, which was also scheduled. He had complained to the nurse, but Mary was glad. It would be terrible if he vomited on top of everything else.

Finally around four in the afternoon, they returned to Dr. Nichol's office. Leroy was in his street clothes.

The doctor seemed more cheerful than he had earlier and Katie took it as a good sign.

"It looks as if the fainting spells were indeed caused by a sudden elevation of your heart rate, Leroy. We'll put you on medication and I'll check you frequently to see if that will do the trick."

"Why does it make him pass out," Mary asked.

"We call it a vasovagal syncope. What happens is the balance between the chemicals adrenaline and acetylcholine, which are produced by your body, becomes disrupted. Adrenaline stimulates the blood vessels, which become narrower, causing the heart to beat faster. But when there's an imbalance, the opposite happens. When the vagus nerve becomes stimulated, excess acetylcholine is released and the heart rate slows down. It's harder for the blood to be pumped to the brain. Follow me?"

"Uh, I think so," Mary said, her brows drawn together.

"Jah, I do," Leroy responded. "Keep going. Then what?"

"Well, the temporary decrease in blood flow to the brain can bring on a fainting episode."

"Well, I'll be. And you figured that all out. You're ever so smart," Mary said, grinning over at the doctor.

"Mary, we need to keep an eye on Leroy though, to make sure we haven't missed anything. It will be up to you to see he takes his medicine. I think I know Leroy well enough—"

"She'll be on me all right. Ain't it the truth, Mary?"

"Oh, jah. He won't get away easy, doctor."

For the first time in two days, Katie heard her brother laugh. "And I'm gonna take over the chores for awhile. You can tell him that, too, Dr. Nichols."

"It would be a good idea, Wayne," the doctor said, looking over at him.

"It's too much for the boy to handle alone," Leroy said with a stiff lip.

"I'm not a boy anymore, Daed. I'll be seventeen in a couple weeks."

"He's a strapping young man, Leroy. Let him help out till we get this thing under control."

"Jah, we'll see. What do I owe ya?"

"We'll send a bill. I'll make out your prescription over the computer and you can pick it up at the desk on your way out. We'll get you back in about two weeks, unless you have any further problems."

The family made their way out to the front office and Mary retrieved the information sheet and the prescription which they filled on their way home. The mood was much lighter on the trip back, and Katie stopped several times to thank the Lord for taking care of her daed.

As they pulled up to the drive, Katie noticed Josiah's horse tied to the hitching post. Then she saw him leaning against the barn, chewing on the end of a stick of hay. He smiled and came over. After he was given the news about Leroy, he offered to stay and help Wayne with the milking.

"I'll take you up on it. That I will."

"Let's go then," Josiah said as he rolled up his sleeves and headed toward the barn.

"Hey, you got them in already from the pasture. Great!" Wayne slapped Josiah on his back and they left the others in order to start the milking.

Entering the kitchen, Katie's heart thumped almost loud enough to hear. Josiah seemed to have that effect on her lately.

Mary smiled over as she went to wash her hands. "Nice of Josiah to offer, jah?"

"It is." Katie stood waiting for the faucet, aware of a blush rising on her cheeks.

"You like him a lot, don't you, Katie?"

"Maybe. But don't tell the others, Mamm. I hate being teased and I can't take rejection again, so I'm taking my time. Right now we're just friends."

"Gut friends, it looks like."

Katie smiled and nodded. "Real gut."

Leroy came into the kitchen, a grin on his face. He came over to Mary and put his arms around her. "Looks like you're gonna have me around for awhile longer, Mary."

She looked into his eyes with a radiant smile. "Jah, looks that way. But you best behave yourself or I'll be telling the doctor about you."

Leroy kissed her forehead and winked over at Katie, who was ever so happy.

Josiah stayed for dinner and when they were done eating, Mary suggested he and Katie take a walk while she cleaned up.

"We'll help clean up first, Mrs. Zook." Josiah said as he removed the few remaining plates from the table and headed toward the sink.

"That's woman's work. Come sit with me," Leroy said, his eyes twinkling.

"Oh Daed, he can help. It won't make him any less a man." Katie realized all too quickly how that had sounded. She glanced at Josiah, who was grinning widely.

"Sure, I don't mind helping the women."

146

Leroy laughed out loud. "Then you can dry and I'll catch up on my journal."

After the dishes were put away, Katie and Josiah went outside and walked over to the pasture where the horses were grazing. Their apple trees were dripping with ripe fruit and Josiah picked one off a low branch and took a bite at Katie's suggestion. One of the horses came over and accepted an apple from Katie's hand.

"Do you like to bake apple pies?" he asked.

"I like to bake all kinds of pies, but I don't do it much anymore."

"Why not?" Josiah leaned against the rail fence and looked into Katie's eyes.

"It's too tempting. I don't want to get fatter."

"Katie, Katie. You are just perfect. Don't lose or gain an ounce." He reached over and touched her nose with his forefinger. Then he tapped her on the cheek. "You have a cute dimple when you smile."

"That's what my daed tells me."

"It's true. By the way, Katie, till your father is well again, I'd like to come everyday and help your bruder. Do you think he would be hurt and think I was hinting he couldn't do it by himself?"

"He might at first, but it does take two men. My brothers are so busy with their own places, plus Mark works at the buggy place..."

"Then I'll mention it to your daed. I wanted to check with you first."

"I'd like it."

"We'd see each other a lot, Katie, at least until school starts again."

"It would be ever so nice."

"Oh, Katie."

She looked into his eyes and she felt a desire to be close to him. She was sure she read the same thought in his gaze. Then Wayne's voice interrupted their special moment. He was headed towards them, carrying old papers for the burn barrel. "Katie, show Josiah what I carved when you go back in."

"What was it?"

"The duck for Daed. It's in the drawer in the kitchen where Daed never goes."

"Oh, I remember. You show him."

"Jah, we'll go back in a minute," Josiah said to Wayne. "Then you can show me yourself. I didn't know you carved things."

"It's the best I ever did. Even Mark said it." Wayne threw the papers in the barrel, which was several yards from them, and they started walking back to the farmhouse.

"Is it for his birthday?" Josiah asked, tossing the apple core off to the side.

"Christmas. I'm getting a head start."

"I'll say. It's only the end of August." Josiah put his arm around Wayne's shoulders.

"Jah, but I like to make everything I give."

"Last year Wayne made me bookends." Katie smiled over at her brother.

"They were cool, weren't they?"

"Jah, cool for sure. They looked like big wooden bricks."

Josiah laughed and took his arm away. "Make me some, Wayne. I have books all over my room making a mess."

"You read a lot?" Katie asked him.

"When I have time. I like history books, especially about the early days in America. Like when the Anabaptists came over."

"It is interesting. I like to read about it in German," she added.

"Me too, as long as it's not too big a book."

Wayne was listening to the exchange. "I like to read about farming. I thought about going into the buggy business with Mark once, but I'd hate to be inside so much of the time."

"Jah, me too," Josiah said. "I like my cows too much."

Katie let out a giggle. "Jah, you do."

Chapter Twenty-Three

Josiah was faithful about helping out and for once Leroy didn't make a fuss. He spent time walking around the property and helped feed the animals, but when milking time came, he seemed relieved to have the extra set of hands available to relieve him of that duty.

The week before school started, Katie had her appointment with the counselor and when they weighed her, she had gained half a pound; but instead of being upset, she shrugged it off.

"I'm proud of you, Katie," Kelly remarked. "I thought it would upset you."

"No. I have a friend and he likes me just the way I am."

"Ah. He. Is he someone special?" Kelly had a knowing smile on her face.

"I hope so. I'm afraid to hope too much, but I think he likes me."

"That doesn't surprise me, Katie. You're a very sweet person."

Katie smiled back and lowered her eyes. "I don't want to be proud."

"Oh no. Of course you don't. But it's okay to get compliments sometimes, isn't it?"

"I guess so. It doesn't happen so very much."

"Then it won't make you proud—just happy," Kelly added, smiling over at Katie.

Katie grinned. "Jah. I don't think I need to come back again, Kelly. I feel ever so much better and I'm not cranky anymore."

"Wonderful. We won't make an appointment then, but you know if you ever want to come back to talk to me—about anything—I'll be more than happy to see you."

The girls embraced and Katie left the office with a spring in her step. Things were definitely improving. Josiah had already asked her to go to the next Sing with him and she saw him every day now. Not for long periods of time, but even if she didn't actually have a chance to talk to him, she loved knowing he was around and helping. Her parents seemed to enjoy his company and he stayed for dinner more evenings than not.

When she arrived home, she noticed Ruth's buggy was there as well as Emma's. Then she remembered they were coming to see their daed and stay for dinner. Their husbands would follow when it was closer to mealtime. Ruth's baby was growing quickly and Katie loved to hold him. When she came through the door, she saw Emma had Nathanael in her arms and he was sound asleep. Katie greeted her sisters and went to wash up before touching her nephew.

"I hear Josiah is helping out while Daed is laid up," Ruthie said to Katie.

"He's been so kind working here everyday. He doesn't even want to take money, but we insist," Mary remarked.

Katie nodded. "He's a strong person. He has gut muscles."

Emma laughed. "Oh my, you noticed, Katie."

"Only 'cause he was lifting something heavy the other day and I saw them bulging a little."

"Mmm." Emma exchanged smiles with her mother and Ruthie.

"Now don't tease me," Katie said with a giggle. "So, Emma, how about you? Are you in a family way yet?"

"Nee. Not yet, but we would be ever so pleased if it happened."

"And the children?" Mary asked. "They would like that, too?"

"I know Lizzy wants a sister sometime in the future. Mervin probably wouldn't care one way or the other. He's playing softball when he's not working. I don't see that much of him."

Nathanael opened his eyes and stared at his aunt. "Look, he's trying to smile at me," Emma said looking down at him.

"He's a contented little fellow. Rarely cries."

"That's the kind I want," Emma stated. "I'll put my order in now."

"Did I cry much, Mamm?" Katie asked as she sat down on the sofa to relax.

"Oh, yah. You cried all the time when you were teething. It drove me a little crazy, but Oma came to help me out a lot. She had a way of quieting you down when even I couldn't."

"Do you like being a Mammi?" Katie asked her mother.

"It's lots of fun. I can spoil them and no one cares."

"I hear someone arriving. Katie, go see if it's Gabe. He said he'd come over early with the children if he could."

Katie opened the door. "Jah, it's him with the kids."

Gabe let the children off and headed back with the buggy. Mervin and Lizzy ran in to get their hugs and hopefully, cookies with fresh milk. Mary kept a supply of oatmeal cookies for just such occasions. Several minutes later, Gabe came in to greet everyone, especially Emma, who received a special kiss on the top of her head, and then he went out to the barn to be with the men.

"You two are so lovey-dovey," Katie said, grinning over at her sister. "Think I'll ever act so silly?"

"It's not silly," Emma said in defense. "We just miss each other when we're apart, is all."

Lizzy came over to see Nathanael and asked if she could hold him.

"Jah, but wash your hands first, Liz," Ruth said. "We don't want to give him germs."

Once she washed up and dried her hands, she sat very still on the sofa and extended her arms. Emma laid Nathanael gently in her arms. Lizzy looked so sweet as she held the infant, a grin as wide as her face. She barely moved.

"Sometimes I wish we could take pictures. Look how cute they are," Ruthie said enjoying the sight.

"Jah, they look adorable together," Mary agreed. "So, Lizzy, you want your mamm to have a boppli for you?"

"She said she will, didn't you, Mamm?"

Emma smiled over at her step-child. "When the Lord's timing is right, I'm sure it will happen."

"How did you say it happens again?" Lizzy asked wide-eyed.

"Oh, child, this isn't the time to talk about such things," Mary said, a flush rising in her cheeks.

Mary's daughters all laughed softly. "Later, Lizzy. Why don't you draw a picture for Mammi? Remember the one you did for me with the ducks?"

"I will, but I forget where she keeps the paper."

"In my top desk drawer, Liz," Mary said, pointing toward the front room where she kept her personal items.

"So, Katie, how is your diet going?" Emma asked.

"I gained a half pound this week."

"Oh." Emma looked over at Ruth. "So you're not upset?"

"Why should I be? Josiah says I'm just perfect the way I am."

Mary's brows rose. "Goodness, I think my Katie is going to get a proposal soon with that kind of talk."

Katie giggled. "It's way too soon, Mamm."

"But you'd like that, wouldn't you?" Ruthie said looking over.

"I'd be lying if I said I wouldn't. He's a real nice guy even if you and Emma didn't think so. I like to hear about cows."

"To each his own," Ruthie said smiling at her sister.

"So where's Daed?" Emma asked.

"He's still resting. He worked too hard this morning, so I made him go lie down after lunch," Mary announced proudly.

"Gut for you, Mamm," Emma said. "You need to be strong."

"He just wouldn't take care of himself without me reminding him," Mary said.

"He must be relieved to know medication will help and he won't need surgery," Ruth said.

"He is, but your daed has always been so healthy, I just think he doesn't know how to handle any problems like this. He doesn't even want to take the medicine."

"Well, he doesn't have much choice," Emma said.

"Maybe he should talk to the bishop about his fears," Ruth suggested.

"I'll mention it, but I have a feeling he'll deny being fearful. Oh, well, let me stir the soup. Then I want to start the vegetables."

"We'll help Mamm," said Ruthie. "Just tell us what you want us to do."

"I'm fine. Katie can help when it's time. You two need a rest."

Emma shrugged. "My family is easy to take care of. Not like having a boppli."

"Still," Mary added, "you and Ruthie should spend time together."

"What about me?" Katie said, her mouth drawn down. "Shouldn't I be spending time with my sisters?"

"Of course, sweetie. I didn't mean that. Jah, I'll call you when I need help. Go sit with them and learn about being a mother."

Katie rolled her eyes as she looked over at Emma. "Like being a teacher to thirty some kids doesn't prepare me," she said under her breath.

Emma laughed. "I'm relieved I can stay home now with my family. School starts next week doesn't it, Katie?"

"Jah. I'm sorry in a way. I like seeing Josiah everyday and I'll miss him when I'm teaching."

"Have you been to the school house to get it ready?"

"Becky and I are going over tomorrow to work on it. It shouldn't be too dirty just sitting there all summer."

"It will need a sweeping, that's for sure," Emma said. "You'd be surprised."

Josiah came in through the back door, removing his muddy shoes first. "I just came to say good-bye," he said, looking around at the group of women.

"I thought you'd be staying for dinner," Katie said with her mouth drawn down.

"I just remembered it's my niece's birthday and I promised her I'd stop by for ice cream and cake. I don't want to disappoint her."

"Of course not." Katie rose and went toward the door where he stood, hat in hand.

"I'll be here early tomorrow, Katie. I'm sorry. I didn't remember until Wayne mentioned his own birthday coming up."

"That's okay. Sure. I'll see you tomorrow sometime," she added, trying to curve her mouth into a smile.

After he left, she began to peel the potatoes while her mother trimmed the fat off the meat and seared it in a Dutch oven.

"Too bad. I know Josiah likes my stew," Mary said.

"Jah, he does."

Several minutes later, while Katie was cutting up carrots, there was a loud knock on the front door.

"Katie, can you get the door?" Emma called in. "Ruthie's in the bathroom and I'm holding Nathanael."

"Oh, jah." Katie set her paring knife down on the counter and rinsed her hands before going to the door. When she opened it, an English man about her age with straggling hair and an angry expression stood with his hands on his hips.

"Jah? What do you want?" she asked.

"I'm lookin' for a friend of mine. Josiah Stoltz. Is he here?"

Katie felt her heart drop. Who was this threatening looking man and how would he know Josiah?

Chapter Twenty-Four

"Who is it, Katie?" Her mother's voice came through from the kitchen. "Show them in."

Katie ignored the invitation and stood, uncertain about how to respond.

"Well? Is he?"

"Nee. No. He's not. Who are you anyway?"

"A friend. So where is he? Are you his girl?"

"It's none of your business." Katie fumed at his impertinence. "I have no idea where he is. Why are you looking for him anyway?"

Katie heard her mother's steps as she came to see who the visitor was. She stopped next to Katie and raised her brows. "So who are you?"

"A friend of Stoltz. I'm lookin' for him."

Mary looked over at Katie, who was frowning. "He's not here."

"I told him already, Mamm."

"I'm sorry, you'll have to leave," Mary said in a steady voice. Katie had never heard her mother ask someone to leave her home. She, too, must feel something is wrong.

"When you see him, tell him Jay's lookin' for him. He'll know why and I *will* find him. Don't worry about that." He turned and stomped over to an old blue Chevy, distinguishable by assorted dents and scratches.

Katie and her mother watched as his tires screeched while exiting their drive with the intensity of a hurricane.

Mary looked at Katie with a frown. "Now I wonder what that was all about. I sure didn't like the looks of that young man. He was up to no gut."

"I'll have to warn Josiah."

"Do you think the man would harm him?"

"It sounded more like a threat than anything, Mamm. I'm scared."

"No, I'm sure there's an explanation. Just talk to Josiah about it. Come, let's join the others. Don't let's worry your daed about it. It's probably nothing."

Wayne and Gabe came through the back door as Katie and Mary returned to the kitchen.

"I heard a noisy car leave our drive a minute ago. Who was here?" Wayne asked as he removed his shoes and headed for the sink.

"Some guy looking for Josiah," Katie said, still concerned. "He scared me."

"Jah?" Gabe looked at his sister-in-law and frowned. "Why was that, Katie?"

"Hard to say. I just know he's not a nice person."

"It's probably the guy he roomed with in Philadelphia," Wayne said, drying his hands on a towel and moving back to allow Gabe to wash up.

"Most likely," Katie agreed. "I guess he didn't leave on real friendly terms."

"Well, it doesn't concern us," Wayne added as he reached for a piece of bread. "Where's Daed?"

"Still resting. He did too much today. You have to stop him, Wayne, before he gets too tired." Mary scowled as she put the butter on the table and began to cut the bread.

"I tried to tell him, Mamm, but you know Daed."

"Jah, I do. Only too well. Go check on him, Wayne."

He went up the stairs and Gabe went over to Emma, sat down beside her, and took her hand in his. "You like your new nephew?" he asked, smiling at her.

"He's wonderful-gut."

Ruthie grinned. "He is that, all right. We're so blessed."

"Jah, and maybe we'll have gut news soon, right Emma?" Gabe beamed at his new wife.

"When God decides."

"Katie," Ruthie called over to her sister who was setting the table. "You look worried. Is it about Josiah?"

"Maybe a little. That man scared me. His eyes looked ever so mean."

"You'll see Josiah tomorrow. Tell him about it and see what he thinks."

"I will."

156

Leroy came down the stairs with Wayne behind him. He went over and kissed Mary on her cheek. "I didn't mean to sleep so long. Goodness, I didn't even know I was that tired."

"It might be the medication, Leroy. Your body isn't used to it. Other than being tired, are you feeling a little better?"

"I don't notice a difference yet, although I haven't been weak in the knees. So what smells so gut?"

"Beef stew is cooking. One of your favorites."

"I thought so. I'm hungry as a bear in spring."

They enjoyed the meal and the evening together. Katie held her nephew for over an hour and he never even stirred. She loved to hold infants and for a minute she pretended he was her own boppli.

That night she had trouble sleeping. The face of the man who came looking for Josiah, the man named Jay, kept popping into her mind and when it did she asked God to take it away and to keep Josiah safe. She woke up once around two and went down stairs to check the doors—just to be sure they were locked. She hoped she'd never see the man again.

Finally morning came and she heard Josiah's voice in the kitchen as he talked with her brother and father. She slipped a dress on quickly and came down to join them. Her mother, who was measuring coffee grinds, looked surprised to see her daughter down this early. Josiah gave her a huge grin and she offered to check the chicken house for fresh eggs. First she went with Wayne and Josiah to the barn. While Wayne started to prepare for the milking, she drew Josiah aside.

"Last night, after you left, a man came by to see you, Josiah."

"Oh, who was it?"

"He called himself Jay."

Josiah moistened his lips with his tongue and looked away from Katie. "I wish he'd leave me alone. First he stopped at my parent's place and another time he checked at the construction site. Both times he missed me."

"What does he want with you?"

"I don't really know. I left money when I took off, which I thought would cover my part of the expenses and then some. If he comes back tell him to leave a phone number and I'll reach him somehow."

"I don't know if it's a gut idea, Josiah. He looked pretty mad about something."

Josiah shook his head. "I don't know why. Please don't worry about it, Katie. It's my problem. I don't want you getting involved. Besides, what could it be? If I owe him for another bill, I'll just pay it, is all. Now go back to the house and have some breakfast. I have to help Wayne. I'll stop in for lunch and we can spend time together, okay?"

"That sounds gut. This is our last weekday together. I start teaching next Monday."

"Jah, I know. I'll miss being with you a lot, but we'll have the week-ends, right?"

"If you want to."

"Miss Katie, I think you know the answer to that one."

She gave her sweetest smile and turned to go fetch the eggs.

"And Katie—" She turned to face him. "I can take care of myself, you know. So I don't want you to worry about me."

"I'll try not to, Josiah, but it's a hard thing to do."

He grinned and tilted his head. "Jah? Maybe I'm more than just a friend, Katie."

"Josiah, hush now. You make me blush."

"Ach, look how cute you are when you turn pink."

Katie walked faster now toward the hen house. She was afraid to continue with this conversation. She would not give her heart away. No, never before the man says something real special first. It would be too humiliating to confess her feelings, only to have them rejected or laughed at. The painful words, 'Weighty Katie,' would never be totally erased from her memory, though she prayed one day they would be.

Sunday night Katie attended the Sing with Josiah and considered it one of her very best evenings with her friends. The girls all gathered around her and questioned her about her relationship with Josiah. She tried to 'play it cool' like an Englisher would do she thought, but her giggles and titters gave it away.

Becky put her arm around Katie. "He's a wonderful-gut guy, Katie. I bet he'll propose before the harvest."

"Jah, he'd better hurry then. It's already September."

Ida Mae grinned. "He was sure to marry a Zook sister the way he went after everyone."

"Ida, that's mean," Becky said, clucking her tongue. "It was God's will that Katie would be the one."

"Oh, that's what I meant," Ida Mae said quickly. "He saved the best for last."

Katie frowned slightly but maybe it was true. Maybe she was the best choice in the end for him. After all, she even liked talking about farm stuff—even cows.

Chapter Twenty-Five

"So, school starts tomorrow. Are you excited?" Emma rinsed the suds out of Lizzy's long hair while she sat in the tub to bathe.

"No, I'm sort of sad about it. I like being home a lot, especially with you here."

"That's sweet, Lizzy. I'll miss you, too."

"Will you miss teaching?"

"Mmm. Maybe a little, but I'm pretty busy now taking care of my new family."

"The house looks ever so gut, Mamm. Always so clean and all."

"Well, I don't mind cleaning and your daed really appreciates it."

"So does Mervin. I heard him say 'wow' one time when he saw his room was all neat and all."

Emma laughed. "Okay, put your head back for the final rinse. Lay the washcloth over your eyes again." Lizzy followed instructions and then Emma dipped a plastic cup in the water and poured it through Lizzy's hair till it was squeaky clean. Then she helped her out of the tub and wrapped a large towel around her as Lizzy stepped onto the bathroom mat to dry herself.

"I have a clean nightie for you, Liz."

"Do you think Merv is jealous you spend so much time with me?"

"Nee. He's always busy with his daed, learning to be a gut Amish man. We still talk a lot when he's in the mood. He knows I love him, Lizzy."

"You love me, too. I know that." Emma helped Lizzy on with her gown.

"Oh, I do. So much. You can't believe it."

"How much?"

"Mmm. More than the stars. Bigger than oceans. More than there are birds in the sky." Emma grinned over at Liz as she towel-dried her hair.

"Me, too. I love you and Daed more than all the dirt even."

"Oh, wow! That's a whole lot, Liz. Danki."

"What if you get a new baby, would you love it more?"

"Oh, honey, we talked about this before, remember? Love is not limited. I would have enough love to cover every single baby or child."

"Promise?"

"Promise. Now get your teeth brushed and I'll still have time to read another chapter before I outen the light."

After Lizzy said her prayers and had her story, Gabe joined them. He and Emma tucked her in and kissed her good night. "I'm glad you got married, Daed."

"I'm glad to hear you approve, little one."

"And I'm real glad it was Emma."

"Oh, jah, me too," he said grinning. He reached across the bed and took Emma's hand. "She's very special, Lizzy. God is gut."

Mervin took care of himself, but stopped in the hallway on his way to bed, long enough to give Emma a hug. She was pleased, but surprised since he tried to act so grown up most of the time. Even a twelve-year-old needs hugs. "Gut nacht, Mervin. Have pleasant dreams."

"Jah, I do now, Mamm."

Gabe and Emma were alone now and it was nearly nine. Though it was time to get some sleep, Gabe seemed hesitant to disrupt their special moment together. They sat at the kitchen table, sipping Chamomile tea.

"Have I told you I love you, Mrs. Kuhns?"

"I believe you mentioned it once, Mr. Kuhns," she said, smiling across the table.

"Gut. I'm glad I don't forget to tell my wife she's ever so special to me."

"Honey, you know how much I love you, too. My life feels so wonderful-gut now. So fulfilled."

"Emma, it's been six months since our wedding."

"Jah. Half a year. And they said it wouldn't last," she said jokingly.

"I just wondered…"

She saw him glance down toward his cup as he stirred another teaspoon of sugar into it.

"Wondered?"

"If there was a problem with…well…like you getting pregnant."

"Oh." It was Emma's turn to avoid his eyes. "It hasn't been so very long. We didn't try real hard in the first couple months, remember? Because of the kids?"

"Jah, you're right. Are you upset, you know, watching Ruthie with the baby and all."

Emma took a deep breath. "How shall I put this. Maybe a little bit, Gabe, but you've been so busy and sometimes when I think it would be the right time…well, I don't like to bother you and all."

"Oh, Emma, sweet girl. You could never 'bother' me. I stay apart sometimes because I'm afraid you're too tired or not in the mood or—"

"Really?" Emma grinned. "I thought you just didn't want me or…something like that."

"You are so desirable, Emma, how could I not want you." He got up from the table and came around to her side. Kneeling next to her chair, he surrounded her with his arms. "You are everything a man could want, and believe me—I want you, my darling."

Emma ran her fingers through his hair, closing her eyes. "Then take me, husband. I believe the time is right."

Gabe stood and reached for her hand. She arose and smiled tenderly at this man she so dearly loved. As they took the kero lamp and headed toward their room, she silently prayed that a new life would grow within her—a bond cementing this marriage and this family.

Monday arrived abruptly and Katie gathered her class plans together, her stomach flipping slightly as she realized the new school year was upon her. The registry showed there would be thirty-eight children this year. She was ever so pleased the board had confirmed Becky as a teacher also. Some districts expected one teacher to handle up to forty students with only volunteer aids, which Katie felt would be way too much for one person. Certainly more than she could manage.

"Katie, you must finish your breakfast before you leave," Mary warned as she poured more tea into her own cup. Katie's half-eaten oatmeal sat getting chilled.

"I can't, Mamm. I'll *kutz* for sure if I try. I made a sandwich for my lunch."

"Ach. You know you'll be hungry in an hour."

"Then I'll take an apple with me, too."

Mary nodded and reached for an apple from a basket of fruit, which she kept in the center of their kitchen table.

Katie leaned over and kissed her mother on the cheek. "See you later, Mamm."

Mary smiled at her daughter. "Josiah got here earlier. He left an envelope for you. It's on the table next to the back door."

"I'll take it when I leave." Katie added it to her notebook and took a *toot* with her lunch. Why would Josiah leave a note for her? Wayne had prepared the buggy, by hitching up her horse and tying it to the post out front. She settled into the driver's seat and opened the note before starting off.

> *Dear Katie,*
>   *I just wanted to wish you a good first day teaching and I was afraid I wouldn't see you before you left. So, have a good day and hopefully I'll see you this afternoon when you get back.*
>   *Your special friend, Josiah.*

How sweet of him. She smiled and tucked it in her pocket. Was she in love? It certainly felt like love. How does one know when it's real and not just infatuation? Maybe time would be the answer. Jah, she'd take her time deciding if he was the one. After all, divorce was never allowed, so she'd better not make a mistake. She knew of cases, hushed of course, where there was little affection between the women and their husbands. They seemed to work out all right, but how sad not to have love.

When she pulled up to the schoolhouse, Becky was already inside and there were two new students, first graders from the Schultz' farm. She knew their whole family and didn't expect any problems from the two boys, who were first cousins.

The children were wound up from their summer vacation, but they quieted down after a few minutes when Katie read the first chapter of Matthew from the Bible. The children repeated the Lord's Prayer together. Some of the new students only spoke in the Pennsylvania Dutch dialect with their families in their homes, so they listened intently while the others recited the prayer in English. They would learn English quickly, since that was the preferred language in the class room.

Then Becky told the children to file up front where they sang three songs from their songbooks. While they sang, Katie finished writing the arithmetic assignments on the board and then prepared for the reading class. It felt like she'd never been away from it. The summer seemed like something out of the remote past. Maybe next year, Becky would be the head teacher. That is, if Katie was married. Oh my. She was getting way ahead of herself.

During recess the younger children played tag while the older girls jumped rope. A couple of the bigger boys just sat and talked. Merv would be leaving school at the end of this year since he would be thirteen and needed on the farm. He had made a turnaround since his father and Emma had married. He was so well-behaved, Katie hardly recognized him.

Lizzy and her friend, Anna, were buddies, though they played well with all the other girls, too. Lizzy was one of the best at jumping rope and patiently tried to teach the new first graders how to hold the rope and turn it. She'll be a gut mother, Katie thought as she watched.

Katie liked having some of her nieces and nephews in class and wondered why Emma wasn't in a family way by now. She'd keep her thoughts to herself. When the time came, Emma would certainly share the wonderful news.

At the end of the day, Katie was surprised at how tired she felt. She and Becky left as soon as the last student headed for home. Katie looked forward to seeing Josiah when she returned to the farm. She was surprised at how much she had missed seeing him. When she pulled in, he and Wayne were taking a break. Josiah came right over to her when she came to a stop. "I'll take the carriage around, Katie. You look tired. How was your first day?"

"Ever so gut. Becky and I work perfect together, but I am a bit worn-out."

"I have to get back to work, but your mamm asked me to stay for supper. Is that okay with you?"

"Of course, you know that."

Wayne was watching the exchange and grinned widely. "You two are so mushy. When are you gonna get hitched?"

"Wayne!" Katie looked horrified at her brother's remark. She heard Josiah guffaw and she didn't know whether to laugh or cry. Brothers!

After Katie got in the house, she sat a few minutes with her parents at the kitchen table. She drank a glass of juice and allowed herself an oatmeal cookie while her parents drank tea. Her father's spirits seemed much better since he was on his medication. She mentioned Wayne's comment and her father laughed heartily. "Maybe your young man needs a little nudge, Katie."

"Jah, like you did, Leroy. I had to push you over the edge."

"I was gonna ask you in time, but you were in a hurry, I guess," he said, as he winked across at Mary.

"Well, I had a lot of young men pursuing me, ja know."

"Oh, jah, you were the belle of the ball."

"Daed, where did you ever hear such fancy talk?" Katie giggled at his expression.

"Can't say I remember. But your mamm was a pretty young thing. The guys took note."

"Oh, mercy, with my limp and all?"

"Mary. Don't. You know that never mattered." Leroy reached across the table to pat her hand.

"Maybe not to you, Leroy, but others probably noticed."

"You had a heart of gold. Gentle and loving to everyone. You even were nice to that young kid with the dirty clothes and broken teeth."

Mary's brows came together. "Otis something?"

"That's the one."

"Poor boy. No one paid him any heed."

"See? You were always the one to be friendly."

Leroy turned to Katie. "You have some of those same traits as your mother, Katie. You're a very sweet girl."

"Maybe Josiah will someday care about me the way you do about Mamm. That would be ever so nice."

Mary nodded and smiled at Katie as she pressed Leroy's hand against her lips. "Jah. Ever so nice."

Chapter Twenty-Six

The next afternoon, Becky and Katie watched as the last of their pupils left the school yard. Becky sat back in one of the pupil's seats and covered a yawn. "I don't know how you do this day after day, Katie. It's really a lot of work."

"It is, but I enjoy the kids, most of the time. Last year was harder because of Mervin and Lizzy with all their problems. So far, things seem to be going okay. You'll get used to it, Becky."

"I hope so. It doesn't make me want to run off and get married and have a dozen boppli of my own, that's for sure and for certain."

Katie laughed at her friend. "Do you have anyone special picked out yet?"

"I'd rather not say."

Katie's ears picked up. "Really? Why on earth not? I'm your closest friend."

"I know, but..."

Katie leaned over and stared into Becky's eyes. "You *have* to tell me now, Beck, or I won't sleep tonight."

"You promise not to tell anyone—not a living soul?"

"I promise."

"You cross your heart and hope to die?"

"Becky, you're so dramatic. Okay." Katie made the sign over her chest.

"Well, I noticed that Wayne hasn't taken Sadie to the Sings the last two times."

"He doesn't talk about her anymore."

"So, if that's the case..."

Katie's mouth dropped open and she sat back staring at her friend. "You like my *bruder?*"

"He is a nice guy, Katie."

"Is he? Oh, my, I hadn't noticed," Katie responded, grinning.

"Why don't you invite me over Saturday to help clean or something and maybe he'll notice me?"

"You poor thing! You must be desperate to like Wayne."

"Katie! Shame on you. He's wonderful. He's smart and cute."

"And a pain in the neck and lazy." Katie sat back and folded her arms.

"Katie, not true. He's always working with your daed. You tell me that yourself."

"Only 'cause he has to. Okay, so he's not lazy, but he's still a pain in the neck."

"That's because you're his *schwester.*"

"Okay, come on Saturday and I'll have you stay for lunch. Otherwise you won't see him. He's outside all the time now."

"You are a dear. I'll never forget this."

"That doesn't mean he's going to like you, Becky. I'm just making an opportunity, is all."

"Jah, I know. Tell me what he likes. What should we talk about?"

"My goodness. Who knows? Let me think. Well, you can always talk about farming. He's gut at softball, though he doesn't get much time for it. And of course, being a guy, you can always talk about how strong he is and how you notice him lifting heavy things. Stuff like that."

"Sounds silly."

"Well, it is, sort of, but guys like it when they feel all strong and tough and we fall all over them and all."

"We're the same age, you know."

"Jah, I guess you are. Do you think Sadie is seeing someone else?"

"I don't think so, but I saw her talking to Benjamin last week and he seemed to laugh more than usual."

"He's nice, but actually my bruder is smarter than he is."

"Oh, Katie, I'm so glad I confessed. I've had a crush on Wayne forever. Even in first grade."

"And you never let on." Katie shook her head in disbelief.

"I've never told a soul. And it has to stay that way. You're the only one, Katie, who knows, so if it gets out..."

"I promised, Becky. I don't go back on my word."

"How about if I come earlier and we work on that quilt you started."

"Okay, come around eleven. We eat at noon and wear your green dress. It looks nice on you."

They both stood up and Becky embraced Katie. "I'll never forget this, Katie. If we get married we'll name our first girl after you."

"Mercy, I think you're jumping ahead a bit."

"I can always hope, right?"

Saturday, promptly at eleven, Katie heard a knock on the front door. Becky stood there, rosy cheeked and hair perfect under her freshly starched kapp. "Hallo, Katie."

"Come on in, Becky. I have the quilting frame ready. I'm sooo glad you were able to make it."

Becky raised her brows and bit her lip. Leaning over, she whispered, "Where is he?"

"Outside. You're safe."

"Whew. I've been a wreck. I had to wear my navy dress. My green dress had a spot on it and there wasn't time to remove it."

"You look gut in blue, too. So, did you bring needles?"

"I figured you'd have extra."

"I do. Mamm," Katie called out to her mother who was upstairs changing sheets, "Becky's here. We're gonna quilt now."

Mary called down to say hello to Becky and went on with her work.

Around noon, the girls heard the back screen door open and Josiah and Wayne entered the kitchen. Wayne looked over, a surprised look on his face. "Hi, Beck. Didn't know you were coming."

"Oh, I wanted to help Katie with her quilt."

"Mmm. So what's for lunch, Mamm?"

Mary removed a ham from the oven and a casserole of scalloped potatoes. "Ham, today. Where's your father?"

"He's coming. He's doing gut today. Even milked with us."

"I guess I'll be out of a job soon," Josiah remarked, looking over at Katie as he headed over to the sink to wash up alongside of Wayne.

"What will you do?" Wayne asked him as he dried his hands.

"I checked with the construction crew, but they don't have anything lined up now. I'm checking out land though and I think I've found a small farm nearby."

Katie's ears picked up. "The one you mentioned to me, Josiah?"

"Jah, the old Bucky Brewster farm."

"I know the spot," Mary said. "Gut fertile land. Has a cute farmhouse on it, too. I was inside once at a quilting bee. Nice kitchen."

"I think I was with you, Mamm," Katie said. "I kind of remember it. The people owned a black car and I was allowed to sit in it."

"Jah, that's right! You were so little, Katie. I'm surprised you remember it at all."

"Want to go with me later, Katie? I'm supposed to go over there and talk to the realtor."

"Maybe. Is it okay with you, Mamm?"

"Why not?"

Katie grinned. "Okay, what time should you be there?"

"I told him around four."

"Becky and I will be done by then."

Wayne looked at his sister. "Since when are you such a devout quilter?"

"I've always like quilting."

"News to me."

Becky and Katie exchanged glances. "So, Wayne, how's it going on the farm?" Becky asked with a lilt to her voice.

Wayne looked over at her as if she had two heads. "Why are you asking?"

"Uh, I just wondered is all."

Mary clucked her tongue. "Wayne, that was rude. Becky's just asking a nice question."

"Sorry. Farming is going gut. How's school?"

"Okay."

Silence reigned. Then Katie broke it. "Becky's a wonderful-gut teacher. She'll be a wonderful Mamm someday, that's for sure and for certain."

Becky rolled her eyes and concentrated on her quilt piece. Katie noted her cheeks were extra rosy. Maybe that was over the top.

Wayne went over to the stove and took an end of meat, popping it in his mouth. "Tender."

"I'm glad," Mary said. "Now where's that man I married?"

"Here he comes, Mamm," Katie said, looking out the window at her father as he headed down the path.

Katie placed Wayne and Becky next to each other, but they barely spoke. It didn't look like things were going well for her friend. Katie tried several paths of conversation, but everything fell flat. Finally the meal was over and the men retreated to the barn. Becky let out a sigh as Mary took dishes to the sink.

"He doesn't even know I'm alive," Becky whispered to Katie.

"Oh, give him time. I'm sure he noticed. Come again next week. Maybe he'll warm up."

"I don't know, Katie. Maybe I should forget the whole thing."

"If you come by often enough, at least we'd get the quilt done. I've been working on it forever. I'm sick to death of it."

"Katie, I confess, I hate to quilt. I only do it because I feel I have to. I mean, all Amish women are supposed to know how to quilt."

"That's silly. Maybe we can think of something else to do. Maybe bake! That's it. Wayne loves raisin pie. We'll make it special for him. In fact, I'll pretend I'm too busy so you can make it all by yourself."

Becky smiled broadly. "You're the best friend ever. Jah, I can bring my own raisins."

"Don't be silly. We have tons."

Mary called in from the kitchen. "Bring in the rest of the dishes, Katie. If you want to be finished with your chores by four, you'll have to hurry."

"I'm gonna head for home when we're done cleaning up, Katie. I'm gonna sew a new dress for next week. I have the material and all."

After Katie was done and her friend had left, she went upstairs and brushed her teeth, washed her face, and re-did her hair. Who knows? Maybe she was about to visit her future home. Her heart skipped a beat just imagining it. Suddenly her whole life looked more interesting. She even admired her new waistline, but reminded herself not to be proud.

Chapter Twenty Seven

Around half past three, Josiah and Katie went off in his buggy to check out the farm. They chatted merrily along about his prospects for owning his own property. Not a word was mentioned about a wedding, though Katie thought of little else.

The farm had laid empty since the death of old farmer Brewster, who passed away almost a year before, alone and in his nineties. His children had all migrated to Ohio and now had listed the property with a realtor.

When they arrived, the realtor was waiting for them beside his car. He was a man in his forties, partially bald and slightly overweight. He introduced himself as Craig Sellers as he led them toward the barn. "Figured you'd want to see the barn first, since you're Amish," he said.

"That's fine," Josiah said, winking at Katie. The barn was large, but needed a great deal of repair. The stalls had broken down and hay was piled everywhere. Some equipment peeked out from under old tarps and broken wheels. Looking up, Katie could see the sky and she was startled by pigeons, which appeared out of nowhere, landing on the rafters.

The milking stalls could probably be used after a heavy cleaning, but most of the doors were either hanging from one hinge or missing entirely. Katie looked over to see how all this was affecting Josiah. She was surprised to see he seemed perfectly fine and quite cheerful.

Craig took them around the perimeter of the property, pointing out the landmarks and even leaned over to scoop up some soil for Josiah to appraise.

"Oh, jah, it's fertile soil for sure. A few rocks too many on the back field, but I can get rid of them, that's for certain."

"So now I guess the missus would like to check out the house," Craig said with a grin.

"Oh, Katie's a friend. I'm sorry I didn't explain. But she's a real gut friend and I wanted her opinion."

Katie was disappointed at the tone Josiah used. Surely he could have made it sound like she was his girl friend, at the very least.

They walked through the back door into a small, but adequate kitchen. There was a square maple table, laden with old newspapers, sitting in the middle of the room. Three straight-back pine chairs were scattered about the room. The imitation brick linoleum flooring had several sections missing, exposing yet another layer of old covering—a pebble design in shades of gray.

It was nice to have a window above the sink, but the window was so covered with grime, one could barely make out the small orchard behind the house. Katie's heart sank.

Assorted pots and pans were all over the counters and when Katie walked over to the sink, she noticed it was filthy and partially rusted through. There was a wood-burning stove with four burners, but everything needed cleaning. Even the few cabinets above the work area would need replacing or extensive repair. The task looked overwhelming.

"Come see the parlor, Katie," Josiah called in to her as he and Craig moved toward the front of the house. "They left more furniture."

Katie was almost afraid to look, but when she did, she was pleasantly surprised to see a tan couch in decent condition and a rocker, which appeared unbroken as it sat in the corner, covered with cobwebs. There were three large windows, allowing the sun to stream through, in spite of the filth. The flooring looked like old pine and there was a large fireplace at one end of the room. With a lot of elbow grease and fresh paint, this room could be nice. There was another room almost identical, though it was void of furniture. There were stacks of old farming journals and cleaning supplies such as an old mop and three buckets. Rather an odd assortment.

The musty smell caused Katie to cough several times and she wished she could open the windows. They went up a flight of stairs, which dipped in the center and creaked loudly, and walked a few feet to a small bathroom—soiled of course. Even Josiah let out a sigh when he checked the footed tub. A stained plastic shower curtain partially hung from a circular bar, which extended to a pipe at the back of the tub.

There were three bedrooms, each large enough for two twin beds or one double bed plus enough space for a small dresser or table, but they were totally vacant, much to Katie's relief. Less to toss out.

174

"Nice place, right, Katie?" Craig asked.

"Needs a whole ton of work," she said in response.

"It would be a challenge," Josiah said as they headed back down to the first floor.

"That's why it's going so cheap. Where else can you find fifty acres with a house at this price?" Craig said as Josiah walked toward the front door.

"Let's check the porch," he said reaching for the doorknob.

"Oh, it's not safe to stand on," Craig said. "We keep the door locked so no one falls through. We can look at it when we go around front from the back door. Did you want to check out the cellar first?"

"Jah. Katie, you want to come down?"

"I guess so." She followed them over to the outside door. The only way to enter the basement at this point, was through the outside cement steps.

"There was a staircase from the kitchen, but something happened to it," Craig mentioned as they walked around the side of the house.

Katie felt so disappointed, she had to hold back tears. How could a woman live there much less bring up a family? It was miserable. Yet Josiah seemed excited as he checked out the other features.

"The roof needs work and probably the plumbing, too. But you Amish don't need much, right?"

"We like nice places, too," Josiah said, his mouth turned down.

"Well, it's a good price, Josiah. And there isn't much else around now in your price range."

Josiah nodded. "I'll think it over. I appreciate you showing me."

Craig reached over and shook his hand and then nodded to Katie. "It won't last long, I can tell you that. I'm showing it again tomorrow, so don't sit on it too long if you're interested. You can always make an offer."

"Jah. I'll be in touch if I'm interested."

They headed back to the buggy, Josiah steering her by her elbow. His chin was firm and he avoided looking at her at first.

Finally when they had ridden nearly half the distance home in silence, he turned toward her. "Well, Katie, what do you think?"

"I think the land is nice, but the house and outbuildings need an awful lot of work."

He nodded. "Trouble is, I don't have much money. I may have to buy it in order to get started. Could you ever live in a house like that?"

Katie swallowed hard. What was he asking? It didn't sound like a proposal, but...

"Well, if it was painted and repaired and had nice furniture and if I was happy with my husband, I guess I could." There, she said it. Now let's see how he responds.

Instead of a verbal response, he looked over at her and grinned. "I think I'll make an offer tonight. Jah, it doesn't hurt to make an offer."

Katie kept her gaze straight ahead. What was she getting into?

Chapter Twenty-Eight

"Things look good, Leroy. Your blood pressure is practically normal." Dr. Nichols smiled across his desk at Leroy and Mary. "I'll keep the medication the way it is and we'll check you again in a month. Of course, if you have any problems, come in before that."

They stood up and headed for the door. Dr. Nichols asked about Katie on their way down the hall to the receptionist's desk.

"She's ever so much better and she's not always talking about food," Mary said.

"I'm glad to hear it. Is she still getting counseling?"

"Nee. She stopped after only a couple sessions, but I think it helps there's a young man in her future."

The doctor laughed and nodded. "I'm sure that makes a difference. Give her my best. Just keep on eye on her and if she begins losing weight too quickly, give me a call and we'll check it out."

On the way back home, Leroy began whistling a tune. Mary smiled over at him. "You seem like yourself again, Leroy."

"Jah, I think the gut Lord is going to let me see more years on this earth."

"I can't tell you how relieved I am that you're doing so much better. God answered our prayers.

He looked over and nodded. "Jah. It's not like I was afraid, but I just didn't want to leave so much for my family to do."

"Well, I was scared," Mary reached across and touched his hand holding the reins. "I would be ever so sad if anything happened to you. You are my darling husband."

"Ach, now I think we'll have many more years together. I should have seen the doctor sooner."

"Oh, jah. You never listen."

"I will next time."

"Sure you will." Mary chuckled and drew her hand back.

"Mary, don't you wonder why Emma isn't in a family way yet?"

"A little, though I think they wanted the children to get used to their being married and all first. It's a hard adjustment."

"I hope that's all it is. Emma seems happy, jah?"

"She is, Leroy. Sometimes it takes longer than other times. God is in control."

"That's for sure. Now that I can go back to my normal schedule, we won't need Josiah. I think our Katie is going to miss him."

"I think you're right, but she went with him to see his property Saturday. I think it may lead to something."

"Did she like it?"

"She didn't say much, but she's been smiling more these days and not so grouchy."

"Jah, I noticed. She's a pretty little thing. Josiah should take notice."

"I'm surprised he came around after being rejected by her sisters."

Leroy laughed. "Katie likes to talk about cows. I think that's why he's sticking around. Not many girls talk so much about animals."

"I remember when we first went out. You talked about a billy goat for a whole evening. I thought I'd go crazy."

"Didn't stop you from dating me again."

"No, because I thought you were pretty cute and a real gentleman."

"I guess I was."

"Oh, my. Where's your *glassenheit?*"

"I'll be more humble when we get home and watch Wayne work rings around me. That boy is strong as an ox."

"He's a gut sohn."

"I'm a fortunate man to have such a gut family." He nodded and clucked to move the horse along quickly, remembering the lemon sponge pie waiting for him.

Becky came by on Saturday as planned, but Wayne barely said hello to her. Katie fumed inside at his indifference and she hated seeing her friend so disappointed. Later as they were cleaning up the mess they'd made baking four raisin pies, Katie put her arm around Becky. "Don't be upset. Someone else will come along. See? Wayne is a pain in the neck."

"I wish I thought so. He probably still likes Sadie. I'm going to try to find out who broke up first."

"I think I know what happened," Katie said. "I heard Wayne talking to Daed a couple days ago and he told him she was getting too bossy."

Becky's eyebrows rose and a twinkling of a smile appeared on her lips. "Oh, she sure is bossy. That's a true statement. I heard her try to boss her own mamm once at a picnic. She has a mouth on her for certain."

Katie nodded. "She looks all sweet and soft, but I think she would be wrong for my bruder. You would be ever so much better."

Becky let out a long sigh. "So what do I do next? I've tried everything."

"Just come around a lot and be sweet to him—even if he looks the other way."

"That's so hard to do, Katie. My feelings get hurt bad sometimes."

"I know how that feels. Well, if you really can't get over him, it's the only thing I can think of. We can bake again next week. Wait, his birthday is Thursday. We're having the family and some friends for cake around six. Come by."

"But he didn't invite me."

"He doesn't have to. I just did."

"Will he be mad?"

"Of course not. He probably won't even notice."

"Oh, danki, Katie. That makes me feel real gut." Becky pouted.

"Oops! I didn't mean it like that. I know! You can bring him fudge. He loves it."

"The dark kind?"

"Any kind, as long as it's fudge."

"Oh, Katie, I make really gut fudge. Everyone tells me that. Okay I'll be here. Do you want me to come early to help?"

"Sure, why not. We'll go together right after school gets out. Thursday morning I'll pick you up in my buggy and then you'll need a ride home. Maybe…"

"Jah, maybe!" Becky's grin lit up her entire face. She was such a sweet girl. Why was her brother so blind?

Just as planned, after school Thursday, they came back to the house in Katie's buggy. Hannah was there helping with lemonade and sweet tea. The children were playing in the front parlor with oversized Lego's. Eight-month-old Joseph was already crawling and he chewed on everything in sight, including the big colorful blocks. It made his mother frantic and she spent most of her time watching over the child, grabbing things out of his mouth.

When Katie and Becky came in, Mary looked up as she spread cream cheese on tea sandwiches "Oh, nice of you to help out, Becky. I'm sure Wayne will appreciate it."

The girls exchanged glances. Katie doubted her brother would even notice her friend's presence, but she didn't offer any comment. Some things are better off not stated.

Around six, the house became crowded with well-wishers. Ruth and Emma arrived with their families and Mark came in with his brother Abram, his wife Fannie and their three little ones. Of course, Mary's parents attended. It was a happy group.

Katie watched for Josiah to show up. He finally arrived on horseback and joined the family. Wayne had slipped past them to go wash up and change, having spent the afternoon in the fields with his father. Leroy had stopped an hour sooner to rest awhile before the celebration, and he remained in his room a few extra minutes to avoid the confusion.

Becky had on her new pale yellow dress and she looked so fresh and lovely that Katie was sure her brother would take notice this time.

When he came downstairs in a fresh shirt and trousers, the group sang the birthday song to him. He blushed and nodded, grinning at everyone. He glanced over once at Becky, and Katie thought he paused a couple extra seconds. Her yellow dress brought out her lovely blond hair and she knew her brother was partial to blue eyes. Gut sign.

As people mingled, Becky scooped a large portion of ice cream into a dish and took it over to Wayne. Katie stood close enough to watch his reaction. He actually smiled at her. Hallelujah!

Josiah motioned for Katie to follow him into the quiet room where they were alone. "I made an offer on the farm, Katie."

"Really? Goodness, that was fast."

"Craig's right. There isn't much around that I can afford. It's a start."

"I hope you get it, if that's what you want."

"Jah, I do and I want it for—"

"Hey, you two, what are you doing in here?" Lizzy asked as she barged in for her coloring books.

"We're just talking, Lizzy," Katie remarked, annoyed at the interruption.

"Your mamm was lookin' for you, Aunt Katie. You have to help serve the cake."

"All right, I'll be right there."

Lizzy grabbed a handful of the coloring books Mary saved for her to use and reached for the box of crayons. Then she stood there staring at them.

"So? I guess we'd better go, too," Josiah said, obviously disappointed.

"Let me know if your offer is accepted, Josiah," Katie said as they followed Lizzy into the parlor.

"I will. I probably won't hear for a couple days, though. Oh, I picked up some work at the farm supply house up the road. Only a few hours a week, but it will help pay bills."

"Week-ends, too?" Katie asked.

"Every other Saturday from eight to four. Of course, not Sundays. We can still go to the Sings together."

"Gut. I'm glad of that. Come on, I'll give you an extra large piece of cake. In fact, you can have my piece as well," she said proudly, realizing it was the first time she ever passed up a three layer cake with butter cream icing!

Josiah stood with the other men while the women kept the punch bowl filled and replaced dishes of ice cream, mostly for the children. Becky and Katie took turns holding Nathanael, who was totally indifferent to the whole occasion. "He's ever so cute, Ruthie," Becky said when it was her turn to hold him. Why, he could be mine with his coloring." She grinned at Katie, who noticed Wayne was in hearing distance. Why did his neck turn so red? Could it be because everyone commented on Nathanael looking like Wayne when he was a baby? Mmm.

It was nap time for Hannah's two little ones and though they tried to get them settled down in Ruth's old room, they continued to reappear until Mark scolded them. There were tears and finally Hannah decided it was time to leave and get her children home where there wasn't so much excitement.

Abram and Fannie left a few minutes later.

Ruth changed the baby and then they left for their home. Eventually, only the immediate family remained and Becky, who was sitting on the sofa next to Katie. Wayne plopped himself down across from them and stretched out his long, lanky legs. "Who made my cake, Katie. It was gut."

"I helped Mamm, but she did the icing."

"Did you like everyone singing to you?" asked Becky.

"It was loud." He let out a grin.

Becky giggled. "It was that all right. You like being eighteen?"

"Haven't been it long enough to feel any different."

"True."

There was an uncomfortable silence. Katie realized Becky had no way home yet. "I'm sooo exhausted, Wayne. Could you take Becky home in a few minutes for me?"

Becky's mouth dropped at the unexpected question.

Wayne squirmed in the chair and ran his fingers through his hair. Without looking at Becky, he nodded. "Jah, sure. It's too far to walk."

"I don't want to cause a problem for anyone. I don't mind walking, really."

"It's not a big deal. I'll stop over at my friend Zeke's on the way back. Ain't seen him since the preaching service. Let me know when you wanna leave, Beck. Right now, I think I'll check the cows. They'll need milking soon."

"That's real nice of you Wayne. I sure appreciate it," Becky said, smiling at him. She sure looks pretty, thought Katie. It would be fun to have her as her sister-in-law.

When he left for the barn, the girls hugged each other. "It's working, Katie. He smiled so cute at me. I'm so nervous. Does it show?"

Katie looked her over from head to toe. "How would 'nervous' show?"

"I'm not too sure, but I think I'd be breathing funny or something."

"You don't look weird and your breathing's fine as far as I can see."

Mary came in from the kitchen. "Oh, Becky, I didn't know you were still here. Leroy can take you home if you'd like. He has to drop something off at the bishop's place and you live right close by."

"Uh, that's okay, Mamm. Wayne wants to take her."

"Oh, jah? Well, maybe your daed can let Wayne drop off the book the bishop wanted then. I'll let him know. He's upstairs freshening up." Mary went up the stairs leaving the girls standing in the parlor.

"What if he finds out he didn't have to take me?"

"Goodness. We'll cross that bridge if we have to later. Maybe we should go get him now before it gets any more complicated."

Katie was relieved when she saw Wayne and Becky head out in the buggy. Mary had given him the book with a note for the bishop and never mentioned that Leroy was preparing to make the trip. So far, so good.

When Wayne returned an hour later, nothing was said. Katie would just have to wait to see Becky to find out what happened. Oh, match making was a chore sometimes.

Chapter Twenty-Nine

Josiah waited for the green light at the corner of the busy intersection in Lancaster before crossing the street. He couldn't believe his offer had been accepted without a counter price. He was anxious to sign all the papers so things could be moved along. His father was giving him the money he promised and the bank would pick up the difference with a mortgage. He hated owing anything, but if he managed well, it would be paid off rapidly. Katie would be so surprised to hear it went through. He planned to casually hand the papers over to her and she'd see his name as the new owner. Then maybe he'd make the next move.

"Hey, Stoltz."

Josiah heard his name called out and turned as a dark blue Chevy pulled up to the curb. The windows were rolled down and the driver, Jay, removed his sunglasses and nodded toward a parking spot off to the side. "I wanna talk to you."

Josiah stood and watched as Jay parked the car, got out of the front seat, and sauntered over to join him on the sidewalk.

Josiah held his hand out for a handshake, but Jay ignored the gesture and motioned for Josiah to go a few feet into an alleyway. When Jay stopped, Josiah did the same. "So why have you been looking for me?"

"You're in trouble man."

"How is that?" Josiah leaned against the brick building and folded his arms.

"Wally's in jail and you put him there."

"What are you saying? How did I have anything to do with it?"

"We know you squealed about our drug business. I'm sure it was no coincidence that the cops came the night you left."

"Look, Jay, I knew about the drugs, yeah, but I never went to the police or anyone else about it. I just wanted out, is all. I'm sorry Wally's in jail. When does he get out?"

"That's where you come in. He needs bail. It's only five grand, but it's more than I have at the moment and since it's your fault that—"

"Hold on! I told you, I had nothing to do with the fact that he's behind bars. You're not getting a nickel from me, so take off."

"You don't sound like an Amish guy, Stoltz. Maybe I can convince you to help. Yeah, maybe if you have a bit of trouble walking tomorrow…"

"That sounds like a threat."

"Does it? Huh. How 'bout that. All right, I'll give you till tomorrow to come up with the cash. I know about that old farm you want, so I'll meet you there at four-thirty. I gotta do some errands first. Don't try to sneak away, dude. I'm gonna be following you wherever you go. Got it?"

"If I weren't Amish, believe me, you'd be on the ground by now."

"Oh, Mr. tough guy. I dare you. Come on!" Jay stepped back a couple of feet and turned his hands into fists, egging Josiah on. "Go ahead. Take the first blow, coward."

Josiah felt his blood pressure rise as the adrenaline surged through his body. In an instant he analyzed the threat. The fists weren't a problem. If he had to, he could take him down, but the bulge in Jay's shirt—that was something else. The metal flashed from the sun striking it and a fist was no match for a bullet. Josiah lowered his arms and shook his head. "You know I can't show force. It goes against everything I believe in."

Jay let out a nasty, evil snort as he pulled back. "You have a choice. Come up with the money and I'll leave you alone or—"

"What's going on down here?" Both men turned to see a man with a trashcan heading their way. He set it down and placed his hands on his hips, glaring at the two men.

Jay answered first. "Nothing that concerns you. Just a friendly talk."

The burly man looked over at Josiah. "Sounded kinda loud to me. Any problem with you, Amish boy?"

"It's okay. I'm on my way." Josiah answered.

"I don't want any trouble next to my store. Go on, take off."

Without looking at Jay again, Josiah returned to the sidewalk and went straight into the realtor's office two doors down from the alleyway. As he entered the stone building, he heard Jay's beat-up car drive off, grinding gears for effect.

He took a deep breath and ran his hands through his long hair and replaced his straw hat. He couldn't give Jay the money even if he was willing to, which he wasn't. Every cent was going toward his new homestead and his future. Just when he could see his way to asking Katie for her hand in marriage, this low life had to come in to ruin things.

He was probably all talk and no bite, but maybe Josiah was in real danger. He would have to avoid Katie's home until things got straightened out. And how that would happen, he had absolutely no idea.

Craig, the realtor, led him into his private office and helped Josiah fill out the necessary paper work. "You got yourself a good deal," he remarked as he filled in some of the information. "I didn't think they'd accept your offer without a counter. God must have been with you on this one."

"Jah, I believe so. It's gonna take money to fix it up, though. Lots of it."

"A can of paint works wonders."

"Jah, and lumber, piping, and gut friends will come in handy." Josiah signed the last paper and smiled over at Craig. "Danki for taking care of all this."

"Well, I do get something out of it," he said with a grin. "Not as much as I'd hoped, since it went for such a low price, but maybe in the future you'll be looking for more land."

"Jah, could be. Keep me in mind if something comes up nearby. Not that I could buy now, but you know..."

Craig stood after collecting all the papers and he placed them in a folder, which he laid on his desk. He extended his hand and Josiah reached over to shake it. "I'll get the paperwork over to the bank and we'll work on getting you your mortgage. Then we'll try to close as quickly as possible. The sellers are anxious to settle the estate."

He walked Josiah to the door and as he left the building, Josiah scanned the cars in each direction. Jay was no where to be seen. He let out a long slow breath, patted his pocket with the papers, and headed for home.

Sleep was not in Josiah's future that night. After lying on his cot for several hours, tossing restlessly, he rose and went into the kitchen. He set up a pot of coffee and sat at the table waiting for it to brew. The rich aroma met his nostrils, but there was no joy in the simple things of life at this point. Everything had looked so promising, but now?

What were his options? So far, he had used only five hundred dollars of his own for the earnest money the realtor had required to start the process. He would soon have an appointment at the bank to finalize his mortgage and the terms would be dependent upon the amount of his down payment.

The rest of the money he'd saved sat in cash under his mattress. The money his father planned to add to it for the down payment, represented his total inheritance. With five sons, his father had known the land couldn't be divided equally to support five more families, so he had saved every dollar he could so one day he could help out financially to provide his loved ones with a secure future. That money had not come without sweat and blood. Josiah was grateful and realized without his father's help it would be years before he could afford his own place.

Now this "friend" had appeared out of nowhere, accusing him of ratting on his buddy and threatening him if he didn't come up with the cash. What were his choices? It wasn't the way of his People to be violent. It was "turn the other cheek" and "give your second cloak" when asked for the first. Do you just hand over five thousand dollars because some criminal thinks you owe it to him? How could he do that? What about the farm and his own future?

If he refuses, what then? Apparently, Jay knew about Katie. He knew where she lived and Josiah couldn't take a chance on her being injured. Never! He'd give up his whole farm rather than have harm come to his sweet girl. It didn't leave him much of a choice. Maybe it was a loan. Yah, bail money is returned when the guy shows up at his trial or hearing or something like that. He was pretty sure that's how it worked. So then he'd get the money back. Did he really believe he'd see the money again? He wasn't that naïve. He knew down deep, he'd never see it, and the bank would probably not issue him a mortgage without that as part of the down payment.

So the choice seemed simple now. Give up your dream of owning your own place by handing over the money or take the risk of getting beaten up or your girlfriend being injured. Didn't seem like there really was a choice.

Josiah poured a mug of coffee and turned off the pot. He took the mug back to the spare room and sat on his cot, sipping it slowly. It helped his head, but not his spirits.

After a while he lifted his mattress and withdrew the envelope containing the remaining money he had earned from working. He counted it out, laying the twenties together, then the ten's and then the fives. After he was done counting, he marked the envelope. It came to three thousand, one hundred and seventeen dollars. Seemed like a lot of money once, but no longer. He knew his brother Amos was a saver. He bragged all the time about his stash, but Josiah had been taught not to borrow. It probably wasn't even an option. Of course, he'd pay him back and his brother would know that.

Placing three thousand in a separate envelope, he returned the remaining cash to his hiding place under the thin mattress, and stuck the envelope with the large amount in his pocket.

What about Katie? He couldn't tell her what was going on. He didn't want her involved at all. Could he trust Wayne? It might get back to Katie and then she'd be worried about him. He'd have to keep it to himself.

Part of him rebelled then. Why? He didn't deserve this. It was—what did they call it? Extortion? Maybe he should go to the police and report it. But then he'd be doing what he was accused of doing. Still...

What he couldn't help feeling was his desire to give the guy a good fight. He actually pictured Jay with a bloody nose and tears begging for release. *Oh, Lord, forgive these images that pop in my head. I know my Bible too well to think that's the right way to go. I see you on the cross, dying for me, rather than fight against your terrible crucifixion.*

Josiah checked the clock. Four in the morning. No point in trying to sleep now. His decision was made. He'd give what money he had and hope that would satisfy Jay. Then he'd ask for a higher mortgage at the bank. If he never saw the money again, well, that's the way it would be. He wouldn't stoop to violence. He'd just have to pray a whole lot for God to keep him calm and not resort to anything physical. *You have a big job on your hands, Lord,* he added as he dressed to attend to the animals.

Chapter Thirty

Katie was surprised Josiah did not show up at the house on Sunday afternoon. She had invited him to come by since her family was having dinner together at noon. It was the visiting Sunday instead of the preaching one. Katie wondered if he was ill and she felt uneasy all afternoon.

"Katie, what's wrong?" Ruth asked when Katie made no attempt to hold Nathanael and instead sat rocking by the front window.

"I'm just concerned is all."

"About?"

"Josiah. He was supposed to come by. It's not like him to forget."

"I'm sure there's a gut excuse. Maybe he was needed at home."

"Jah, maybe," Katie answered unconvinced. "I'm sorry if I've been grouchy."

"No, it's not that. I just hate to see you look so sad."

Katie forced a smile. "I'll do better, honest. I wonder if he's over at the farm he wants to buy."

"Maybe. Sure, that's probably it. Maybe he's checking out the barn and making notes on how much it will cost to fix it. You said it needed a lot of work."

"Too much, in my opinion. He's limited moneywise."

"Aren't we all," Ruth said with a grin.

"Maybe I should go over and see if he's there."

"Katie, he might think you're chasing him and besides, Mamm wouldn't like you to leave while the family is all here."

"I guess." Katie felt tears forming and bit her lip, determined to remain optimistic. An unwanted thought forced itself upon her mind. What if he changed his mind about her? Maybe he was upset that she didn't rave about the house. Or perhaps he noticed her waist wasn't as slim as he once thought. Oh, mercy. Why did she allow such thoughts?

Around four Sunday afternoon, Josiah rode his horse over to the property he planned to purchase. Whenever he heard a car, he looked over, wondering each time if it was Jay. Did he really follow him? He must have—to have spotted him in Lancaster. It gave him a weird feeling to know someone could hate him this much and he wondered why Jay wasn't behind bars himself. Josiah was actually sorry he hadn't reported their activities to the police. It just hadn't occurred to him. Now he's blamed for it and didn't even have the satisfaction of seeing justice done.

The realtor had given him a key to the house and told him he could hide it under a milk can sitting by the barn door when he left. Josiah walked around the perimeter of the barn first and visualized it once it was finished. He smiled as he envisioned his life down the road in a few years. He pictured Katie picking strawberries in her garden with a couple toddlers running about chasing each other. He could almost smell the lilacs he'd plant for her. She always exclaimed over their perfume-like scent when they passed by the lovely bushes. He let himself in the back door and walked around the first floor, taking in the vast amount of work it required.

A crushing of tires on the gravel driveway broke his mental picture and he looked out. The now familiar blue Chevy was making its way toward the house. His horse was startled by the racket and swished his tail.

Jay climbed out of the car and headed toward the house as Josiah went out the back door and came around to meet him. He didn't want that guy to enter what hopefully, would one day be his home and haven.

They stood about ten feet from each other. "Well? Got it?" Jay asked. He placed his hands on his hips—a little too close to the bulging handgun.

"I don't have five thousand. I can't come up with it, but I'll loan you three," Josiah said, hating every word coming from his own lips. Was he a coward?

"I told you five."

"Look, this is the best I can do. Take it or leave it."

"Not good enough. I'll take it, but you owe me two more. I can give you another twenty-four hours to come up with it. But that's it." He patted his pocket where the gun was wedged.

Josiah's heart rate quickened, but he remained calm on the outside. "Be fair. I'm telling the truth when I say I didn't blab to the police or anyone else about the drugs."

"Sure. I believe you, right? What do you take me for? I've got a brain, you know."

Josiah had a perfect retort for that one, but bit his tongue. He reached in his pocket and handed the envelope with the money. "Count it."

"I don't need to. If it's wrong, you'll hear about it. I'll be by here tomorrow, same time. Don't disappoint me Stoltz." He turned and got in his car, drove off without another word.

Josiah slammed his fist into the palm of his hand. It smarted from the intensity and it shocked him to realize how angry he was and how frustrated. Where was he going to come up with more money? Now Jay even knew where he was going to live. Perhaps notifying the police was his only solution. Or get a loan from his brother. Then the whole thing could come to an end and everyone, especially dear Katie, would be safe. She would never have to know what kind of people he knew in his past life and she wouldn't need to fear for her own safety.

He locked up the door and placed the key under the milk can. His enthusiasm was gone. All the excitement he had felt on having the offer accepted and the anticipation of showing Katie the paper with his name as future owner—all that was gone. He had an overwhelming desire to sleep. He barely made it home. Then he collapsed on his cot and tuned out the familiar voices of his family as they went about their activities. He'd decide tomorrow whether to go to the authorities or ask his brother for the rest of the money. Right now, he was brain dead. He fell asleep the moment he laid down his head.

During school hours on Monday, Katie forced herself to avoid looking out the window, searching for a certain person, and instead concentrated on her students. During recess, Becky and she sat eating their lunch while the children took advantage of an exceptionally warm and sunny day by playing outside. Becky looked over at her friend.

"You're awful quiet today. Are you feeling okay?"

"Uh huh."

"So, what's wrong?"

"Oh, Becky, I'm worried about Josiah. He was supposed to come yesterday for dinner and he never showed up. I thought he'd come by sometime today to explain himself, but…"

"You're not worried about him changing his mind about you?"

"I don't know what to think. Of course, that's gone through my mind."

"I'm sure that's not the case. I'm real certain there's an explanation. He'll probably come by today to tell you himself. Cheer up, Katie. Everything will be just fine."

"I wish I had your confidence. If I don't hear from him, I'm gonna stop by the farm he wants to buy. He may just be checking it over again. He said he wanted to figure out how much it would cost to fix it up."

"Would he bother going over there, if it wasn't gonna be his for sure?"

Katie nodded. "He's cautious, Beck. That's one thing I like about him. He wouldn't just jump into it without thinking it through. At least, I don't think he would. And maybe he's re-thinking his feelings for me."

"Nonsense. What's to re-think? You guys are great together."

"You really think so?" Katie's face lit up.

"I do. I hope that will be me and Wayne someday. He smiled at me at the birthday party and we talked all the way to my place when he drove me back. I even made him laugh once."

"See? Things are getting better."

"Jah, that's for sure and for certain. Well, we'd better call the kids back in. It's getting late."

"I can't wait until this school day is over. I'm having a hard time thinking."

"I'll teach the German class, Katie. Take a break."

"I'll take you up on it. Danki."

The time dragged on, but finally school was dismissed. Katie got into her buggy and the horse tried to return to her farm, but she pulled lightly on the reins and directed him in the opposite direction. "Not today. We're going somewhere new," she said aloud as she headed toward the land and farm she might one day share with Josiah.

Chapter Thirty-One

Josiah stood watching the road for the blue car. His brother had wanted to think over the loan and Josiah did not want to alarm him with the urgent need. He probably would have insisted on going to the police instead if he'd known. Jay would just have to give him more time. That's all there was to it. Surely, a few more days wouldn't matter.

While he waited, he took measurements of the front porch, which would have to be replaced almost immediately in order to avoid having someone injured. He decided to extend it by three feet in the front in order to allow more seating. While writing the dimensions down, he heard wheels on the drive, but when he looked up, it was a buggy. Who could it be? No one, besides Jay, even knew he'd be here at this time. He watched as it came closer. Not Katie! Not now! His heart took a leap. He walked quickly over as she pulled to a stop just a few feet from the patch of overgrown lawn in front of the house.

"Katie, what are you doing here?"

"That's a nice greeting," she said, hurt by his solemn expression as well as his words. "I came to see you. I figured you'd be here."

"But you can't stay."

"What's going on? Why didn't you come by yesterday? You told me you would be at my place. I waited all day." Katie began to fight back tears, but one escaped and rolled down her cheek.

"Oh, Katie, I'm sorry—"

He looked over her shoulder as the blue Chevy rolled down the drive. What should he do? This could be dangerous.

"Katie, I want you to go home now. Please. I'll explain later."

"You don't have to explain. It's pretty clear," she said as she turned to get back in the buggy, now crying without holding back. Her heart was breaking.

Jay got out of the car and came over to them. "So here's the girlfriend again. I forget your name."

"You don't need her name. She's leaving right now," Josiah said firmly.

"Hey, what's up, Stoltz? You have the pretty little thing in tears. Is that any way to treat a girl?"

"Go home, Katie."

"Oh yeah, it's Katie. Yeah, you'd better go before you see your boyfriend get beat up. Of course, maybe he's smart enough to come through with our deal."

Katie turned, stunned, to see if this horrible stranger was serious about his threat. He had a smirk on his face. She looked over at Josiah, whose jaw was clenched and brows furrowed. She'd never seen him like this and it was frightening. Josiah turned his attention to her. "Please, Katie." His voice was stern.

She climbed in and turned the buggy around, barely able to see through her tears. Was he in danger? Josiah seemed so sure of himself, she figured it was just friends having an argument. But what had he told her about the friends he had in Philadelphia? They sounded more like hoodlums. Okay, he wanted her to leave, so she would. Josiah was strong and could handle that horrible looking man without her. She shouldn't worry. She told herself she *wouldn't*.

She snapped the buggy whip in the air and encouraged her horse to move swiftly back to the road. What kind of awful people did he know?

The two men watched as the buggy went out of sight and then Jay extended his arm with his palm upward. "I'm waiting."

"Look, Jay. I'll have it, but it was impossible to get it today. I guarantee somehow I'll get it, but you have to give me a little more time."

"I could take care of you right now, buddy, but I'm a nice guy. I'll give you exactly two weeks to get the rest. I have commitments at home. You're lucky this time, Stoltz. Put it on your calendar. Two weeks from today. And if you don't have it, well…I know where that pretty little Amish girl of yours lives." He sneered as he got back in his car and tore out of the drive.

Josiah stood motionless, watching the dust cloud the car left behind. Poor Katie. How it grieved him to see her so upset. He wanted so much to explain, but would it further endanger her if he did? If he just waited until the money was exchanged, even though it was two whole weeks away, then she'd be safe and they'd be back together again. It seemed like his only option. If he told Wayne or her father, or anyone else, it would involve them. He couldn't take that chance. No, as painful as it was, in the end it was the right thing to do. He would stay away from Katie and her whole family until this thing was resolved.

He went back to measuring for the new porch. His hand was shaking so hard he could barely read the numbers. He snapped the metal measuring tape back in his pocket and called it a day.

"Katie, *dochder,* what's wrong?" Leroy was cutting back weeds from the sides of the parking area when Katie pulled up in the buggy. Her eyes were puffed and red from crying.

"Oh, Daed," she cried as she jumped down from her seat and surrounded her father with her arms.

"Honey, what's happened? You can tell your old daed." Leroy patted her head as he held her.

"It's over between Josiah and me. He doesn't care about me. I should have known all along he couldn't love me. I'm just too fat and ugly."

"Oh, Katie, Katie. Stop with the nonsense. Come in the house and talk to your Mamm. We wondered why you were late coming home. Where did you go? Never you mind. Don't talk now. Settle down first, honey."

Katie allowed her father to lead her into the kitchen, his strong arm supporting her from collapsing. The tears refused to stop. Mary stood, mouth agape as Leroy settled his daughter down on a kitchen chair.

"Katie, what's wrong?" Mary knelt beside Katie and took her hands in hers. "Has someone hurt you?"

Katie nodded. "It's…Josiah. He's hurt me."

"Oh, my," Mary said, horrified. "What did he do? Don't tell me he…" She stopped half way through her sentence and stared at her daughter waiting for some hint or explanation.

"Not that way, Mamm. He'd never…no, he hurt me here in my heart," Katie said as she pulled one hand away and held it against her chest. "He doesn't care about me. He told me to leave."

"I'm so confused. Leave from where?"

"From the farm he wants to buy."

"Katie, please explain. Why were you there?"

"Because he didn't come yesterday. I was worried sick. I knew I'd find him at the house and I wanted to know what was wrong, but then when I got there he told me to leave."

"Just like that?" Leroy scowled.

"It was when that Englisher, Jay, came up in his car. He looked so mean and he was threatening."

"Goodness, should we call the police? I remember that man and he looked like nothin' but trouble." Mary's concern was written all over her face.

"I don't know. I don't know anything anymore. All I know is Josiah wanted me out of there and he didn't smile or look happy when I pulled in. He hates me. I know it."

Leroy shook his head. "Something ain't right with this whole thing. I'm gonna ride out there myself and see what's goin' on."

"No, Daed, please. I'll get over him. He said he'd take care of himself. So, let him. If he doesn't care enough to explain, then I don't want him around anymore. I'll find someone else someday. Maybe." She burst into tears again and Mary stood and folded her arms, shaking her head.

"My, my. This is strange goings-on. He got mixed up with bad people, I can see that. Maybe he sold drugs, too."

"He'd never do that," Katie said in his defense

"Well maybe you're jumping to conclusions too fast. Give the young man a chance to explain himself," Mary said.

"I don't know, Mamm. In a way, I'm scared for him and in another, I'm just mad at him."

"Well, pray about it Katie. We'll all pray that everything turns out gut. Now go wash your face and rest for awhile. I have supper under control."

Katie obeyed her mother and tried to be optimistic, but all she could see was the cold, scary eyes of the man named Jay.

Chapter Thirty-Two

October was spectacular. Golden, rust, and brilliant reds abounded on the deciduous trees throughout the hills beyond the fields, but Katie barely noticed. It had been nearly two weeks since she'd made that disastrous trip over to see Josiah. No one had heard a word from him and he had not attended the preaching service. His other family members were there, but no one said a word about Josiah. Obviously, he was still alive and functioning or there would have been talk. The very fact nothing was said proved in Katie's mind that he had no excuse to behave the way he did. It was just his way of ending things. She found herself delving into fresh batches of cookies with new vigor and cared little that the scales were tipping the wrong way. She mentioned once to Ruth that her clothing felt tight, but it didn't seem to bother her. At least that was what she wanted others to believe.

Katie was grieving.

During this busy season, the men spent hours harvesting their crops. It had been a fruitful season and spirits were high though days were long and tedious for the men in the families. They worked from sunrise till sunset.

Mary spent hours canning and preserving, along with Ruth and Emma who came by nearly everyday to work with her. Katie helped when she could, but her heart wasn't in it. It was difficult to teach, feeling rejected the way she did. Nothing Becky said seemed to help and the whole family was aware that their Katie was most unhappy.

One Sunday in mid-October, Emma prepared for church service by setting out clean clothes for Lizzy and Mervin. Then she went into her bedroom to change to a fresh apron, when she suddenly felt light-headed. She sat at the end of the bed as Gabe came in to change his clothing after feeding the animals.

"Honey, what's wrong? You're so pale." He came over and sat on the bed beside her, reaching for her hand.

"I'll be fine in a minute." Emma leaned against Gabe's strong frame. "I think I have gut news for you."

"Jah? Is it what I'm thinking?"

"Depends upon what you're thinking." She looked up into his smiling blue eyes. "Oh jah, I can see you already know. I'm three weeks late, Gabe. I'm never, ever late."

"Sweetheart, I just knew. I really did. I don't know how, but I'm not surprised by your wonderful news." He lifted her chin and kissed her gently on the lips. "Danki, Mrs. Kuhns, for being my wife and carrying my child."

"I'm so excited, Gabe. I wanted to tell you sooner, but I wanted to be absolutely sure."

"Should we tell the kids?"

"No, not yet. It's way too early. It will seem like forever in their little minds if we tell them now."

"Jah, and it's fun to have this time to enjoy our little secret. How about your sisters and parents?"

"Ruth and Katie will know before I tell them, I'm sure. Oh, jah, and Mamm. She has a sixth sense about boppli. I still will wait a while before telling the world. Do you want a boy or a girl, Gabe?"

"I don't care. I have one of each already, so whatever the Lord gives us, I will be happy."

"Jah, I feel the same. I hope it's a healthy child, is all."

"His mama is healthy."

"Oops, you said, 'he'," she said, giggling.

"I did, didn't I? But I hate to say 'it' you know."

"I'm teasing. I think I'm fortunate not to be sick like poor Ruthie was. I feel real gut except a little light-headed once in a while, especially if I get up too quick."

"Are you up to going to church Emma?"

"Of course. Goodness me, I'm only pregnant—not sick. Amish women have babies like most women have haircuts."

"Mamm, Daed," Lizzy's voice came through the bedroom door. "Time to go. I don't want to be late. Annie's saving a seat for me."

"We'll be right there. Have Mervin bring the buggy around."

"Jah, okay."

They heard the quick steps of Liz as she headed down the stairs. "The kids will be thrilled, Emma."

"I know. Especially Lizzy."

"Jah, if it's a girl."

Emma laughed. "She'll love having a brother *or* a sister. She's a natural born mamm. Her bunny is proof of that. No one's been hugged more than that poor creature."

"You're right. Let's go, sweetheart. I hate to be late," he said. Then he took her in his arms and kissed her. "You will be a wonderful-gut mamm. You know your husband loves you so very much."

"Jah, and it's returned a hundred fold." They went down the stairs, their new secret bringing special joy to their hearts.

"Katie, you need to go back to your counselor," Mary said as she mashed sweet potatoes after the service. "You eat too much one day and not enough the next. You're going to make yourself sick again."

"I'll be okay, Mamm. Just give me time."

"It been almost two weeks now, Katie, and you're still not yourself."

"It's so hard. You have no idea. I really think I was in love with Josiah. And here I thought he loved me the same." Katie was finally able to discuss it without the tears, though when she was alone at night...

"I thought so, too, the way he looked at you sometimes. I don't understand it at all. Maybe you should have a talk with him."

"Never! I'll never put myself through that again. I'm upset I even went over there. And the people he knows. That Jay guy was scary."

"But you didn't think he was happy to be with that man, right?"

"He stayed with him when he was in Philadelphia. He must have liked him somewhat. Josiah claims he never took drugs. I doubt he would, but I can't imagine staying with people who not only took them, but sold them as well."

"Well, he did leave Philadelphia to come back to the Amish way."

"I know all that. I don't want to talk about it, Mamm. I don't want to hurt your feelings. I know you're trying, but I'm just trying to get over it. Please don't nag me about my eating."

Mary nodded, but she looked ever so sad. Her frown upset Katie and she went over to her. "I love you, Mamm. Try not to worry so much about me. I'm strong. I'll get over it." She wondered if it was true, but then people eventually got over all losses—even losing loved ones to death. Surely, she'd survive a broken heart.

Josiah's brother, Amos, paced the floor while he explained the situation he was faced with. "So you see, Josiah, with my in-laws facing so many medical bills and the expense of putting a new *dawdi haus* up, I simply don't have the money you need. I'd give it to you if I had it. Why again do you need it so fast-like?"

Josiah shook his head. This had been his last hope. He'd scraped the last two week's wages together after expenses, and it only amounted to three hundred and five dollars. Not enough to satisfy Jay. "Okay, I'll tell you, Amos, but it must not go further. I'm in trouble."

Amos looked at his younger brother in bewilderment. "What kind of trouble? With the law?"

"No." He explained the situation with Jay and Wally. "But I didn't go to the police or tell anyone. I realize now I probably should have. He doesn't believe me. Problem is, he carries a handgun and I don't think he'd be afraid to use it. People have the idea Amish people are so separated from the rest of the world, that they don't get involved with police or visa versa, which means he could hurt me or even worse, and there'd probably be no consequences."

"Of course that's not true. How on earth did you get yourself involved with criminals like him?" Amos asked with a stern expression.

"I met him at a job a couple years ago and he seemed okay to me then. I ran into him a few months back and he said they needed workers at the factory where he worked. When he told me how much money I could make, I figured out I could make enough to come back and buy my own farm. I'd need the money Daed offered me, too, but I'd be able to get started with my own place ever so much sooner."

"So he seemed okay when you first met him?"

"Jah. I didn't know him well, but I didn't expect the guy was a drug-dealer. That's one reason I came back early and of course, I didn't make the money I had expected to since I wasn't there that long. Now I won't even have what I did set aside. You have no idea how hard it is for me to turn the other cheek. My flesh wants to strike out at him. His lies."

"Jah," Amos nodded. "I know how it is. I've felt that way, too, sometimes. It's a battle, bruder, but we can't give in to our carnal desires. You're right to accept the wrong he's doing you."

"Katie's suffering because of it. If only I could tell her I still care. I saw Wayne the other day but he barely spoke to me. I know he's upset. I'm so frustrated." He held his head in his hands, elbows resting on his knees.

Amos went over and laid his hand on his brother's shoulder. "Maybe if we all put in some money we can come up with enough to satisfy this Jay guy."

"No. I'll deal with him myself. I'm meeting him tomorrow around four at the farm I was hoping to buy."

"Just hoping? Won't they hold off for a while and give you a chance to come up with the money?"

"I went to the bank a couple days ago. They'll see what they can do. The realtor told me he's checking with other banks, too, so I haven't given up hope yet."

"So what will you do if Jay isn't willing to wait for the money?"

"I don't know. Appeal to his better side, I guess."

"Maybe he doesn't have one."

"I can hope."

"Jah. I'll pray about this, Josiah. You too. Maybe the Lord will have a solution we haven't even thought of."

"He'd better hurry. The clock's ticking." Josiah's eyes were cast down.

"In the end, it's all in God's timing, jah?"

Josiah nodded and looked up at his brother. "That's what I'm counting on, Amos."

After Josiah left, Amos went out to the barn to round up his brothers. Maybe he could give God a hand. After a discussion, the brothers took off in different directions as he headed on horseback to his neighbor's house and then on to the Zook farm where he found Wayne working alongside his father.

"What brings you here, Amos?" Leroy asked, wiping his forehead with his sleeve.

"I think we need to talk. Just the men folk."

"That include me?" Wayne asked.

"Jah, it does, boy. We have ourselves a problem, but it must stay in our man's world. Understand?"

Wayne's grin gave his answer. "Oh, jah!"

Chapter Thirty-Three

Becky worked with the group of children studying the multiplication tables while Katie checked the Arithmetic scores of the older students. She was pleased to see how Mervin excelled in all his studies. What a turnaround from last year. Lizzy was always a good student and this year was no exception. Emma must be happy to see how much her influence had helped her young stepchildren. Gabe seemed unusually cheerful when they were together Sunday, and Katie wondered if her sister was in a family way. Gabe had seemed more than solicitous to her sister's needs. And perhaps one day, it would be Katie, married to a man who adored her, preparing for her first boppli. At least, that was Katie's dream.

Once classes ended, she wiped down the blackboard as Becky took out the trash. Then the two sat down to plan the next day's schedule. Katie seemed distracted. Finally Becky asked what was wrong.

"You've been so down lately, Katie. Can't you get over Josiah?"

"It's not that easy, Becky. For heaven's sake, wait until you get rejected someday."

"I already was and by your own bruder. Remember a couple months ago? He totally ignored me."

Katie shook her head and clucked her tongue. "That's not the same."

"Well, I've liked him forever, you know."

"Becky, I know it hurt when he didn't notice you, but it's not like when you think a guy might be in love with you and he takes you to see a house he's buying and all and holds your hand and—"

"All right, I agree. It's not quite the same. I'm sorry. But maybe Josiah's just been too busy and—"

"Right, for weeks? No, I've accepted it. We're done."

"I think you've given up too quickly. If I were you, I'd give him one more chance to explain. Maybe you should go over to see him at his house, pretending to need something."

"Like what? A plow?"

"Don't be silly. I don't know. Maybe you can pretend you lost something and you're not sure if it was left in his buggy. Like a hanky."

"Very weak. But you do think I shouldn't give up totally?"

Becky nodded. She pushed her assignment book away and leaned toward her friend. "If you care as much as I think you do, you need to find out what happened. Otherwise you may regret it some day. That's what I think."

Katie puckered her mouth and gave it some thought. "I bet he's at the farm he wants to buy. He may even have bought it by now. If I go by after I leave here, maybe I can just stop to say 'hallo.' What do you think?"

"I think you should. Definitely. And for Pete's sake, stop eating so much candy. All the work you did to lose weight and boom! Like that—it's all going to pop back."

"I know. I can't seem to help myself, but that's just an excuse. I do it because I feel sorry for myself. You're right. Why should I gain back all the weight just because of one man! I'm going to go, Becky. I have to know what happened."

"Gut. Now let's finish up our plans. I'm beat."

Josiah was headed over to his farm when he nearly ran over a golden lab puppy running loose on the road. The pup was trailing his leash and it caught on a low tree limb causing the poor thing to practically strangle himself. Josiah pulled his horse to the side of the road and looped the reins on a tree while he freed the pup from his noose. "There you go, fella. Let's see if you have an address." The puppy danced about while Josiah tried to read the words on his collar. With that, he heard a young girl's voice coming from across the road. "There he is. I've been looking all over for Dusty."

Josiah recognized the little girl. She was preacher Smucker's youngest child. The freed dog darted across the road toward his mistress, dragging the leash. "Danki for getting a hold of him," she said to Josiah. "I was afraid he'd get hit by a car. He took off when I went to help Mamm hang sheets."

"Glad to help. Poor little guy was strangling himself on his leash."

Josiah spotted her father, Malachi, heading his way. "Josiah, it's gut to see you. Missed you at the preaching service. Have ya been sick?"

"Nee, just workin' hard and helping with my *grossdaed*."

"Oh, jah, I heard he was walkin' off sometimes. How about a glass of lemonade. Ellie just made some."

"I have to be somewhere by four, but I could use something to drink."

"It's only three-thirty," Malachi told him.

"I guess I have time."

He led the horse across the road and tied him to a fence railing. Malachi's wife was hanging up sheets when she saw them coming toward her. She stopped and greeted him and Malachi stepped on to his porch and poured each of them a glass of lemonade. He pointed to a bench, where Josiah and he sat, enjoying the autumn sunshine. They began talking about the puppy his daughter was hugging, as she scolded him for running off.

Malachi laughed as he watched his daughter. "You have to keep him tied up. He's still a pup, dochder. He hasn't learned to behave yet."

The men talked about the harvest and before Josiah realized it, it was nearly four o'clock and he was a good fifteen minutes away. He stood up and shook Malachi's hand. "Danki for the drink. I appreciate it." Then he turned to the child. "Take care of your pup."

Malachi walked with him to his horse and waved as he left. Josiah clucked at his horse to make up for lost time.

Katie got to the farmhouse early. It was nearly four o'clock. It didn't look as bad as she had remembered it, but it still was not her dream house. She pulled the buggy off to the side of the drive and looped the reins around a tree. Even though she saw no signs of Josiah, she figured she'd walk around the grounds. It was one of those perfect fall days, just a hint of a breeze, which shuffled the fallen leaves about as she walked. She loved the crunch of the dry leaves underfoot and thought back to her earlier days when she and her sisters would jump in the piles her brothers raked off the lawn. What fun.

As she headed toward the back of the house, a blue car came up the drive. Certainly Josiah didn't drive a car and then she recognized the man getting out of the driver's side. The horrible man, Jay—who spotted her almost immediately. The buggy was a giveaway. She couldn't have hidden even if she'd had a chance.

"Where's your boyfriend?" he called out as he ambled in her direction.

"I…I'm not sure." Goodness, this was not part of her plan at all.

"He's supposed to meet me here. Is he hiding?" he asked with a leer.

That got her dander up. "Hardly! Josiah is no coward! He's just not here—yet," she added hoping he'd think he was on his way.

"This your place?"

"No."

"But your boyfriend's buying it?"

"I'm not sure."

"You don't know much, considering you're his girl."

"Uh, I know a lot, but I don't feel like telling you everything I know." Katie stood a little taller. He wasn't going to intimidate her.

He walked closer to her and she backed up a couple of feet, but he gained ground by taking two strides forward. For the first time, she felt fear. Real genuine panicky fear.

"I never kissed an Amish girl before. I've always wondered what it was like," he said, lowering his voice and taking another step toward her.

"I…I don't think you should try anything with me. I don't want to be kissed."

"No? Doesn't Stoltz take care of you? I would take real good care of a girl like you." He reached out and took hold of her arm. His grasp was rough and he gripped her upper arm like a vice. She felt she might faint as her fear immobilized her. In the distance she could hear horse's hooves galloping toward the house. She looked past Jay's shoulder and saw Josiah heading toward them. *Thank God!*

Jay dropped her arm and turned toward Josiah as the horse made its way to the couple. Josiah jumped down and quickly stood between Jay and Katie.

"What do you think you're doing? Whatever business we have doesn't concern her." He turned toward her briefly. "Katie, wait in the house. Here's an extra key to the back door. I won't be long."

Katie took the key, her hand trembling. She was breathing so quickly, she felt she'd faint, but she headed toward the side of the house and leaned against the building. "Lord Jesus, help us. Please." Black spots danced before her eyes and she felt woozy. Then she slumped to the ground in a faint.

Chapter Thirty-Four

"Leroy, where do you think you're going?" Mary spotted Leroy mounting his horse and he hadn't even had his afternoon rest yet. It was already close to four. And behind him, Wayne was holding a pitch fork and a long-handled shovel in one hand, while holding his saddle horn with the other.

"We'll be back in a few minutes, Mary. Don't ask so many questions," Leroy said, authority resounding in his deep voice.

"I'll have my tea without you then." Mary stood firmly on her two feet and folded her arms.

"Mamm, don't worry about us."

"Well, I wasn't worried until you said that. Just where do you think you two are going, carrying tools like that. Hunting today, Leroy? Isn't that your shotgun under your blanket. My goodness, you two look foolish."

"No time to talk, Mary. See you in a bit. Save my tea."

The two trotted off quickly. Mary stood and watched while her heart pounded. Then she saw Mark, Jeremiah, and Abram at the end of the drive on their horses, forming a group. The neighbor men across the road joined up with them. What on earth was going on? Everyone had something with them. Either a tool or a shotgun. Something big was about to happen. And where was her Katie? She should be home by now. "Lord, protect my family and all my friends."

Something caught her eye and she looked toward Abram's farm next door. Fannie was nearly running across the field toward her. Little Sammy was trying to keep up with his mother, who had Isaac in her arms. Mercy, what was happening? Was there a war going on in the United States? For once, she wished she had a television. Once she reached Mary, Fannie put her child down and leaned over to hug her mother-in-law.

"I have no idea what's happening, Mamm, but I'm scared."

"Jah, me too. Come in and we'll pray together. I don't know what else to do."

"Where's Katie?"

"Still at school I guess. She should be home by now, but sometimes she stays with Becky and they work on test papers."

"Then we'll include her in our prayers, since we have no idea what's going on. Men can be so secretive sometimes."

"Jah, when they don't want to worry us. Trouble is, it makes us worry ever so much more."

Fannie nodded and they went inside with the children to pray. What else could they do?

Josiah stood facing Jay, dreading the moment when he'd learn there was no more money to be had.

"I'm waiting. Where's the dough?"

"Jay, we were friends, jah?"

"Till you ratted on us."

Josiah shook his head. "Not true."

"I need the money. Now."

"I don't have it."

"Just like that. 'I don't have it.' And you think I'm gonna say 'it's okay. Have a nice day?' You think I'm stupid?"

"Look, be reasonable—"

"You don't expect me to walk away, do you Stoltz?" Jay removed his jacket and threw it on the ground. Then he edged closer to Josiah, who was standing his ground. Before Josiah had a chance to step back, Jay arched his arm and slapped Josiah across the face with the back of his hand. It stung so badly, Josiah nearly lost his balance.

"What's the matter? Too scared to fight back? Are you Amish nuts or what? Or just cowards?"

"We're not cowards." Josiah removed his straw hat and swirled it to the ground a few feet away. With deliberation, he rolled up his sleeves and stood, feet apart, arms in a protective position, but he didn't attempt to strike back.

"Yeah, you're a bunch of violets. You gonna turn the other cheek?"

"If I have to."

"Hey, I like your girl, but I don't think you're takin' good care of her. She wanted to kiss me."

"You're a liar! Leave her out of this."

"Oh, I hit a tender spot. Don't worry, when I'm done with you, I'll take care of her. Real good care, if you know what I mean."

"That's it—I've had it." Josiah swung his fist and socked Jay so hard, he fell to the ground. Jay picked himself up immediately and took a swing at Josiah, who ducked and came back at him with his knuckles. After several blows, they grabbed hold of each other and ended up rolling on the ground.

Katie found herself slouched over on the ground against the side of the porch, but after a few slow breaths, she recalled what had happened and ran back to the front of the house, just in time to see a group of about forty men riding on horseback, all with straw hats and dark clothes, headed their way. It was quite a sight to see as they galloped toward the drive, tools and guns swaying as they rode.

Josiah and Jay were so absorbed in their wrestling match, they didn't even seem aware of the crowd approaching. Just as the first man jumped from his horse, Jay rolled over to his jacket on the ground and reached toward the pocket, where Katie could see something glimmering. Something metal. Without a thought, she ran and kicked the jacket at least five feet away from the man. Jay tried to grab her ankle, but Wayne had arrived and he stomped on Jay's arm, causing him to scream out in pain. The group of men surrounded Jay and stood menacingly with their objects aimed toward his head. Not a word was spoken. Wayne removed his foot, but held a shovel above Jay's head. He was motionless.

Josiah, stunned by the last blow he'd received, remained seated on the ground. No one moved for several moments and then Jay dusted himself off, pushed the shovel aside, and stood up, blood dripping from his nose. He turned around in a complete circle, obviously evaluating the whole situation.

In the meantime, Leroy went over to Jay's jacket, removed the weapon, dumped the bullets, and stuck the gun in his own pocket. Then he folded his arms and stared at Jay.

He shrugged. "I guess you have me. All right. I'm leaving."

"Wait a minute," Amos stepped in front of his path. "You owe my brother some money."

"Get out of here. He owes me, jerk."

"I don't believe that's correct. Is it Josiah?" Amos asked without moving his eyes away from Jay's.

"Nee. I guess he made a mistake."

Amos held out his hand, waiting for money to be placed there.

"I don't have it on me, Amish man," he said with a sneer.

"I'll take an I.O.U. then." Amos turned to his younger brother, Benjamin. "Got a paper and pen like I told you to bring?"

Benjamin supplied them and Amos handed them over to Jay. "How much was it he took, Josiah?"

"Three thousand."

"Okay, with interest, let's make it thirty-three hundred."

Jay threw the pen and paper on the grass. "What, are you guys *nuts?*"

Silence again. Each man took one step closer, closing the circle around the man. Their expressions were somber, even threatening.

"Here," Jay said, angrily as he reached in his pants pocket and drew out a wad of bills. "Take this!" He threw it on the ground and Amos picked it up and counted it out slowly.

"That's only twenty-five hundred."

"That's all I've got. Take it or leave it. Let me out of here!"

"Well, we can take an IOU on the rest."

Josiah spoke up from his seated position. "Let him go. I'm glad to get any back."

"Okay, but we don't want to see your face again in Lancaster County," Amos continued. He looked around at his friends. There were a few nods and grunts.

"What about my thirty-eight?"

"Jah, nice handgun. We'll keep it for you."

"You're Amish men! You're not supposed to act like this! What about turning the other cheek?" Jay seemed outraged, but it was obvious he was out-numbered.

"Sorry if we don't fit your description. Guess you can leave now, boy."

Jay gritted his teeth and edged his way through the crowd. He climbed into his car and gunned out of the drive, scaring two of the horses, but none of the men. Leroy shook his head. "That boy needs a trip to the woodshed." The others laughed and patted each other on their backs.

"Say, Leroy, think you really would have used your pitchfork on that critter?" asked one of his friends.

"Can't really say, but it sure did slow our friend down to see us lookin' so fierce."

"Glad the Bishop didn't show up," Wayne said, grinning over at his father.

"We never touched the man, Wayne," Leroy said. "Can't help it if we scared him though. Poor guy looked white as a newborn lamb."

Gabe laughed as he stuck his shot gun in his saddle. "Forgot my bullets, anyway."

"My goodness, so did I," Abram said, grinning over at his brother-in-law.

"Now let's take care of our boxer," Amos said as he leaned down to check on Josiah, who was still sitting on the ground, counting and arranging his money face-up.

Chapter Thirty-Five

After Katie kicked the jacket, she remained in the background, watching the crowd of friends and family protecting Josiah. It all happened so fast, she didn't have time to process it. Thankfully, Josiah was safe, though badly bruised, and whether they ever resumed a relationship seemed unimportant at this point. She was ever so grateful to God for protecting him. It had not occurred to Katie yet, that she too had faced danger.

Josiah's brothers and father were offering him sips of water from a flask as Wayne made his way over to his sister. Leroy followed behind and took Katie in his arms. "Katie, what on earth were you doing here?"

"Oh, Daed, I just came by to see Josiah. I had no idea that man would be coming here."

"I saw you kick his jacket, Katie. That was pretty fast thinking. You may have saved Josiah's life by that move."

"Really?" Katie moved back to study her father's expression. "Are you serious?"

"Jah, there was a loaded gun in there."

"I figured it was a gun. I saw it shining in the sun and I didn't even think—I just did what I knew I should do. I'm so thankful everyone is okay."

"We're going to get you home, young lady. Wayne, take your sister in the buggy. I'll lead your horse behind mine. There ain't no hurry now."

"Okay, Daed. Come on Katie."

"Wait, I want to talk to Josiah first."

"He's hurtin' bad, Katie. It can wait."

She followed her brother and glanced over at Josiah as she passed the group of men standing about, talking in their dialect about the events that had just transpired.

"Oh, Katie," she heard her father call out to her. "You don't have to mention all this to Mamm. No sense in upsetting her."

Katie felt a smile coming on in spite of the seriousness of the event. "Jah, okay. I'll let you explain what happened."

"Just needed to straighten out a man's thinkin' is all."

"Oh, right. That you did, Daed." Wayne climbed in the driver's seat as Katie pulled herself into her seat.

"What a day." Katie rested her head on the seat and thanked the Lord for the outcome as the horse clip clopped toward home.

Once they arrived, Mary and Fannie ran out of the house and headed over to greet Wayne and Katie. Wayne glanced over at his sister before they reached the buggy and reminded her to let their father explain what transpired.

"Oh, mercy, we've been so worried, Katie. Wayne, how did you end up in the buggy with your sister?"

"It's a long story, Mamm. Daed will fill you in."

Mary looked over at Katie waiting for some answers. "What's happened? Is everyone okay?"

Katie climbed out and gave her mother a hug. "Everyone is fine, Mamm. Not to worry."

"It's a little late for that. I saw everyone taking off. Where did you go? Don't leave me in the dark, Katie, for Heaven's sake."

"Daed wants to tell you himself."

"Well, I'll be," Fannie remarked. "Such secrets!"

"I'm exhausted, Mamm," Katie remarked. "I could use a cup of tea."

"There's enough left in the pot for one cup, Katie. Come on. I can see I'm not going to get any information from my children. May as well finish my tea before it's ice cold. Fannie, see what you can learn from Abram when he returns. He is returning isn't he, Katie?"

With this they heard hooves on the road and looked up to see several of the men returning home. Leroy, Jeremiah, and Gabe galloped down the drive, elated expressions on their faces. Mary put her hands on her hips and looked as stern as she was able at the returning victors. "My, my, if it ain't my Amish family. Did you bring the scalps with you?"

Leroy laughed as he dismounted and wrapped the reins around a stump. "So, you think we're warriors returning home, is that it, Mary?"

She shook her head, clucking as she waited. "You look mighty pleased with yourselves. I hope you didn't use your haying tools on some poor soul."

"Nope. We didn't have to lift a finger. Not one finger!"

The men laughed together and that was the end of the discussion. Mary knew there would be no further explanation. At least not until she wore Leroy down with her inquisition. But that could wait. Right now she was just grateful no Amish blood was shed—or anyone else's, for that matter.

Katie was too exhausted to talk about her experience. Though she was relieved no one was seriously injured, she was sorely disappointed at having to leave before talking with Josiah. Had anything changed after the day's events? She still had no idea why Josiah had been avoiding her. If she had indeed saved his life, then surely he would come by himself to thank her. That was the very least he could do. And if he didn't see fit to show his appreciation, then he was not worth caring about. This would be her test.

Mary put more water on to boil as the men remained outside, laughing together and speaking in low tones, so as not to be heard by the women-folk. She shook her head. "I must say, they certainly are a proud group. I wonder what the Bishop would think."

Katie sipped her tea and started to reach for a chip cookie, but withdrew her hand.

"For goodness sake, Katie, treat yourself to one. You look like you've seen a ghost."

"I'd like to tell you what happened—"

"Jah?" Mary and Fannie both leaned in waiting for information.

"But I mustn't. Daed said."

"Oh." Fannie and Mary exchanged glances and returned to their tea. The children were jumping on the furniture and had to be reminded to settle down. When Katie finished her cup, she asked to be excused.

"I think I'll lie down a while. I'm exhausted."

"I guess." Mary puckered her lips and avoided looking at her daughter.

"Mamm, please. I *can't* tell you!"

"Mmm. Well at least you're safe. For that I'm grateful. Jah, go take your rest, Katie. You can help with supper later."

Once Katie got to her room, she took off her cap and apron and pulled the pins out of her hair. It flowed down and she laid on her pillow, eyes closed, reliving the events of her day. It seemed surreal. She had never experienced anything like it and hoped never to again. Josiah had fought for her honor, this she knew. She had heard enough to know it was only when her name was brought up that Josiah allowed himself to fight Jay. It had indeed pushed him over the edge. She hoped there would be no consequences for his actions. She knew of a case where a man was shunned for hurting another man. Surely, there were exceptions. What if he was shunned? And still cared about her? Would she give up her Amish roots to marry a man separated from his People? She would cross that bridge if she had to, but at this point, there were way too many unknowns.

Katie allowed herself to doze off and she slept for two solid hours. It was dark out when she awoke. She went downstairs with the realization she had missed supper entirely. Mary and Leroy looked up from their books as she came into the parlor. "We didn't want to wake you. You looked so exhausted."

"I can't believe I slept that long. Where's Wayne?"

"He went to see Becky," Mary said.

"Becky? Really?"

"I figured you might need a day off from teaching after your father finally explained what happened, so I told him to go tell Becky she would be alone tomorrow. That way, if she needed someone to help out, maybe she'd have time to get one of her sisters."

Leroy looked over his glasses at his wife. "He's been gone a long time, Mary."

"Jah, he has." She smiled and then looked over at Katie. "Are you hungry? I saved some soup for you and rye bread."

"Maybe in a while. I feel dopey from my nap. When I woke up, I wasn't sure what day it was."

"Oh, Josiah came by a while ago," Leroy said without looking up. "I told him you were sleeping."

"Why didn't you wake me up?" Katie asked, devastated to have missed his visit.

218

"I offered to wake you, Katie, but he wouldn't hear of it. He'll probably stop by tomorrow." Mary closed her book and sat back in her seat. "He had a black and blue eye."

"Mmm. I'm not surprised," Katie answered, wishing she hadn't taken a nap at all. How could she wait until the next day to talk to him? Was he just there to say thank you for saving his life? And then he'd shake her hand and be off? She could have gone to school to teach tomorrow. Her parents shouldn't have made that decision for her, but she knew they just had her best interests at heart.

An hour later, as her parents were about to retire for the night, Wayne came through the back door.

"Took you long enough," Leroy said to him.

"Becky wanted to gab. Plus she makes really gut fudge. I had five pieces."

"You'll get cavities," Mary said. "That's too much chocolate."

Katie smiled over at her brother. "Becky is a gut cook all right. She's pretty, too, don't you think?"

Wayne's neck reddened. "I didn't notice."

Leroy laughed out loud. "Come on, sohn. Since when don't you notice the girls?"

"She's cute enough. She likes to talk about softball. I like that."

"Oh, jah," Katie nodded. "She sure loves softball. Talks about it all the time."

"You were really conked out, Katie. I heard you snore when I walked by your bedroom."

"Oh, no. I don't snore!"

"Jah, you do. I bet Josiah heard it from outside." He grinned at his sister and went into the kitchen for another snack.

Mary shook her head. "He's such a tease, Katie. Don't pay him any heed."

Katie smiled. "In spite of his teasing, I'm glad he's my bruder."

Since she didn't have to teach the next day, Katie finished a novel she had started a month before. Maybe she'd just happen to pass by the farm tomorrow, since she'd be free all day and perhaps,

Josiah would be there alone. She smiled as she closed the book and snuggled into her quilt.

Chapter Thirty-Six

After a late breakfast, Katie decided to take the open buggy for a ride. "It's nice to be free to do what I want just this once," she told her mother as she washed her plates from breakfast and set them in the drain to dry. "I'll help you clean later, Mamm."

"It's not necessary," Mary said as she kneaded bread for supper. "You go have a nice time. Are you headed anywhere special?"

"I'm not sure yet. Maybe I should check with Becky to be sure she's okay. After sleeping more than twelve hours, I'm ready to teach again."

"Let her be," Mary said. "She's very competent. After what you went through yesterday, I think you should spend the day relaxing."

"Jah, and thanking the Lord for the outcome."

"I've been praising him all morning, Katie. It's scary to think what could have happened."

"I know. Okay, I'll do as you say."

"Going over to the Brewster place?" Her mother had a knowing smile on her face.

"Maybe."

"Josiah mentioned he'd be coming over this afternoon, but he wanted to do some more measuring for wood at the farm. I guess he thinks it will be his or he wouldn't be spending so much time there."

"I guess now that the threat is over and he got most of his money back from that bad guy, he expects the mortgage to go through. Maybe he'll know more today. So since he's there now, probably, I'll just drop by on my way to the market. Do you need anything?"

"No, we're fine, unless they have mushrooms at a gut price. Your daed loves mushrooms with his eggs sometimes."

"I'll check." Katie came over and kissed her mother's cheek. "See you later, Mamm."

Mary nodded and smiled. "Just be careful if you are alone with Josiah. We don't want people talking."

"I'll be careful." On the way over, Katie prayed about the whole situation. *And Lord, if it be your will, let Josiah love me.* She knew God had a lot to do, but this was so important to her. As she pulled up to the drive, she saw Josiah's horse grazing in a small pasture—the only area with a standing fence. She brought her horse to a stop and got down. Josiah was no where in sight. She called his name, but heard no response. Then she tied the reins to a post and walked around to the barn. She peeked through the open entranceway. She saw movement in the area of the milking station and headed over. Dry hay crackled underfoot and Josiah stood up and turned toward the noise. "Oh my goodness, it's you," he said, removing his hat and standing motionless while she approached.

"Jah, I was just riding past…"

"It's out of your way, no? Aren't you teaching?"

"It doesn't look that way, does it?" she said, tilting her head coquettishly.

He laughed and walked toward her. "I came by last night."

"Jah, I know."

"You were sleeping."

She nodded.

"I just wanted to thank you for what you did."

"Oh. You're welcome." It felt so awkward. She wished she had waited for him to come to her in the familiarity of her own home.

"Katie, maybe now I can explain."

"Explain about what?"

"You know. Not coming by and all."

"Oh, jah. That." She looked down at her hands and joined them together, wondering what to say next.

"I wanted to see you. Very much."

"I missed you, Josiah."

"I know and I'm sorry. I didn't want you to get involved in my problems."

She nodded and continued to look down at the ground.

"Come, let's go sit in the sun together. It's a wonderful-gut day out. Warm, even."

He took her by the hand and went with her to the back stoop which was in full sun. They sat down and Katie reached for a blade of grass, running it through her fingers.

"Did you get the farm?" she asked.

"I'm not sure yet, but it looks like I will now that I have most of my money back. My realtor stopped by this morning to look for me and he seemed optimistic everything will go just fine."

"So, you have a lot of work ahead of you." Katie looked around at the unkempt grounds.

"Jah, that's for sure. I'll probably need help along the way."

"Gut thing you have a big family."

"I meant help with cooking and stuff like that."

"Mmm. Maybe your mamm will—"

"Actually, I was thinking more like a wife maybe."

"Oh, jah, a wife could help you, that's for sure."

"I have someone in mind."

Katie couldn't bring herself to look up. She'd give too much of her feelings away. She plucked a second blade of grass and continued to stare down. "Anyone I know?"

"Jah, I think you know her real well."

Oh, dear, that didn't sound gut at all. She hesitated before asking. "What's her name?"

"Katie."

She looked up into his eyes. He reached for her hand. "It's you, Katie. You are the one I want for my wife. To love you forever. Will you marry me?"

"Oh my. Jah, I believe so."

He reached for her other hand and they stood up. He released her hands and placed his arms around her waist, looking into her eyes. "May I kiss you?"

Katie nodded, unable to form words.

Josiah drew her closer and bent his head down, reaching her soft lips with his. He pressed gently as he closed his eyes. She caught her breath and then returned his kiss. This was truly happening. It was not her imagination. Josiah loved her and she loved him and this was the start of something very special. God had drawn them together and no one could break that bond.

"I love you, Josiah, and I want to be your wife and the mother of your children. I just hope I never disappoint you."

"You couldn't, Katie, even if you tried. You are everything I want in a woman. I don't know how I could have been blind so long and not realized you were the sister for me. Now, how about if we decide what we should do with your kitchen." He held onto her hand as he led her through the back door, which was barely hanging on one hinge. She looked at it and saw a palace.

THE END